EYES WIDE OPEN
THE OUTLAW CHRONICLES

EYES WIDE OPEN

THE FULL STORY | BOOKS 1-4

TED DEKKER

WORTHY
PUBLISHING

Library of Congress Control Number: 2013954255

ISBN: 978-1-61795-273-9 (trade paper)

This book is a work of fiction. Names, characters, places, and incidents are the product of the author's imagination or are used fictitiously. Any resemblance to actual events, locales, or persons, living or dead, is coincidental.

Published in association with Creative Trust, 5141 Virginia Way, Brentwood, TN 37027.
www.creativetrust.com

For foreign and subsidiary rights, contact rights@worthypublishing.com

Cover Design: Pixel Peach Studio
Cover Illustration: Pixel Peach Studio

Printed in The United States of America
14 15 16 17 18 LBM 8 7 6 5 4 3 2 1

www.teddekker.com

BOOK ONE
IDENTITY

MY HEART sounds like a monster with clobber feet, running straight toward me. It's pitch dark. I'm lying on my back, soaked with sweat from the hair on my head to the soles of my feet. I'm lying perfectly still, but my hands and knees won't stop shaking.

I'm in my grave, and I know I'm going to die here.

It's only about eighteen inches high, and my forehead is bruised from hitting it more than once. I can feel both sides with my hands if I reach out. Just longer than me, maybe by a foot. I'm claustrophobic. Very claustrophobic.

I saw the coffins. I saw them, and now I'm in one, buried under tons of concrete. It's all I can think, over and over, and I can't stop thinking it.

Breathe. Just breathe, Christy. Close your eyes and breathe.

It's not like this. It can't be like this. It's all a mistake. I have to calm down or I'm going to have a heart attack. It's all a mistake. They'll find me. This is Boston, not Africa. People in Boston don't die like this. People don't die like this *anywhere* in America. It's all a mistake.

This *isn't* my grave.

I close my eyes and try to slow my breathing. Try to think different thoughts—not the old ones that keep shoving me under tons of smothering earth. Good thoughts, like the fact that I'm still alive. Like the fact that my imagination has always been my biggest enemy.

Like the fact that it's all a mistake.

But that's not true, is it? My whole *life* is a mistake—one tragic error after another, and this one's going to be my last.

I'm in a grave, and I'm going to die.

My heart sounds like a monster with clobber feet, running straight toward me. It's pitch dark. I'm lying on my back, soaked with sweat from the hair on my head to the soles of my feet. I'm lying perfectly still with my eyes closed, trying to think new thoughts, but my hands and knees won't stop shaking.

How did this happen to me?

———

IT ALL began with a little heart-shaped silver locket, the kind that typically holds a small picture of a smiling boyfriend or a perfectly framed family at its best, frozen in time on photo-reactive paper to be forever cherished.

Christy Snow's locket held no such image because she had neither a boyfriend nor a perfect family. No family at all, in fact. No mother, no father of her knowing. She was an orphan, age seventeen, disturbingly in the dark about her entire existence prior to age thirteen, when she entered the orphanage.

The picture in her locket was the same black-and-white placeholder that had come with the necklace when she bought it for $19.99 at the Target on Steel Street two years earlier—a constant reminder worn near her heart, a promise that she would one day at least know who her real mother and father were. Maybe even recover her childhood. How could she love herself if she didn't even know who she was?

It wouldn't be beyond a psychiatrist to suggest that the silver piece had become her identity, that she was lost in the deeply held fear that she didn't belong. Not to a family, not to a man, not to a friend, not even to herself.

Christy, like the image in her locket, was only a shadow, living as a fraud. Although she did her best to pretend that she was happy with her life, she secretly hated herself for being forgotten by family, by anyone who might have said she belonged or had value.

She took the necklace off only when she went to bed because she tended to toss and turn in fitful nightmares of being thrown away as a child. Twice she had broken the chain in her sleep. But last night, when she'd reached for the necklace around her neck, it was gone.

A thorough, frantic search of her studio flat had turned up no sign of the locket. She remembered glancing at it before heading out to meet Austin late in the afternoon. The chain must have broken somewhere along the route they'd taken to the old storage room, or in the storage room itself. She would retrace her steps as soon as she woke.

The sun was already well up when Christy woke at nine—no reason to get up any earlier. She'd graduated from high school six months ago and was still trying to figure out what to do with her life. The trust fund had kicked in when she'd turned seventeen, so getting a job wasn't critical. Two thousand dollars a month wasn't exactly pay dirt, but the anonymous account turned over to her by the orphanage she'd entered when she was thirteen was enough to buy her time.

She decided to walk the three miles to the hospital in case she'd lost the locket on the street somewhere. She pulled on a pair of jeans, slipped into a red blouse, pulled her hair into a ponytail, and forgave herself for avoiding any makeup before heading out.

No one to impress; she was searching for her locket, not a man.

Truth be told, she wasn't interested in men if the ones she'd known were representative of the entire species.

Despite an ugly overcast sky, the day was already unusually hot by the time she reached the south end of Saint Matthew's Hospital. She wasn't in the best shape, maybe even fat if ten pounds too much was the rule of men. And it was; so, yes, she was plain fat and she secretly hated every one of those ten pounds. She was sweating now because of them.

But she wasn't there to be seen by anyone, or to be judged and found lacking. She was there to find her locket.

The south end of the building was called the old hospital. It was made of red brick and adjoined the much larger new construction. One block north, the streets and landscaping looked pristine, but approaching from the west as Christy was, few would guess they were approaching a hospital.

Quincy Street was home to several shops—everything from antique stores to Bill's Round Bar at one end. A dirty yellow taxicab rolled past on dirty asphalt, followed by an ambulance. The street was otherwise vacant, except for an old bum slouched on a bench under a picture window just ahead.

Someone had dropped sections of the morning paper along the sidewalk without bothering to use the trash bin on the corner. If her locket had fallen off here, some vagrant had surely found it and taken it to the pawnshop for a few dollars.

The world was ill, she thought. Building a hospital in the middle of that sickness didn't change all the suffering. If anything, the building was only a sad reminder of the fate that awaited every soul helplessly born into such a cruel world.

A wave of emptiness washed through her chest as she passed the man on the bench. He wasn't dead yet, but he'd given up on life, and isn't that what inevitably awaited everyone?

She wasn't any different from him, not really.

Christy turned into the alleyway that ran between the old hospital and the shops. No sign of her locket. She kept her eyes down, searching for any flash of silver on the ground around the base of the four large green dumpsters that hugged the wall to her right.

Nothing.

The door to the hospital's storage room was made of metal, covered by mottled gray paint, dented in several places as if someone had taken a bat or hammer to it.

Two years earlier, during a discussion with a doctor about how medical equipment had advanced so rapidly, Austin had learned about the old artifacts all but forgotten in the storage room. Curious, he'd broken in and found a haunting space that became a bit of an obsession for a few months. Its secrets still drew him from time to time.

Christy angled for the door. Austin had gone to the trouble of jimmying the lock so it could be opened with a key of sorts, which he hid in a crack between two bricks.

Picking up a splinter of wood, she pried the key out of the crack, then walked up to the door, glancing left and then right to make sure she was alone.

She inserted the thin metal piece into the keyhole and wiggled it until the lock sprang. With one last glance both ways, Christy opened the door, slipped through, and shut herself inside.

She found the switch and flipped it up. The single incandescent bulb strung from the ceiling filled the room with passable light.

For a few moments, Christy stood still, taking in the silence, aware that she'd just broken some law likely punishable by time in a jail cell.

The thought fell away as she scanned the room. Twenty feet wide by ten deep, Austin had said, and he was dead accurate about such things. Two wooden wheelchairs, some rusted IV stands, dirty bottles, and some wheeled trays in the corner to her left. A bookcase filled with old medical books stood along the wall beside them, spines wiped of dust. Austin had scanned most of them. He stuffed his mind with more information than most people could read in five lifetimes.

A gurney and two hospital beds were stacked on the wall in front of her, along with some old crates full of medical stuff of some kind.

The west side of the storage room had interested Austin more. Another old wooden wheelchair, wiped clean of dust by the seat of

Austin's pants. He liked to balance on two wheels and think. An old writer's desk hugged the far end, complete with old writing pens and an inkwell supplied by Austin.

He was a writer. The desk had drawn him. Of all the artifacts in the room, she understood this attraction the most because she, too, was a writer of sorts if filling journals counted as writing. Sometimes she thought she was trying to make up for her forgotten childhood by writing down every detail of her life now.

Four old, plain wooden coffins were stacked in pairs along the wall. Yesterday she'd sat on a fifth casket and leaned against the wall for an hour, talking with Austin.

A quick scan of the grime-smeared concrete floor revealed no sign of her locket. She walked over to the desk, searched it quickly, and then crossed to the coffin.

Nothing on its surface, nothing along its base. Her heart began to sink. She was about to turn away and search the floor near the desk—she'd spent some time there, sitting in Austin's wheelchair, flipping though a medical journal—when she saw the gap between the coffin and the wall.

Christy bent over the casket, supporting herself with one hand. Peered down the crack. Too dark to see, so she pulled out her cell phone.

The tiny battery icon in the corner of the screen glowed red. She'd have to charge it when she got back. Should have plugged it in last night. She thumbed to the flashlight app and brought the bright screen up to the gap.

Her silver locket lay along the base wall, glinting like a tiny star. Her heart soared.

Shoving her phone into her back pocket, she grabbed the wooden box, found that it was quite light, and tugged it back from the wall several feet. It was strange how finding the little $19.99 piece of jewelry affected her. This was her life, caged in a silver heart: a fake picture.

How lame was that?

Christy hurried around the coffin and stepped behind it to retrieve her necklace. She was already leaning down with her right arm extended when she planted her foot on the wooden floor.

One minute she was reaching for the locket, the next she was falling. Forward and down. Through a trapdoor in the floor.

But it wasn't the initial fall that got Christy. It was her survival instincts.

In that first split second, she knew that she was too far off balance to abort her fall, but she impulsively threw both arms wide anyway, grabbing for the coffin on one side and the wall on the other, hoping to stop herself from going through.

Her head slammed into the wooden trapdoor that had opened under her.

The impact elicited another knee-jerk reaction, this one to save her head. If she hadn't grabbed for her head, she might have stopped her fall.

She free-fell less than a second before landing on hard concrete with her hands and feet first. She grunted and rolled onto her right shoulder, still pushed by adrenaline and the basic call for survival.

The trapdoor slammed shut above her, plunging her onto darkness. She saw it from the corner of her eye halfway through her roll.

Half up and reeling, she crashed into a wall and dropped hard to her seat.

For a brief moment, Christy didn't know how to process what had just happened to her. She'd fallen into a basement or hole of some kind.

Then her brain reengaged and started spinning. Thoughts of sewers and broken bottles and snakes scurried through her mind like frightened mice.

Terror set in and flashed down her spine. Ignoring any thought of what the fall might have done to her bones, she scrambled to her feet and backed against a concrete wall, where she stood frozen by dread.

It was too dark to see. The room smelled stale, dry not wet. Not a sewer. No sound of rats. The silence was as thick as the darkness.

"Hello?"

Only silence answered her.

No light through cracks in the wooden floor above her. Austin said the old hospital had once been a hotel in the early 1900s. Maybe this was a part of the old building. But none of that mattered. She had to get out.

She grabbed her back pocket and felt a stab of gratefulness as her hand closed around the familiar shape of her phone. Thumb and forefinger trembling, she jerked it out and blinked when the screen emerged blazing with light. She'd left the light app on.

Christy turned the screen into the darkness and saw that she was in a square room maybe eight feet to a side. Cinderblock walls rose to the wood floor. A hinged, spring-loaded trapdoor rested shut ten feet above her. The old rusted latch that held it closed was broken. As was the rope that had once been used to pull the panel down like an attic access.

There were several six-inch crates along the far wall, a handful of empty bottles, and scattered sections of newspaper that looked as old as the room. Nothing looked remotely useful. Even if she stacked the crates on their ends, she didn't stand a chance of reaching the trapdoor.

Slowly the nature of her predicament settled into her mind.

Stay calm, Christy. Breathe. It's all a mistake.

But the mistake was that she'd illegally broken into a hospital storage space. For that, she blamed Austin, because Austin didn't know the first thing about following the law like ordinary people.

Fighting back fear and frustration, she tried to think of a way out short of calling for help. Austin was auditing a class at Harvard this morning, and it would take him an hour to reach her. The idea of spending an hour in this dark pit terrified her.

Only then did Christy see the six-foot plank pressed against the wall at floor level. It was held in place by channel irons that ran a good eighteen inches up the wall on both ends, as if the heavy board was designed to be raised. A two-inch eyehook was screwed into the center of the board.

Why someone would build such a device, she didn't care—she only wanted to know if it hid a way out.

She tilted her phone up and saw the pulley bolted into wood where the ceiling met the concrete wall. A rope, long gone, had once been used to pull the plank up.

Hope lit her mind, replaced almost immediately with an image of crawling under the hospital in old ducting overrun with rats. Maybe it would be better to call Austin and wait.

But her battery wouldn't last long, and the thought of waiting in darkness until Austin could get to her was more than unnerving.

She had to move.

Christy stepped over to the board, grabbed the big eyehook, and pulled up. The board budged but was too heavy to move with one hand. So she set her phone on the ground, wrapped both hands around the hook, and tugged.

The heavy plank slid up with grating protest and falling debris on either end. She got her fingers under the wood and dropped to her knees.

An opening just over a foot high and six feet wide gaped to show darkness beyond the board. Too dark to see how deep it ran.

Wedging her knee between the plank and the floor, she reached for her cell phone, shone the light inside, and bent for a better look.

It was a concrete causeway that ran four or five feet in and ended at what looked to be a plywood plank. Maybe a utility room in the basement. That would make sense, right? The room she'd fallen into was probably some kind of abandoned plumbing room or something.

She stared at the opening for a good minute before deciding she would prop the plank open with one of the crates and at least see if the wood on the far side could be pushed out. The passage was dry. No rats. If she got into the basement, she could just exit out of the hospital, come back around for her locket, and be gone as if nothing had happened.

It took her some maneuvering to shove one of the small crates under the plank to brace it open. Sweat had turned the dust on her arms into a brown mess, and the condition of her red blouse would be hard to explain if she got out, but she didn't care.

She had to get out. That was all. Just out.

Christy lay on her belly, cell held tightly in one hand, stared into the opening for a few seconds, and gathered her courage.

You can do this. It's not that small of a space. Just five feet, check that wall, and back out if it's not open. You can do this.

She hesitated.

You have to do this.

She took one last deep breath and scooted forward slowly.

Head to foot, she was just over five feet tall, but with her arm extended she was over six, and she reached the far end with her feet still dangling out next to the crate. The plywood board refused to budge when she pushed with stretched fingers. But she couldn't get enough leverage to apply any real force.

She glanced back, saw nothing had changed, then scooted in farther, so that her head was up next to the board. A harsh shove still produced no movement.

Maybe if she called out, someone on the far side would hear and come to her rescue.

"Hey!"

Her cry filled the small space and sent a shiver down her spine.

"Anyone there? Hey!"

She listened for the slightest sound but could hear only her own pulse. She was alone. Buried under tons of concrete. She had to get out! Back out where she could at least breathe.

In that last moment before retreating to the larger room, Christy gave the wood plank in front of her one last, grunting shove, using all the leverage she could muster, with more frustration than hope it would pop open.

She wasn't aware of her feet moving as her body clawed for the leverage.

Didn't mean to place the sole of her right foot against the crate that supported the plank behind her.

She didn't know she was in danger until the heavy board struck her shoe as the crate slid free.

Christy did what her body told her to do: she jerked her foot out from under the crushing weight. The board dropped to the concrete with a solid thump that echoed through the narrow passage.

She froze. What had just happened?

But she knew very well what had just happened, and she clawed around to get that board back up, bumping the back of her head as she twisted in the tight space.

The next thirty seconds produced a flurry of frantic activity. She tried to dig her fingers under the board, and when her attempt with one hand failed, she dropped the phone and tried with both. Fingernails, fingers, palms, it didn't matter. No effort managed to budge the plank. And none would without much more leverage.

She was sealed inside.

Christy slammed the board with her fists, screaming out for help. But the sound of her voice was trapped in that crushing space with her and only pushed her terror deeper.

She stopped screaming and lay sweating, trying to still herself. She had the light, she had the light...

And then she didn't, because the light on her phone went out, leaving her in utter darkness.

Christy rolled to her back, breathing hard, stabbing the main button with her thumb to get the phone back up. She had to call Austin. She had to. If she couldn't make the call...

The menu came up in dimmed color. Battery-save mode. *Thank you, thank you...*

She had difficulty navigating to the call log because her fingers were shaking, but she managed. Austin Hartt, 4:35 p.m. yesterday. It was now 10:36 a.m. She tapped the screen and brought the phone to her ear.

Ring... Come on, please... Just ring.

It rang.

Pick up, pick up, pick up...

"You've reached me. Do what you do." Click.

Voice mail. *Oh please...*

"Austin..." Her voice sounded like it belonged to someone else. "I'm trapped in your..."

The tone that cut her off might have been a sharp stake that did not stop at her ear. She knew it too well: the descending tone announcing that her phone was now dying.

And then dead.

She dropped her arm to the ground and stared up into pitch darkness, aware of the concrete only inches from her forehead.

No one knew where she was.

No one could hear her.

She was in her grave.

Christy was familiar with panic attacks, but she had never faced the kind of fear that now settled over her like death itself.

She was going to die.

2

SPIKES OF morning light nailed Austin Hartt's eyes shut. His hand fumbled for the stack of books he'd sneaked out of the old hospital the night before. His fingers bumped against his sunglasses. Grabbed them. He slipped them on, swung his legs over the edge of his mattress, and pushed unsteadily to his feet.

The glasses mercifully dimmed the world and he blinked the sleep from his eyes. The digital alarm clock's scream echoed from the countertop across the living room, placed there so he would have to get out of bed to shut it off.

He crossed the floor and slapped the alarm button. 10:26. He'd slept through the alarm and would now be late for ten o'clock class.

Just what he needed.

It hadn't always been this way. Until recently, he'd never set an alarm, never even owned one. He'd simply lie in bed, eyes shut, and repeat seven times what time he wanted to awaken, as if programming his mind. Without fail, his eyes would snap open precisely when he'd decided. Or at least close enough.

That was before the headaches began. The pain meds he now needed to sleep dulled his mind, which he despised. His mind was everything. In every other way he was quite average: average height, average weight, average athleticism.

But his mind set him apart.

I think, therefore I am. The mantra cycled through his thoughts. It was a mental anchor for him, a beam of light that burned through the fog. With each syllable, he rhythmically touched his right thumb to each of the fingertips on his right hand. It was a compulsion, he knew, but it somehow grounded him.

He drew a deep breath, fingers moving. *I think, therefore I am.*

He stood at the window of his fourth-floor apartment and squinted at the thick bruise of clouds festering over Boston. The dull throb thumped at his temples, keeping time with his pulse.

He crossed the living room, sidestepping the twin mattress in the middle of the floor. The pillow lay askew and the blanket was shoved to the foot in a bunched heap. Other than the forty-two-inch flat-panel TV hanging on the wall and a black leather chair he'd bought online, the makeshift bed was the only furniture in the place.

Christy thought it strange that he slept in his living room, but it suited him. When he wasn't in a library or attending a class, he was here in his sanctum, devouring books and thinking. Always thinking.

He'd chosen the two-bedroom loft for its proximity to Harvard, but its open floor plan was the clincher. It was a practical consideration, because he needed every inch of the twelve hundred square feet.

The living room was a yawning space with painted concrete floors and stark white walls, almost monastic in its plainness. Two thick beams rose from the floor and seemed to prop up the entire building. Near the front door, an L-shaped granite countertop hemmed in the small kitchen of stainless-steel appliances that he rarely used, except for the refrigerator, which was stocked mostly with flats of coconut water and Red Bull.

Except for a six-foot-wide passage that connected the rooms, nearly every inch of floor space was occupied by neatly stacked columns of books—thousands of them arranged meticulously by subject. He had read every one, many of them multiple times, from philosophy to religion to advanced scientific theory. The apartment was one part library, one part temple. If he had a religion, it was Knowledge.

The landlord had first refused to rent the space to him. Being only seventeen, Austin couldn't legally sign a contract, she said. His offer to pay the first year's rent up front in cash, however, changed her opinion.

He scanned the room, looking for the prescription bottle.

Where are those pills?

Kitchen.

He plucked a gray T-shirt from a laundry basket on the floor and pulled it on. Rounded the kitchen counter and picked up one of the dozen amber medicine bottles lined up next to the sink. Three left. He emptied the tiny pills into his hand and tossed them back, swallowing them dry.

The headaches had started a month ago. They always began as a niggling pinprick at the front of his skull, like an insect burrowing deep into his brain. Lately, the pain was only bearable with a steady dose of Imitrex. He was supposed to take only one at a time, but two barely made a dent.

Two MRIs, two CT scans, and three doctors later, the headaches hadn't improved. Austin hoped Dr. Bishop would have some answers today.

Why hasn't he called yet?

It had been four days, one day longer than promised. He checked his cell phone. Nothing. Pocketed it. All he could do was wait. Wait and hope his brain wasn't rotting from the inside out.

Austin snatched a Red Bull from the fridge and shrugged into his backpack. Campus was within walking distance, and he could still make the last half of the lecture if he hurried.

With a last look behind him, he pulled the door closed and joined the land of the living with his mantra pushing him forward.

I think, therefore I am.

A LIGHT rain fell as Austin pushed through the twin doors of Abraham Hall and found lecture room A13. The newest addition to the campus was named for the distinguished alumnus who'd recently been considered for a Nobel Peace Prize.

Austin paused at the door, heard the muffled drone of a professor's voice beyond it. He would slip into the room and find a seat in the back, hopefully unnoticed.

He leaned into the door, opening it just enough to pass through the narrow gap, then eased it shut as he entered.

Four tiers of seating, occupied by thirteen students, arced around the room and converged on a small platform at the front.

Dr. Thomas Riley paced slowly at the front, obviously making a point to the class. He glanced up and his eyes met Austin's briefly before the professor continued his talk.

Austin descended the steps to an empty seat two rows from the back, feeling more conspicuous than he liked on his first day in a graduate class, never mind that he was only auditing it.

He'd just slumped into the seat when a loud marimba ringtone cut through the quiet. His phone. He'd forgotten to silence it. The doctor?

Dr. Riley stopped pacing. Several heads turned in his direction.

Austin fished the phone from his pocket, muttering apologies. "Sorry. Sorry."

He looked down at the screen as he thumbed the button to silence the ringer. CHRISTY.

He pressed the button a second time, sending her call to voice mail, and then shoved the phone back in his pocket.

When he faced the platform, all eyes were on him. "Sorry."

A young woman with fat blond curls that fell to her shoulders smiled. He averted his eyes. His face felt hot with embarrassment.

Without missing a beat, Dr. Riley drew the class's attention back to himself.

"As we survey the observable world of phenomena, what is it that truly sets *Homo sapiens* apart from the rest of the animal and plant kingdoms? This is a cornerstone issue, the answer from which rise our personal and communal ethics, our perceptions of life's value, and our own sense of meaning. What is it, then, that comprises our deepest selves and gives us worth?"

He leaned on his podium and waited.

A male student with close-cut dark hair spoke up. "Your question presupposes a position that neither science nor philosophy can afford if it hopes to be objective."

"Which is?"

"That humankind *is* unique and that such a thing as intrinsic worth exists in any absolute sense. Centuries of scientific inquiry have proven that humans are genetically no different from the rest of the animal kingdom. We may be more developed, yes, but that's thanks to billions of years of evolutionary mistakes that, thankfully, worked in our species' favor."

Dr. Riley paced to his right. "Then the universe is a lottery and we've just happened to hit the jackpot."

"If it's helpful to think in those terms, yes," the student said. "The universe is a harsh place and we just happen to be at the top of the food chain. For now."

An agitated young woman in the third row lifted her hand. "I couldn't disagree more. It's precisely that line of thinking that has been used to justify mass genocide and a whole host of other atrocities throughout human history. What makes us human isn't simply a matter of genetic coding or our dominion over lesser forms of life."

"Then what does?" the professor asked.

"Our ability to love. Compassion. Our yearning to feel, to inspire and be inspired, to admire beauty and creativity—those make us human. We are the only species with a soul, and the only one that seeks transcendent meaning."

"Those are all evolutionary developments we've used to our advantage," the male student said. "Religious myths, creativity, beauty—all of those exist only because they serve our long-term survival. The truth is, we're little more than carbon and water, no more valuable to the universe than a clod of dirt. We think we're important because we want to be."

"Said the Ivy League grad student," she replied. "I wonder how valuable you'd think life is if someone had a gun to your head."

Austin scooted forward in his seat.

Irritated, the man began to speak but Dr. Riley cut him off. "Interesting points, and passionate. I like that." The professor shifted his eyes and looked at Austin. "Mr. Hartt? What would you say?"

Austin felt his palms go clammy. He swallowed.

"What makes us human?"

"Yes. Speak up, please."

Austin cleared his throat. Given the choice between being with books or people, he'd always choose books. You could always tell what a book thought without needing to have a confrontation. People, on the other hand, defensively clung to their need to be right no matter how flawed their thinking.

"Consciousness enabled by our particularly well-developed brains is what sets us apart," he managed. He continued with a little more confidence. "*Homo sapiens* have a uniquely evolved neocortex, prefrontal cortex, and temporal lobes that make us capable of abstract thought, language, problem solving, and introspection."

"Our awareness makes us human then?"

"No. It's not simply a matter of passive awareness. Even slugs and plants have a level of sentience. It's our ability to harness the power of our minds to gather knowledge, organize it into something relevant, and advance to a more evolved state. Our thoughts are the gateway. We think, therefore we are."

"And how can we trust our thoughts?"

"It's a matter of intelligence and careful observation. You said yourself that ours is a universe of observable phenomena. The only barrier to apprehending the truth is our own unwillingness to see the world as it is instead of how we prefer it to be."

The professor's lips nudged into a smile. "Perhaps. Well said, Mr. Hartt." He turned toward the class. "Our time's up today. For next class, please read chapters twenty through forty-five. And"—he glanced up at Austin—"be sure to arrive on time for the discussion."

Austin nodded as he stood.

"Mr. Hartt, a word with you please?" Dr. Riley said, stuffing his papers into a leather briefcase as the class filed out of the room.

Austin approached the platform. "I'm sorry about the phone."

The professor waved off his apology. "No need. I'm just pleased you're attending my class." He stared at Austin's sunglasses. "Are you feeling all right? It's a cloudy day, you know."

"Yes sir. I know. Migraines."

"I see. I've heard quite a bit about you."

"Heard about me, sir?"

"A colleague of mine, Dr. John Ferriss, spoke highly of you."

"I sat in his quantum theory class at MIT last semester."

"You made quite the impression. He said you're the most gifted mind he's seen in a long time."

"He's the one who suggested your class."

The professor smiled. "I had to see for myself. So tell me, what kind of young man with a GED and perfect SAT scores audits quantum theory at MIT and graduate-level philosophy at Harvard?"

"A curious one, I guess."

"Young man, you have the kind of gift this world needs. I'd like to help you develop that gift. Assuming you're interested."

"Help me how?"

"Attend Harvard as a full-time student. I can see to it that finances aren't an issue. I'll make sure a course of study is designed for you that will unlock your full potential. You can't waste this gift, Austin. Minds like yours come along but once in a generation."

"Thank you, sir. I don't know what to say."

"Start by saying yes, or at least think about it. You don't have to decide today."

"Okay. Thank you," he said, feeling self-conscious for the awkward way the words came out. "Thank you."

The professor handed a business card to Austin. "Call my office and we'll schedule a time to meet. All right?"

"Yes sir."

"Good." He pointed to Austin's pocket. "You should get back to whoever was calling you."

"Right. Thank you, sir." He shouldered his backpack as he walked up the stairs.

Attending Harvard officially? He smiled at the thought and pulled out his phone.

Austin pushed the voice mail button then pressed it to his ear.

"Austin… I'm trapped in your…"

The frantic sound of Christy's voice was cut short. Was that the whole message? Two seconds? Strange. He listened a second time. Her voice seemed distant, hollow, like she was in a bathroom. Or a tunnel.

Christy was always the emotional type, but she'd never left such an urgent message.

He quickly pressed the call-back button and waited for her to pick up, but her phone went straight to voice mail.

Something was wrong.

Trapped in your… His what?

His phone suddenly vibrated and he glanced at the screen, thinking it was her.

Dr. Bishop. A prick of dread needled the back of his mind.

He took a short breath and answered. "Hello?"

"Austin Hartt?"

"Yes."

"This is Melinda at Dr. Bishop's office. I'm calling because your MRI test results came back." A beat. "The doctor would like to meet with you as soon as possible to review them."

There was concern in the woman's voice. He could hear it through her practiced professional monotone.

"Is there a problem?"

"I'm not qualified to discuss that information with you. Dr. Bishop would like to go through the test results with you himself. Are you available today?"

The needle in his mind pushed deeper. The only thing he could think was *tumor.* There could be nothing worse. Just last night he'd read the case study of a physicist in Switzerland who'd been diagnosed with an inoperable tumor. It had ravaged his brain in a matter of months.

"Mr. Hartt?"

"I'm sorry, I'm here. Of course I can meet with him today. When?"

"His last appointment just canceled. I can slot you in, but you'll need to come within the next forty-five minutes. Otherwise we'll need to schedule two weeks out when the doctor returns from vacation."

His heart pounded like a fist against his ribcage. Something wasn't right, not just with him. Christy's call gnawed at him.

"Can you make it in the next forty-five minutes?"

"I'll be there."

BREATHE. *Just breathe, Christy. Close your eyes and breathe.*

How many times had she told herself that in the last half hour? She was trying to trick her mind into thinking the thick fog of fear would lift. That light would suddenly stream into the darkness in the form of a flashlight held by Austin, who had come to her rescue.

But she kept remembering that it was only a trick. In reality, light wasn't going to come. She really *was* trapped in a grave of her own making. She didn't even know if her short call to Austin had gone through.

Her head was bruised from banging it on the concrete ceiling during a particularly bad panic attack. She'd tried to kick out both ends of the grave more times than she could remember. Her body was soaked in sweat.

Christy now lay on her back, feeling another wave of fear wash through her body from head to toe, as if it was the breath of death itself. Her mind spun through memories of the last four years, the only ones she had.

She couldn't remember her first week at the Saint Francis Orphanage. The first month was mostly a haze. They told her that she'd been picked up wandering the streets without any identification. The nuns and the counselor who cared for her and the other eleven children, most of whom were younger than she, were kind and affectionate and repeatedly assured her that her condition wasn't so unusual. Clearly, she'd faced some kind of trauma, but knowing its nature wouldn't necessarily ease her passage into a well-adjusted life.

She'd formed a bond with Austin in her third month, after learning that he, too, suffered from amnesia. Being the consummate cerebral junkie, he dismissed his past as an aberration that had no bearing on his future. He gave it no more attention than a shrug. She, on the other hand, obsessed over her identity, which only made her more insecure.

In her grave now, she wondered if this particular death was her karmic obligation. Maybe this was how she was supposed to die.

The fear riding her breath began to descend into that familiar space that spawned panic attacks. The thought that she might suffer even deeper terror than she already had shifted her emotions.

Anger welled up in her gut. Anger at her parents, whoever they were. Anger at herself for being so weak. Anger at the anger itself.

And then it wasn't just anger… It was rage.

Without thinking, she swiveled on her backside, screaming full-throated, eyes shut tight in the darkness. She slammed her heels against the plywood barrier with every reserve of strength her legs still possessed. Then again, fists clenched, not because she had any illusion of breaking what she'd failed to break before, but because she could.

And still again, and again, using her heels, not caring if she bruised herself or scraped her back on the hard floor.

Something popped on the seventh or eighth strike. At first she thought it was one of her bones. But it wasn't.

The wood?

Christy jerked up and hit her head again, but the thought of getting out overrode the pain. She twisted and saw dim light outlining the long, thin panel that had sealed her in.

She kicked again, frantic to be out. The bottom of the door popped open several inches before striking something that blocked it from the other side. But that something had moved as well, filling her grave with a distinct scraping sound.

She scooted her butt closer for more leverage and pushed out again. This time whatever was blocking the exit slid noisily and the plywood swung up and open on hinges behind a row of large steel drums. Fresh air flooded the small space.

She blinked. She'd broken through!

Scooting feetfirst, she placed her heels on one of the drums and shoved it into the room beyond, then slid around and crawled out the same way she'd first entered—like a crab, this time scuttling for her very life, hardly aware of the tearing sound of her blouse as it caught a sharp edge and tore right down the back.

The moment she cleared the door, she clambered to her feet, panting. The door dropped shut behind her.

Free.

Christy spun and saw the plywood door that had resisted her kicking for so long. The screws that had anchored a sliding lock on either end had popped out of the concrete. Each of the large metal drums was stenciled with red letters: ST. MATTHEW'S.

She didn't care what it all was for, only that she had escaped with just a few scrapes and bruises.

She turned and took in what appeared to be an old boiler room, judging by the large hot-water tanks and labyrinth of pipes along the unpainted concrete walls. It was old but still in use by the looks of it. She must be in the basement of the hospital. The door from the boiler room was closed to her right.

Her course now was plain. She would cover her tracks here, exit through the hospital, return to the storage room for her locket, and put the whole incident behind her as if it had never happened.

She quickly shoved the drums back into place to cover the door and its broken latches.

Christy crossed to the door, found it unlocked, and pushed her way through. She was halfway to a door topped by a sign that read STAIRS before any thought of her appearance entered her mind. She glanced down.

Sweat mixed with dust stained every inch of her shirt, not to mention the large tear in back. Walking down a hospital corridor looking like she'd crawled through a sewer wouldn't go unnoticed. Her face must also be a mess. Maybe she could clean herself up in a bathroom.

She hurried to the first of two doors on her right and peered through a small glass window. Inside, stacks of linens and a sink. A laundry? She pushed the door open and stepped in.

Five stacked washers and dryers hugged one wall; the other was lined with racks of neatly folded uniforms, towels, and linens. Several bulging cloth laundry bins beside the washers awaited processing.

It took her less than a minute to strip out of her filthy, torn blouse, discard it in a waste can, and shrug into a light blue smock from one of the bins. Her blue jeans had fared better than her shirt, and a damp washcloth made quick work of the dirt on her knees.

She cleaned her hands and arms in one of the two sinks, then her face. Did her best to fix her hair. A bruise darkened her forehead—her bangs hid the worst of it. What a mess.

She stepped back and looked at herself in the mirror above the sink. For a few seconds her mind, however relieved at having escaped such a harrowing ordeal, took time to notice her imperfections.

A red pimple on her right cheek had tenaciously resisted the acne medication she'd applied over the past three days. Her neck was fat and her nose too stubby. She'd left her flat without a trace of makeup.

Austin had once said that her obsession with body image was patently absurd. How could anyone have fingers that were too short? They worked, didn't they? And long nails only got in the way. Better to chew them off.

What did a left-brained male who'd yet to open the cover of *Cosmopolitan* know about body image anyway? She was too fat, plain and simple. Ten pounds might as well be the weight of the world. He could never understand that.

Christy turned from the mirror feeling disgusted. And foolish for feeling disgusted. Maybe Austin was right; maybe she really was a basket case.

At least she wouldn't stand out like a street urchin now.

She entered the stairwell and took the steps at a run, mind on her locket.

The stairs emptied into a short, vacant hallway. The distant sound of voices reached her. She crossed to a large door operated by a crash bar and pushed into what looked like a standard hospital corridor. A glance in either direction revealed no exit sign.

An older female patient with wispy gray hair, wearing a smock similar to the one Christy now wore, ambled toward her aided by a squeaky walker. Beyond her, the hall ended at a sign that read ADMINISTRATOR.

"Don't you worry, honey," the patient said, smiling toothless, "just stay away from the Froot Loops. They're poison. Rot your teeth right out of your head."

Christy gave the woman a slow nod. "Can you tell me where the exit is?"

The woman stopped in the middle of the hallway and stared at her as if she hadn't heard. "You drink coffee?" she said. "Cause it'll rot your gut and give you gas." She paused. "I got gas right now." She proved it without breaking eye contact.

Clearly no help. Christy turned to her right and headed to the far end of the hall, which jogged left toward what was hopefully the exit.

Twenty feet ahead, across the hall, a door swung open and a man with brown hair and square glasses, wearing a white doctor's coat, stepped out of a door marked ADMISSIONS. He led a young patient out by her arm. Blue smock with name tag: ALICE RINGWALD. Shoulder-length dirty blond hair hung around her apprehensive face. The girl's eyes met Christy's for a brief moment before Christy looked down.

She angled across the hall and walked past them, keeping her attention averted, hoping she didn't look out of place in her jeans.

She'd never spent time in a hospital herself—only visited twice, once with Austin when he'd gone for an MRI. Her own self-consciousness seemed absurd in a place like this. Her heart went out to the young girl, who was probably contending with testing and procedures and questions of life and death.

All while Christy worried about a single pimple on her cheek.

The sound of a door opening behind made her wonder where the man in white was taking the girl. She glanced over her shoulder and saw them step through the same door she'd just exited.

"Can I help you?"

Christy jerked her head around and pulled up sharply, three feet from a nurse who stood in her path, clipboard in hand. The door beside the woman whispered shut.

"No, I'm good." She started forward.

"You sure?" The nurse, Linda Roper by the brass badge on her red blouse, took in Christy's jeans.

"I was just leaving."

"Leaving?"

"I was just visiting." Christy looked down the hall. "That way, right? I got a bit turned around."

The nurse smiled. "Don't we all? We don't have visiting hours in here, dear. That's what the lounge is for, Britney."

Christy glanced down at the name tag on her blue smock. How was she going to explain this without looking like a fool? She was busted, pure and simple.

She smiled apologetically. "It's not mine. I…" What was she supposed to say? She couldn't think of anything but the truth. Kind of.

"I got lost and ended up in the basement. My shirt ripped and I found this shirt down in the laundry."

The nurse studied her as if trying to decide if she would buy such an unlikely story.

"Crazy, I know, but I'm not stealing it. I swear, if you have anything else I could wear... I just didn't know what else to do."

"It's okay, dear. Crazy things happen to the best of us." She stepped forward, gently rested her hand on Christy's elbow, and turned her back the way she'd come. "Come with me."

Christy turned with the woman. "Can I just bring it back? I don't live far; I swear I'll bring it right back."

"Of course. But it's property of Saint Matthew's psychiatric ward. I wish I could let you leave with it, but I can't. We'll find you something more appropriate."

"You have something?"

"I think we can find something."

Good. It was all going to work out. She'd left the storage room unlocked. What was the chance that some bum would get in there before she could retrieve her locket? Her mind spun through the possibilities as they headed down the hall.

The nurse led her into the administrator's office and nodded at the receptionist, who sat filing her nails behind a desk.

"Can you pull up a file for me, Beverly?"

The receptionist glanced at Christy's smock. "Sure."

"Status of Britney Hunt?"

The receptionist set her file down, brought her long nails to the keyboard, and clacked away.

"That's not me," Christy said. "I'm just wearing the shirt."

"We just need to check on her status, dear," the nurse said. "Protocol. Patients tend to misplace themselves, you understand."

She didn't, not really. She was in a psychiatric ward. Images of the two patients she'd seen earlier now made more sense. They also quickened her need to put this all behind her.

"Britney Hunt is in 401." She picked up her phone. "I'll have the station attendant check her room."

"Thanks, Bev." To Christy: "What's your name again?"

"Christy," she said. "Snow."

"Driver's license?"

Christy blinked. She'd left her purse at home.

"Not on me."

"No?" Linda nodded at the receptionist. "Anything on a Christy Snow?"

Clack, clack, clack.

"No Christy Snow."

"Of course not," Christy said. "Do you have anything else I can wear? I feel a bit stupid in this shirt now." She felt her face flush.

"As soon as we check. I'm sure it'll all be fine, but we simply need to run some checks. If you had your license this would be quicker. Any other identification?"

Her cell phone. It had her name on it.

"My cell phone?"

"Might help."

Christy brought her hand to her back pocket. No phone. Her heart spiked. She'd left it in the space under the foundation.

"I..." She hesitated, thinking she should just tell them the whole story. But she would also have to explain why and how she'd broken into the storage room.

"No?"

"Well... I, no. I must have lost it when I..." She couldn't quite bring herself to betray Austin's secret.

"That's okay," the nurse said. "I'll tell you what. Why don't you just explain this to the administrator."

She addressed the receptionist. "Is Kern available?"

The receptionist made a quick call, then hung up the phone.

"Go on in."

Christy's mind was reeling as she followed the nurse around the receptionist's desk into an office with a golden placard that read ADMINISTRATOR. The way she saw it, she had no choice but to tell all now. And there was no reason why she had to bring Austin into it. They would probably lock the storage room up tight, but she saw no other way.

The administrator sat behind a large, shiny wooden desk, scanning the contents of a file through narrow reading glasses. His eyes glanced over the wire frames for a moment, then back down to his file.

"I'll be right with you."

Dressed in a dark blue suit with white shirt and red tie. His finger traced what he was reading as Christy sat in one of the two stuffed chairs facing his desk. Books lined the case behind him, most of them psychology journals and textbooks. A family portrait, which showed him with his wife and a young adolescent boy, sat on the desk.

Kern Lawson, Administrator. She looked up from the nameplate at the edge of the desk and met his light-blue eyes as he set the file down and sat up.

"So. What seems to be the problem"—his eyes darted to her smock—"Britney?"

"Apparently she's not Britney," the nurse said. "We're checking now."

The administrator's phone rang and he scooped it up. He listened for a moment before thanking his receptionist and hanging up.

"And apparently she's right," Lawson said with a kind smile. "Britney Hunt is in her room. So that would make you...?"

"Christy Snow," she said.

"I have to get back to my rounds," the nurse said.

"Thank you, Linda." The administrator dismissed her with a nod and folded his hands under his chin.

"Christy Snow. You're new here?"

"No, I'm not here at all!"

"You're not?"

"I mean I'm not supposed to be here."

"And where are you supposed to be?"

"At home, where I was this morning, on Blanard Drive. I came in this morning, trying to find my locket, and I got stuck…"

The look in his eyes said he'd heard a thousand similar stories from patients looking for a way out. She had to tell him everything. He would check the basement, find that she was telling the truth, and that would be that.

"Look," he said before she could speak. "This isn't rocket science. If you are Christy Snow and we have no record of your admission, then you can be home within the hour. But we have to know; I'm sure you can appreciate that. Many of our patients have very deep imaginations."

"There's no record of a Christy Snow in admissions. They already checked. Please, this is a bit ridiculous."

"Yes, of course. Still, you have no identification, I take it?"

"Not on me, no. But you'll find my cell phone in the basement."

"All right. Do you mind telling me how you came to be in the basement?"

She swallowed, nodding. So here it went.

"I lost my locket last night."

"Your locket?" he made a note of it on a scratch pad. "Where?"

"In the storage room. Off the alley."

Lawson peered at her. He set his pen down and sat back, crossing his legs.

"Go on."

She told him everything, from the time she woke up until the time she entered the main corridor, sparing no detail.

"So, yes, I probably broke the law by breaking into the storage room, but I can assure you that I'm not a patient here. I just want my cell phone and locket, and if you want to report my crime to the police, that's fine. Either way, I don't belong here."

He nodded, jotting down more notes. "Don't worry, I have no interest in your breaking in. I wasn't aware there was a trapdoor under those caskets. We'll have to take care of it."

She exhaled, letting her anxiousness fall away. "Someone could get hurt. I could probably sue the hospital." She thought better of it. "Course, I won't. I just want my locket back. That's all."

"I understand. I'll have to check this out, naturally. You can see how this could look differently."

"Not really, no. How?"

He shrugged. "For all I know, you're a recent admission whose name is Jane Doe and you found a clever way to attempt an escape. Failing, you returned with a clever story—it's not unheard of. This is, after all, the psychiatric ward. All kinds come to us and many are quite intelligent."

She thought about it and saw his point.

"Then check it out. You'll find the entrance I told you about, and inside, my phone. Christy Snow, cell number 555-7897. I live at 456 Blanard Drive. Trust me, that's me."

"I'm sure it is. Procedure requires that I account for all patients to make sure no one is missing. When that comes up whole and we check out the basement, you'll be free to go. Shouldn't take too long. Fair enough?"

She thought about it and again saw the reason in his being thorough.

"I suppose. Can you please have them bring me my locket as well?"

"Sure. Can you describe it?"

"A silver heart."

"Photograph inside?"

"Yes."

"Of? Boyfriend? Parents? Maybe they could help us out here."

"No. Nothing like that."

"Then what?" he asked. "It would help us identify the locket as yours."

She hesitated. The standard picture had the small words *Sample Only* printed on the side of the image.

"It's just the picture the locket came with. I don't have any parents."

Dr. Lawson looked at her with kind eyes for a few seconds.

"I see. Not knowing who your parents are can mess with your identity. An all too common phenomenon these days, but in reality, most people have no idea who they really are. Do you know who you are, Christy?"

The question threw her into a momentary tailspin. A part of her wanted to tell him everything about herself—maybe he could help her. But she put the compulsion aside and took a calming breath.

"I'm Christy Snow. I live at 456 Blanard Drive, and I need to get home to feed my cat."

He smiled. "All right. I'll get you home. You can wait in our lounge while we run a quick inventory and check out your story."

AUSTIN HESITATED as he approached the alleyway. Glanced at his watch. *Thirty-two minutes.* It'd taken longer than he hoped to get here, but there was time.

He'd decided to check the storage room because it was, one, on his way to his doctor's office in the hospital and, two, a logical context for her urgent call.

He'd eliminated his apartment quickly. Or hers for that matter. It was possible she'd hurt herself and couldn't reach a landline or cry out for a passerby's attention, but highly unlikely.

Given the fact that they'd been at the storage room last night, and its relative isolation, he would at least check. That her message had been cut off midsentence concerned him the most. Probably a dead battery, but what if someone had taken the phone from her?

If there was one person that he identified with, it was Christy. They were about as similar as fish and fowl, but they were both loners and they shared a similar history.

Truth was, he found her emotional approach to life more interesting than annoying. She was one person he honestly felt he could help. The fact that she was attractive didn't hurt. The thought of harm coming to her unnerved him as much as the thought of the tumor in his head. Assuming he had a tumor.

He looked down the street.

Saint Matthew's Hospital was in sight, just two blocks away. The sprawling complex rose above the madness of city life. The austerity of its modern steel-and-glass exterior was simple but impressive, an architectural citadel of reason that gazed upon the world with detached indifference. Inside, the finest minds in medical science relentlessly pursued empirical facts.

Like Austin, they valued data above all else—radically impersonal and objective answers, however harsh they turned out to be.

He could attest to that himself.

Fact: His headaches had become more intense and frequent in the past seventeen days, and meds had a decreasing impact on his symptoms. Likely the result of a tumor forming beneath his skull, but that wasn't yet fact.

Fact: All diagnostic tests had been inconclusive until now, but inside in his doctor's office sat a man about to tell him if he was going to live or die.

Fact: Christy had called him, but he didn't yet know why.

He veered left, leaving the sidewalk, and entered the alley that separated the shops from the hospital.

"Austin… I'm trapped in your…"

The desperate sound of her voice hung in his mind. He passed the dumpsters and angled for the door.

With each step the pain in his head grew worse. How long had it been since his last meds? An hour? The intensity was likely psychosomatic, a result of obsessing about his test results. Put under continued stress, the mind could create physical conditions within the body to match the thought patterns—a sort of self-fulfilling prophecy.

Screw it.

He stuck his hand into his jeans pocket and withdrew two pills, which he didn't bother bagging anymore, then swallowed them.

He pulled up in front of the old battered door and fingered the crack where he kept the makeshift key.

Gone?

He peered into the crack, suddenly alarmed. Christy was the only other person who knew where the key was.

Austin reached the door and tested the knob. It twisted easily in his hand. He leaned into the door and pushed into the cold room. It fell shut behind him.

Austin scanned the room. The light was on. He was meticulous about shutting it off every time he left. Someone was here, or had been.

"Christy?"

His voice echoed.

A swirl of dust motes orbited the light bulb overhead. No sign that anything had been disturbed, except for...

The stack of caskets beside the far wall drew his attention. The one Christy sat on last night had been moved. However stoic he might be, logic didn't preclude the sudden rise in his concern.

Austin slowly approached and leaned over the coffin, half expecting to see the worst. Nothing but a wooden floor. And a piece of jewelry he could hardly mistake.

He reached down and plucked the object from the floor. Christy's locket.

Austin held it in front of him. The small heart dangled from the thin silver chain and swung under his hand. She must've dropped it last night and come back for it. So then, where was she?

He looked again and only then noticed the hairline seam in the floor.

Setting the locket down, he knelt behind the casket and traced the splintered boards with his finger. A trapdoor?

His mind cycled through the scenarios. It was possible that she had fallen through, but into what? What was below? He'd never moved the caskets before.

He braced one hand at the edge of the trapdoor and, with the other, gave the floor a sturdy shove. It opened downward. Spring-loaded.

He leaned close, careful not to fall forward.

"Christy?"

His voice disappeared into the smudge of shadows below.

Again he called her name, this time louder.

Silence.

She could've been trapped or might be lying injured in the darkness. Unconscious.

He pulled his hand away and the door snapped back into place. He had to assume that she'd gone down. He also had to assume she was hurt. Or worse.

Moving with urgency now, Austin hurried to the corner of the room where an old wooden extension ladder leaned against the wall behind the cluster of IV stands. He could use it to prop open one side of the trapdoor and climb down, assuming the old ladder wasn't rotted through.

It took him less than a minute to haul it over to the trapdoor, shove it down and through to prop the door open, and descend carefully, testing each rung as he lowered himself to the floor below.

Light filtered in from above and illuminated the small concrete room around him. It was some sort of abandoned storage room. No sign of Christy.

He dug his apartment key out of his pocket and thumbed the attached penlight with RadioShack logo. He'd purchased this two years ago and never used it. Still worked.

"Christy?" He walked to his right, sweeping the bluish-white circle of light from one side to the other. Crates of dust-covered bottles. Scattered newspapers. To his left, a large timber with an eyehook on it—a sliding door to a storage compartment maybe. Christy wasn't here but someone had been recently: prints covered the dusty concrete.

He peeled one of the old newspapers off the ground.

December 18, 1923. A paper from the Prohibition era. The old hospital had been a hotel then. Someone had built this room to store and move illegal moonshine.

His light zeroed in on the thick sliding timber in the wall. A way to pass illegal alcohol in and out of the building.

He tilted his light down at the base of the wall. One of the bottle trays lay beside the tracks on the floor.

The thought that he might miss his appointment hardly mattered to him in light of the unfolding evidence. If she'd fallen in, she'd also managed to get out, and the only way he could see was past that board.

Austin held the light between his teeth, squatted, and gripped the bottom of the plank. It slid open with some effort, but it wasn't terribly heavy. Christy could've managed.

He nudged the crate into the gap with his foot and lowered the beam, wedging the crate between it and the floor.

He shone his light inside what appeared to be a crawlspace that connected this room to another. The far end of it was covered by plywood. A sliver of light edged its perimeter. A way out. But it was the cell phone on the concrete floor inside that snagged Austin's attention.

Christy's. The yellow case was plain enough.

He reached in and grabbed the phone. Pressed the power button. Dead. But why leave it behind?

It had been a long while since Austin felt the kind of concern that swept through him as he considered the possibilities.

He crammed her phone into his pocket and crawled inside, moving as quickly as the low ceiling would allow. She'd probably made the frantic call from here before managing to kick her way out the other end.

At the far side he shoved the plywood into something that blocked its path. Another grunting shove and the wood slid, pushing several large barrels out of its way as it opened.

Another worry crossed his mind as he pushed the drums aside and stood. Someone had taken the time to slide the drums back in place. Christy, trying to cover her tracks? If so, why?

He stood in a boiler room, no doubt belonging to Saint Matthew's Hospital. Rows of thick pipes hugged the left wall and ceiling.

If she made it this far she'd probably found her way to the main lobby and was already on her way home. But why hadn't she returned for her locket or her phone?

He looked at his watch. Already late. Dr. Bishop was as punctual as they got. Austin would have to rebook the appointment.

He stepped toward the exit, hitting dial on his phone as he moved. The call connected to voice mail. He left a quick message saying he'd been delayed and would like to rebook as soon as possible.

Pocketing his phone, he slipped out of the boiler room and headed for the exit sign. He surged forward, passing beneath banks of fluorescent lights that buzzed in the ceiling.

He'd reached the exit, taken one step into the stairwell, and was already releasing the door when he heard the distant but unmistakable sound of a woman's voice speaking urgently enough to stop him. A male voice rumbled through the walls, just barely audible. Again, fairly urgent.

For a moment his mind spun through a reasoning cycle that led him to the thought that this might be Christy. She hadn't returned for her locket. She hadn't called from a landline to say she was all right. She'd essentially broken into a hospital.

She was being detained?

He left the stairwell, eased the door shut, and crossed to the other side of the hall, letting the speakers lead him. The exchange became less urgent. The voices were coming from beyond the last door on his right. SUPPLIES, a black plastic sign read in print and braille.

He leaned close to the door and listened.

The girl's voice came again. She was crying?

42

Austin twisted the knob quietly and slipped inside.

To his left, large gray cabinets lined two walls. A squat metal desk was shoved against the third. A single banker's lamp, the only light in the room, cast an amber halo across the tabletop. Straight ahead, the room faded to a patchwork of shadows and a drawn curtain that hung from a track in the ceiling.

"And if I say yes?" He could hear the girl's soft words clearly now, just beyond the curtain. It wasn't Christy's.

"I'll let you out," a gentle male voice said.

"I already know the way out. I've been there. I've seen it. I know."

"You've seen nothing, Alice."

"I've been there. I've seen it. I will get out."

"Not unless I allow it, which I won't. I just explained the rules. Or weren't you listening?"

"I don't care about your rules."

"Then you'll suffer."

"I'm used to it," she said.

Austin felt his heart rate surge as the low voice chuckled. The old hospital was now a pysch ward. All he could think was that he was overhearing some craziness between two patients. It wasn't Christy—he should just leave.

And he was about to, but what the man said next stopped him cold.

"If I say you'll suffer, you will, make no mistake."

Austin turned toward the curtain, reacting only to that part of him that overrode common sense. This wasn't his business. Christy was. This wasn't Christy. Therapists had their ways… this might just be one of them. A good one, for all he knew. Mental illness sometimes brought cycles of suffering that could only be broken through atypical therapy. Was he a psychotherapist? No.

But none of that held him back. He approached the curtain carefully, walking as if the floor was made of cracked glass. They'd stopped talking.

He turned his head and listened intently. One second stretched into five. A faint ripping sound. What, he had no idea.

Leave, Austin. Find Christy.

The movement of the curtain being swept open on its tracks sealed his course.

Austin jerked back and blinked as light stuttered to life overhead. A man in a white coat stood before him, regarding Austin without expression.

Austin took him in with a single glance.

He was tall, six-two, with close-cropped hair. Brown. Sure eyes stared through black-rimmed glasses that perched high on his angular nose. His facial features were chiseled and square. He was meticulously groomed from his starched white dress shirt and perfectly Windsor-knotted crimson tie to his pleated gray slacks, the hem of which fell perfectly to the top of his coal black shoes. A badge with his picture and name clung to the lapel of his white lab coat.

DOUGLAS FISHER, it read. Below his name: ADMISSIONS DIRECTOR.

Austin drew a breath and tried to calm his startled heart.

"Lost?" the man said calmly.

Austin searched for the right response. Nothing presented itself, so he just said, "Yeah."

For a long time the man looked at him like someone watching a common animal in a zoo. There was nothing threatening about Douglas Fisher, nothing that seemed out of place. Only the exchange that Austin had overheard.

A smile slowly formed on Fisher's face. "You strike me as the kind of person who thinks he knows what he doesn't."

"No, not really. I'm looking for a friend who's missing."

"I see. And what would your name be?"

His mind spun, but he saw no reason not to answer. "Austin."

"Austin?"

"Hartt."

"Austin Hartt. That's strange. I don't think I know you. Being the Director of Admissions, I should at least be aware of everyone in our care. But I don't recall an Austin Hartt." He paused. "And you say you're looking for a friend who's missing?"

His own predicament settled into his mind. He wasn't exactly eager to explain his path of entry. Giving his name had been a mistake.

"Yes, but I must have taken a wrong turn and wandered into the ward. She's probably in the main hospital. I'm sorry, I didn't mean to cause any trouble."

"No, I'm sure you didn't. Strange how easy it is to miss the right door." The man's smile said he was congenial but the circumstances weren't adding up. Fisher must know that Austin had overheard part of their conversation. And yet he seemed unworried, which could only mean that what Austin had overheard presented no problem for Fisher.

He shrugged. "True. I should be going," he said, and as he spoke, he glanced past the man. A white porcelain sink with exposed plumbing was bolted to the wall. A wooden stand in the corner next to it. A bar of soap, a glass with a toothbrush sticking out. A six-inch handheld mirror, resting against the corner.

In the mirror: An image of a girl with brown eyes and dirty blond hair sitting on what appeared to be a gurney, staring directly at the mirror, seemingly unconcerned.

There was gray duct tape over her mouth.

Austin's eyes flickered back to the director of admissions, who'd turned his head and was looking at the same mirror.

Fisher faced him, one eyebrow cocked. For a moment, they stood still. Then the man took one step toward the sink, retrieved the mirror, and returned. He lifted it and looked at his own image. Stroked his chin as if checking his shave.

"Interesting things, mirrors," he said. "You see something that isn't real. It's only reflective glass, and yet it reveals something entirely new."

Austin was telling himself that he should run, but the man was so calm—so precise and reasoned in his demeanor—that Austin found himself caught off guard.

Fisher flipped the mirror around so that it faced Austin. "What do you see?"

All he could think was: *I just saw a girl with duct tape on her face. I've just stumbled into something horrific and I don't know what to do.*

"Hmm? Your face, right? But the mind easily deceives itself." He set the mirror on top of a cardboard box to his right, lifted his hand, and motioned *come* to his right without removing his eyes from Austin.

"You think you saw something in the mirror that took the red out of your face," Fisher said, still relaxed.

The girl stepped into view and stood beside Fisher. Maybe seventeen or eighteen. There was no duct tape on her face.

"And yet the tape was there, just a few seconds ago." He looked down at the girl and smiled kindly. "Wasn't it, Alice?"

She kept her eyes on Austin and slowly nodded. No expression.

A wadded up ball of tape slipped from her fingers and plopped on the floor. She'd taken the tape off herself.

"Go sit down, Alice," Fisher said.

She turned and retraced her steps.

"You see, Mr. Hartt, we employ some rather unusual therapies at Saint Matthew's. Very effective, I might add. We take some of the hardest cases and produce results other facilities only dream of."

"I can see that."

"Can you?"

"Sure." Half of him couldn't, but the other side knew that science had few limitations, if any.

"Then feel free to see yourself out. The stairs are just down the hall.

If you run into any trouble just follow the exit signs. They'll lead you out to the main hospital."

His mind still trying to makes sense of what he'd seen, Austin gave the man a short nod, backed up a step, and turned toward the door.

By the time Austin saw the man's sudden move in his peripheral vision, it was too late to avoid him. A fist crashed against the side of his head with the force of a sledgehammer.

Austin's head snapped sideways, and his legs collapsed beneath him. He crumpled to the ground. Thick shadows swirled and crowded the edge of his sight.

He felt a sharp kick in his side. The force rolled him flat on his back.

Austin's eyes fluttered as Fisher stood over him, then the world grew dim as he felt himself being dragged across the floor.

The girl said something but her voice faded, replaced by a high-pitched ringing that he was sure would kill him.

Austin felt a sharp sting in the crook of his arm and a warm sensation rushed through his body.

His eyes drifted closed, and he surrendered to the darkness.

THE LOUNGE they'd led Christy to while they cleared up the confusion was located near the administrator's office. It was a typical waiting room with two groupings of blue cushioned folding chairs set around oak coffee tables, several large ficus plants, magazines, and a counter that offered coffee and water.

The round white clock on the wall had clicked off forty-three painful minutes, and still, no one had come for her. Why everything concerning doctors took so long, she would never understand.

One of two doors led into the administrator's reception room, where Christy had met Beverly, Kern Lawson's secretary. The other led into what appeared to be a larger patient lounge or recreation room.

She knew this because she'd opened it, poked her head through the door, and looked around the room for a full minute before retreating to the relative security of the lounge.

There had been about a dozen patients in the room, half gathered around a television, the rest either sitting at one of the tables playing games, or seated alone, some still, some repeating obsessive behavior. All wore blue smocks.

She'd watched Linda, the nurse who'd found her, talking quietly to a woman seated cross-legged on the floor, hands shaking incessantly. The patient's abject fear reached Christy like a wave of unseen energy that seeped into her bones. She'd withdrawn and closed the door softly.

Her own problems seemed absurd next to what some people faced.

She should be grateful for her life. Sure, she had her issues, but she wasn't destitute or homeless. It was all a matter of perspective. After this, a calm settled over her for a while, but her anxiousness slowly returned as the minutes stretched.

She consoled herself with the confidence that Austin would eventually track her down, and they would laugh about being in such an unlikely mess. All because of a cheap locket from Target.

The door suddenly opened, and Christy unfolded her legs. Beverly faced her, unconcerned. Just another day at the office.

"You can come back now, honey."

Christy stood and crossed the room. "It's all good?"

"It is." She smiled. "Kern just wants a word."

She stepped into the reception room, waited for the secretary to close the door, and followed her to the administrator's office, where Beverly turned.

"Anything I can get for you? Some water?"

"No thanks."

"All right." She ushered Christy through and shut her in.

Kern Lawson removed his feet from his desk and tossed a toothpick in the waste bin. He'd loosened his tie and rolled his sleeves up. The day was getting on.

"Have a seat. Just going over what we have here. You need anything? Water?"

"She already asked. I'm fine, thank you."

"Good. I'm sorry to keep you waiting, but as you can imagine, taking inventory when the patients are up and around isn't as simple as when they're asleep. You caught us during a shift change to boot."

"But all's good, right? I really need to get back home."

"You're at 456 Blanard Drive, right? Yes, we checked on that too. Rented by one Christy Ray Snow, just like you said."

"Just like I said."

He clicked his mouse, eyes on the monitor. "You understand why we check these things. Not that we really need to—anyone who knows where Christy Snow lives could claim to be her. But we like to cover all of our bases. Lawsuits these days can be a real pain."

Something about his demeanor triggered her concern.

"It's fine. As long as it's all cleared up, I'm fine."

Lawson's eyes peered over his reading glasses at her. He took them off and set them down.

"Well, that's the problem we're having. Everything's not quite fine. We've confirmed that we have a patient missing. Until we find her, we're prohibited by hospital rules from releasing anyone from the wing."

Christy sat up, alarmed. "That's ridiculous!"

"My words exactly. I ordered a second count. We have one patient unaccounted for."

"That doesn't mean I'm her. Give me a break. It's obvious I don't belong here!"

"I understand. But protocol is protocol. What really concerns me is this other bit."

"What other bit?"

"They searched the basement, like you suggested. Problem is, we found no cell phone."

Christy felt the blood drain from her face. "They checked the door behind the drums?"

"They did." He picked up his glasses and wiped the lenses with a Kleenex. "I didn't know the door was there. This place was once a hotel during Prohibition. Moonshine runners. Crazy thing."

"And they couldn't find my phone? Tell them to search again!"

"There's no sign the door was breached. Certainly no cell phone. If you came in that way, you did one heck of a job covering your tracks. But it's the no-cell-phone thing that doesn't add up. So you see how this is looking—"

"This is crazy!" Christy blurted, jumping to her feet. She knew that she was losing it, but she made no attempt to calm herself. "They're lying. I was there!"

"Sit down, Christy."

She remained standing, beside herself with frustration.

"Or should I call you Alice?"

"Alice?"

"Alice Ringwald. The name of the girl who's missing. The new arrival. You can see how easy it is for me to conclude that you tried to escape through an old crawlspace in the basement, found a dead end, and then came up with a clever story using the name of a girl you knew from the outside."

She did follow his logic, which only made things worse.

"Please sit down," he said, this time with less patience.

She sat. "I don't know what's happening or who took my phone, but my name is Christy, not Alice." The name echoed in her ears. "Alice Ringwald?"

"Alice Ringwald."

"I saw her in the hall! Blond, right? She was with a doctor, I saw her! You're saying she's missing?"

"Seems so."

"And you really think I'm her?"

"I'm not saying that. She came to us this morning. I'll know more when they bring me her file. The director of admissions is processing it now. Should be here shortly, but I didn't want to keep you hanging. In the meantime, I would like to know more about you. Just a few questions. Sound fair enough?"

Christy felt trapped. Not by Lawson, but by what was clearly a series of tragic errors compounded by the fact that someone had found her phone but didn't report it. Why would anyone do that? For a two-hundred-dollar phone?

Stay calm, Christy. It'll all work out. Just do what they say and this will all work out.

"This isn't right," she said. "What about my locket? Did you search the storage room?"

"No locket, I'm afraid, though it's clear someone's been in there. Unfortunately, this isn't exactly the safest neighborhood."

She could think of nothing more to say.

"Fine. Ask your questions. I've got nothing to hide."

"Good." He pressed his intercom button. "Beverly, can you come in?" The door opened a few seconds later.

"Please take our guest to Dr. Wilkins. She's waiting in room two."

Receiving parting assurance from Lawson that this wouldn't take long, Christy followed Beverly yet again, this time to a room two doors down the main hall on the left. The sign on the door identified it as a counseling room.

Christy was ushered in and introduced to a young woman, maybe in her late twenties—a professional type wearing heels and a skirt with a white satin blouse. She wore her dark hair up and studied Christy through wire-frame glasses.

"Have a seat." She glanced at an open folder on her side of a table. "Christy. Christy Snow, correct?"

"Yes."

The room was plain, with white walls, a darkened window that Christy thought might be one-way glass—maybe for observation in the event a patient got violent? One six-foot table with four simple chairs.

"Nancy Wilkins." She extended a hand that Christy took. "Please sit."

Christy sat opposite the woman. "The administrator said you need to ask me some questions. What kind?"

"Just a standard profile. Apparently there's been some kind of mix-up. I'm sure you're eager to get this all cleared up."

"Dr. Wilkins—"

"Call me Nancy," Wilkins said with a genuine smile. "I'm not your doctor."

Christy settled, warmed by Nancy's casual tone and demeanor.

"You know about the mix-up then?"

"No. I've only been asked to run a standard profile on you. Just a few questions. It's nothing, really."

Christy nodded.

"I can see that you're tense, but I'm only doing what I do. I could be a waitress for all you care. I just get to know you a bit. That's all."

"All right."

"Truth is, most people don't really know who they are. And I think that includes me. We do the best we can, more often than not stumbling along in the dark. And that's okay."

The gentle words came to Christy like a soothing balm. The events of the morning flashed through her mind. Being trapped in the crawlspace, being mistaken for a missing patient... It was all a tragic comedy of errors. She really had no reason to be so uptight.

She felt herself relax.

Nancy smiled, eyes warm and inviting. "That's better. Let's get you out of here, shall we?"

Christy gave up a shy smile. "No argument from me."

"So let's start with the basics."

Nancy asked a series of innocuous questions about Christy's current living situation, her education, work experience—the typical kind of questions that might fill out a résumé. It was more like a conversation than an interview, and Nancy offered up some interesting facts about her own life in the mix.

She once thought she would be a professional dancer before an injury ended the dream. She'd become so distraught about having her dream yanked out from under her that she'd fallen into a deep depression. Her interest in psychiatry began then. Seven years later, she became a professional with a doctorate, albeit one who consumed shows like *So You Think You Can Dance* as if they were crack.

Like Christy, Nancy had no boyfriend. She, too, lived alone and was a little surprised that Christy was so independent and well adjusted for being only seventeen. Nancy was thirty-two.

They both had cats. They both listened to Coldplay and Mumford & Sons. They both were neat freaks. They both dreamed of having children one day. They both wanted to fall in love. Today if possible, and that made them both laugh.

Nancy's occasional glance at her watch brought Christy back to the fact that she was in a pysch ward, possibly mistaken for a girl named Alice, but talking with Nancy rooted her in more important things that mattered outside these walls.

Twenty minutes became thirty and then forty, and still no one came for her, probably because the interview wasn't finished. But the urgency she felt earlier had dissolved.

She found herself wondering if becoming a psychiatrist might be a good career path. She could tell the story one day of how losing her locket and crawling into a basement set her on the path to a whole new life.

She said as much to Nancy, who tilted her head back and laughed.

"So this all began with a missing locket?"

Christy told her the story in short summary.

"No wonder you were so anxious when you came in," Nancy said. She made a note in her folder. "Tell me about this locket, Christy. Why is it so important to you?"

She explained and the tone of the conversation turned more somber.

"So your locket really represents a missing childhood," Nancy ventured. "A part of you is missing. You're searching for yourself."

The room grew very quiet.

"I guess so."

"I can understand that." Nancy leaned back and folded one leg over the other. "I'm going to ask a few questions and make some observations that might trigger some feelings in you, is that okay?"

She shrugged. "I guess."

"When you look in the mirror, what do you see?"

"Me."

"And do you like what you see?"

A pause.

"No."

"No? What don't you like about what you see?"

"I don't know." She shrugged again, feeling suddenly awkward. "I could lose some weight."

"What else?"

"Specifically?"

"Specifically."

"Well… My neck is too fat. I have a stubby nose. Ten pounds could come off my stomach."

"What else?"

"My fingers could be longer. My hair gets too frizzy."

"Do you hate the way you look?"

"Sometimes."

"More often than you like it?"

Much more, she thought. "I guess."

"Do you feel misunderstood by society?"

"I guess."

"Don't guess, Christy. Just say the first thing that feels true."

"Yes."

"Of course you do. We all do at times." She smiled. "What kind of dreams do you have?"

Christy blinked. A slight chill washed down her back. "Not-so-good ones."

"Nightmares?"

"I think so. I can't remember them, but I wake up sweating and I don't sleep very well."

"Considering your history, it's no wonder. Such large-scale memory suppression can only be triggered by intense trauma. Usually severe prolonged distress."

The chill down her spine doubled back, now laced with anxiety. She found she couldn't address that last statement.

"How much of the day would you say you spend wondering if you measure up?"

All the time, she thought. But saying it sounded stupid so she only said, "Quite a bit."

"You feel lost. Missing, just like the real photograph for your locket."

Christy hesitated, which was answer enough.

"In fact, a day doesn't pass without you suffering some kind of deep anxiety linked to your true identity."

The turn in the conversation had taken Christy from a state of relative ease to one of smothering fear.

"Even now you feel a kind of terror, and the worst part of it is that you can't figure out why. It's just there, like a monster lurking behind your brain."

She still couldn't seem to find the right response. She felt naked, disrobed by a few simple words.

"You hate being so weak," Nancy said. "You can't understand why you hate yourself and think no one else could possibly be as bad off as you. Is that true?"

Christy's face was hot. Sweat had beaded on her forehead—she could hardly pretend that she hadn't been exposed.

"Yes."

"Yes. It's okay. We all get to discover who we really are at some point, and when we do, it can be quite unsettling."

Christy felt her eyes misting and averted her stare. She wasn't sure what to say. It was true, she thought. All of it.

"There's a part of your mind that's shattered. You feel isolated and lost. You don't know who you are, so you try to be what they say you should be, and that leaves you incapable of coping, hating yourself, hating those who want you to be someone you aren't—even though you yourself don't know who you are. You've lost your true identity and are desperately looking for a new one even though that's impossible."

The volume of disquiet that swept through Christy's mind and heart at those words could not be properly expressed. She felt desperate to run from the room, but there was nowhere to go.

"You live alone and keep to yourself because you're broken. Your mind is fractured. Even at your best, you suspect that something is wrong, because it is. The only time you feel good is when you're able to pretend that you feel good, but deep down you hate everything about yourself. The way you look, the way you feel, the way you think, even the way you sleep, because that time that should be peaceful is full of nightmares."

Christy's fingers began to tremble ever so slightly. She lowered them to her lap. She recognized the onset of a panic attack, and none of her attempts at self-reassurance put a dent in the one rushing up to meet her now.

"My observations bother you, don't they, Christy?"

Her throat was frozen shut. She managed a soft, "I guess."

Nancy addressed her in a kind voice laden with compassion, but the words could not have been more upsetting.

"You see the world through broken glasses, Christy. Your mind is wounded."

She wanted to cry. She wanted to scream. She wanted to run.

But she could only sit as tears leaked from her eyes.

And she hated even that.

The door opened, jerking her from her thoughts. Kern Lawson glanced between them, then nodded at Nancy, who smiled congenially at Christy, thanked her for being so vulnerable, gathered her files, and stepped out with the administrator.

Christy wiped her eyes and quickly gathered herself. Nancy's words still buzzed through her head. Austin had once suggested that a good therapist might help her find tools to deal with her despondent emotions. Maybe he was right. Her reaction to Nancy's observations bothered her more than the words themselves.

Five minutes later Lawson walked in wearing a congenial grin. He sat in the chair Nancy had occupied and folded his hands together.

"Nancy tells me that you were very cooperative."

"She seemed nice enough."

"Yes. Nice enough. And now it's time to put this behind us so we can both get back to our lives. We have a nice room ready for you, Alice. I'm sure you're going to like it. The staff is very excited to learn of your safe return."

Christy felt gut-punched. His words slammed into her like the crushing fist of God himself.

She stood, knocking her chair back and over. "This is insane!"

"We don't prefer that expression on this floor, Alice. *Challenged* is more becoming."

"I'm... not... Alice!"

"The charade is up, my dear. There is no cell phone, no locket, nothing but your own delusion, something that comes quite naturally to you based on the history in your file, supported by Nancy's assessment. Your name is Alice Ringwald, dark hair, five foot two, 121 pounds, brown eyes. You were processed this morning. Welcome to Saint Matthew's."

For a moment the thought that she might actually be hearing the truth spun through her mind. If she was delusional, everything she remembered from this morning could be a kind of wild fabrication. Something about the possibility rang true.

Something deep in her mind snapped, and Christy found herself running for the door, desperate to be out. Anywhere but here.

She flung the door wide and threw herself forward, aware that the administrator wasn't reacting to her flight.

She collided with a guard, who grabbed her arms and tried to calm her, but she was powerless to suppress the panic, powerless to still her thrashing arms and quiet her scream.

A second guard assisted and a sliver of reason told her she had no hope. No escape. She'd been here before, maybe, and knew what to do now.

She stopped her thrashing and stood still, breathing hard. Mind swimming with confusion.

"All right," she said, staring through the door at the administrator, who still sat, watching calmly. "All right. I'm fine. Let me go; you're hurting my arms."

The grip on her left arm eased and she jerked it free.

For a moment, Lawson just looked at her.

"Take her to her room," he finally said.

THE ROOM they'd taken Christy to was small, no more than ten feet side to side and maybe fifteen feet deep. White walls with a single metal bed supporting a white-sheeted mattress, one tiny wooden desk with chair, no windows, one empty closet. Hardly the kind of accommodations that matched the staff's jovial attitude.

It didn't matter. Christy had no intention of spending the night.

She'd used the last reserves of her energy to manage her panic and suppress her need to make them understand that they were making a terrible mistake.

A counselor named Mike Carthridge had ushered her to the room, assisted by one of the two guards stationed outside the interview room. She'd tried one last time to make her case to the young man, but he'd only nodded and offered his sympathy. Clearly none of them believed a word she said.

The worst of it was her own words, whispering through her mind, asking the impossible: *What if they're right, Christy?*

Fighting back the dread riding her mind, she'd made a decision: She would play along, earn herself some space, and then go. She didn't know how to get out, but she was going to go. She had to, if only to know that she wasn't crazy. Eventually Austin would track her down, but she wasn't going to wait for him. For that matter, if they'd locked up the storage room tight, there was always the possibility he might not find her.

She'd spent the last twenty minutes sitting or lying quietly on her bed, mind drained and frenzied at once. Her skull tingled, screaming for relief, and her face was flushed. She wanted to move, to pace, anything to work off her nervous energy. But she wanted to appear defeated in the event anyone came to check on her.

She could make her way to the cafeteria or lounge whenever she felt up to it, Mike had told her. They didn't seem concerned about her leaving the room, which didn't help. They obviously were confident in whatever security measures they had in place.

Still didn't matter. She had to try.

No cameras in the room that she could see.

Christy sat up, heart pounding. No sign of anyone outside. If she entered the hall and met any of the staff, she could always tell them that she was headed for the lounge, right?

She stood and steadied herself. They placed a plastic band on her wrist that identified her as Alice Ringwald. It had her number and a few letters—SAD, PD—whatever that meant. Maybe her diagnosis. The blue smock they gave her had no name tag. Said they would get her some clean clothes later.

It was now or never.

Christy walked to the door, opened it slowly, and slipped her head out. The hall was clear. Same hall she'd first entered, along the same wall that opened to the stairs to the basement, only two doors down from the administrator's office.

She gathered herself for a few seconds, listening to the silence. No sign. She would get to the far end of the hall and take the corner. It was really the only way she could go.

Just walk easy, Christy. Nothing wrong. Nothing wrong.

She stepped into the hall and turned to her right. Still no one.

Breathe. Don't run.

She headed down the hall, feet numb, eyes on the end where the

62

hall turned to the left.

The patient rooms all had small windows, six by twelve inches, allowing a clear view of the interior. She cast a glance into the first room she passed and saw that it was empty.

Still no sign of traffic. She picked up her pace.

Passed a third room and glanced in as she passed. Patient asleep on the bed, facing the door She was glad they hadn't sedated her. If they had she wouldn't have—

Christy pulled up sharply, the image of the sleeping patient she'd just passed large in her mind. She spun back and peered through the narrow window.

A male. Dark hair. Restrained at the wrists.

Austin?

But...

She blinked away the image, but the face refused to change. How could Austin be a patient in the same ward she was in? And in restraints? Nothing made sense.

Was she losing her mind?

Christy didn't think to check the hall again. She twisted the knob, slipped into the room, and stood trembling, facing the apparition before her.

Only it wasn't an apparition.

It really was Austin.

"WAKE UP! Wake up!"

A sharp pain set fire to Austin's cheek. Spread into his jaw.

His eyes fluttered open. Drifted to his right where Christy's face hovered over him, eyes puffy and red. Her dark hair was pulled back in a ponytail that struggled to keep her tousled locks in check. Beads of sweat glistened on her forehead.

He blinked. "Christy?"

She looked at him with fear-fired eyes. "Tell me you're real. Please, just tell me I'm not imagining this."

"Where am I?"

She hesitated. "The psych ward."

He was flat on his back with his arms at his sides. In bed?

His attention flitted between her and his surroundings. He tried to force the world into focus, but his mind was sluggish. He was in a white room with cinderblock walls. Windowless.

"How...?" Christy looked frightened. "You're real, though. Right?"

"Of course I'm real."

"Then how did you get here?" She jerked her head toward the door. "They could be coming soon. We have to hurry!"

"Hold on." His chest and his heart surged. "Just hold on."

Thoughts raced. He had to stay calm. *Think, Austin.* His mind cycled through what happened in the basement. With Fisher. With the girl.

Fisher.

He scanned the room and tried to sit up, but his attempt to rise to his elbows was stopped by the thick padded restraints that secured his wrists to the steel bedrails. The metal chain links clinked in protest. He tugged at them.

"Where is he?" he asked.

"Where is who?"

"Fisher. Where is he?" He knew the man was nearby. Had to be.

Christy was confused. "I don't know who Fisher is."

"Okay, listen to me."

She muttered to herself. Held her head in her hands. "They're coming."

"Look at me. *Look* at me."

She faced him.

"I need you to get me out of these." He pulled at the restraints. "Can you do that?"

Her trembling fingers fumbled with the fat leather straps. Her breathing was shallow. After several tries she managed to free his right hand.

He slipped it out of the leather cuff and reached across his body. His fingers made quick work of the second restraint and he sat up. Excruciating pressure bloomed in his head with the rush of blood.

He grabbed a fistful of the bedding. Clenched. Waited for the pain to settle to a dull roar.

"Are you okay?" Christy asked.

"I'm fine." He wasn't though.

Austin scooted to the foot of the bed. He dropped his feet to the floor and stood.

Fueled by a potent mix of pain and adrenaline, his mind crackled with renewed clarity. It might be temporary, he knew that. He had to think quickly.

"Christy..."

He turned and saw that she'd closed the distance between them. She slipped her arms underneath his, around his body, and laid her head on his chest.

He stood there for a moment feeling her body tremble.

"I knew you would come," she said.

He held her gently. They were alive and together—that was good.

They were in a psych ward. As patients. That wasn't so good.

Her shoulders heaved.

"Hey, listen," he said softly. He pulled back and held her at arm's length. Fat tears carved trails down her cheeks. "It's gonna be okay."

"Are you sure?"

"It will be. We just need to figure this out."

She bit her lower lip, on the edge of a cliff somewhere in her mind. What had they done to her? He needed to keep her head in the game.

"Good," he said. "We have to reason our way through this. Right? Don't go crazy on me."

Her eyes narrowed. "Crazy? You think I'm crazy?"

"Bad choice of words. I need you to get hold of yourself."

"I'm not crazy."

He checked the door with a glance. "Keep it down. Of course you're not crazy."

"I'm not." This time her words came out as barely a whisper.

"But you're obviously stressed out, and you're not thinking straight. The only way we're getting out of here is if we stay calm and figure this out."

"You're right." She ran her hands through her hair. "You're right. I'm sorry."

He paced across the room. With each passing moment the cloudy layer in his mind burned away.

"Tell me *everything*. Focus. What happened to you this morning after you got here?"

The story spilled out of her in one rush of ragged emotion. The panic she felt in the passageway. Her phone call to Austin. The run-in with the hospital staff. The mix-up that led to her admission. Lawson. All of the pieces clicked into place for Austin.

"You had no ID on you?" he asked.

"No. I left everything at home."

He noticed the blue plastic wristband on her left hand. He reached down and twisted it. A series of numbers were printed on it. Next to the numbers, a name: RINGWALD, ALICE.

Alice.

Austin jerked his left hand up. A similar band snugged his wrist. The name on it: CONNELLY, SCOTT.

A pang of terror rose in his gut.

"What?"

"Of course," he said. "Fisher."

"Who's Fisher?"

"After I got your call, I traced your steps to the storage room. I found the way into the hospital that you took. While I was in the basement, I stumbled onto something I wasn't supposed to see. A hospital employee was down there. A man—Douglas Fisher. His name badge said he's the admissions director. He was performing some form of therapy on a young girl. Whatever he was doing, I wasn't supposed to see it."

"He did this to you?" she asked.

"He injected me with some kind of sedative. That's the last thing I remember."

"Oh no."

Austin churned through the possibilities, but there were too many to process so quickly. He was midstride when he saw the red folder peeking from a wall tray next to the light switch.

His folder.

He covered the distance in three steps and pulled the chart out. Flipped it open. His finger traced the record as he scanned it.

"Scott Connelly. Age seventeen. Paranoid delusional." He closed the folder. "Same name on my wristband. This is me."

"What?"

"You've got to be kidding." Fisher was smart. Dangerously so.

"What?"

"Keep your voice down."

"What is it?" she asked for a third time, this time in a whisper.

He held up the folder and spoke quickly, his own urgency rising. "He admitted me as a patient. That's what he did after he knocked me out."

"But you're not a patient. How can he just... *do* that?"

"Fisher's the admissions director. Think about it. He has access to the system. He controls the records. After the basement he must've taken my phone, my wallet—everything that proves I'm Austin Hartt. I had your phone on me too. He has both of them now."

"But why? Why would he do that?"

The realization steamrolled him. "Whatever I saw him doing was dangerous enough that he couldn't simply let me walk away. It had to have been illegal, probably some kind of experimental therapy that the hospital would never approve. Something that would cost him his job. That has to be it."

"Then we'll just find a phone and call the police," Christy said. "It's all a mistake. They'll see. It's all just a mistake."

"There won't be any outgoing lines except in the offices." He tapped the folder against his open palm quickly, thinking. "Besides, this isn't a mistake. It's a calculated move. We're patients in a psych ward. No one's going to believe anything we have to say."

"Of course they will. They have to."

"Why? He stripped me of my identity." Another realization dawned on him in that moment. "And he took yours too." He motioned to her wristband. "You said they think your name's Alice, right?"

"Right."

"And why do they think that?"

"Because she's the patient who went missing."

"Precisely. Look at it from their perspective. You show up inside a secure facility with no identification. No phone. Nothing. Think about it. Who breaks into a mental facility? No one. And who would be in charge of a patient population? Fisher—director of admissions. But Fisher suddenly finds himself in a tight spot because he's been found out. By me. He's got to cover his tracks."

A beat.

Her face went slack. "He has to get rid of the real Alice. She knows too much."

"Exactly. She knows what he did to me. But he can't just get rid of Alice because Alice is in the system. Instead, he turns you into her. She was just checked in. You are her. End of story. No missing patient."

"So he turned us both into mental patients…" she said.

Austin didn't bother responding. It seemed plain enough.

"If he's willing to do that, what's to stop him from doing something worse to us?" she said. "What's to stop him from killing us?" Her voice escalated.

"Calm down," he whispered through clenched teeth. "They'll hear us."

She pressed, this time in a harsh whisper. "What's to stop him from killing us?"

He hesitated. "Nothing."

"Wait. Alice. She's the key, right? All we have to do is find her. She knows the truth. You said she's in the basement, right?"

"*Was*. Fisher's not stupid. By now, he's cleaned up whatever evidence was down there and has put Alice somewhere else. Or worse."

There was a long silence.

"So we're trapped," Christy said. "What now?"

"We've got to get out of here. We get out of here and we go to the authorities. We tell them what's happening here. Whatever I saw goes deep. Deep enough that Fisher's willing to falsely admit two perfectly sane people into a psych ward to cover his tracks."

"But which way is out?"

"How did you get in here?"

"I walked down the hall."

"Your door wasn't locked?"

"No."

"Were there guards in the hall?"

"Not that I could see."

"Are you sure?"

She nodded. "I'm sure."

"They must have some other security measures in place. Video cameras probably, which means we have to move fast."

"Don't they lock these sorts of places down? It's not like we can just walk out of here."

"We have to try. There's got to be an exit somewhere."

"What if they see us?"

"We've got nothing to lose. Fisher probably thinks I'm still sleeping off the sedative." He grabbed Christy's hand and led her toward the door. "What did you see in the hallway?"

She glanced through the door's narrow window. "There's an administration office to the left. It dead-ends there."

"To the right?"

"Just more hallway."

"Where does it go?"

"I don't know."

"That's fine. It'll lead somewhere. We'll follow it until we find a door. We'll find a way out." He squeezed her hand. "You ready?"

She nodded.

"We run and we don't look back, understand?"

"Okay."

"No matter what you hear behind us, keep running forward."

Austin pulled the door open gently. Peered out. Except for an old woman with a walker, the hallway was empty.

"Okay, let's go."

They turned down the hall and started to run. Doorways lined the hallway on either side every ten feet or so. Patient rooms.

They skirted past the old woman, who shuffled slowly in the middle of the hallway.

She smiled a crooked smile and waved. "Don't touch the whiskey, you hear? Stuff'll rot you dead."

They both ignored her.

"Hey, kids," she said, "got any whiskey on you?"

A plastic sign hung next to a fire extinguisher. A fire evacuation chart.

"Over here," Austin said. They pulled to a stop in front of it. A rough schematic of the facility was etched into it. The psych ward was U-shaped. They stood where the left side of the U met the bottom.

He glanced down the hall. "Down that way and to the left. Main exit. Hurry."

They followed the hallway until it jogged left again. Took the turn at a run.

Deserted except for two patients: One, a bald Asian man who stood in a doorway doing nothing. Just beyond him, a teenage boy sitting in a wheelchair backed against the wall. He watched them without expression. Just another day for a patient without much of a mind.

Austin veered to the left side of the hall to keep distance between them. "Keep going, don't stop," he whispered.

The Asian patient lifted his arm and pointed at them as they passed but addressed the boy in the wheelchair. "Jacob. Look, Jacob. Two birds running. I hear the wolf snap-snap-snapping at their heels. I hear him. Do you hear him, Jacob?"

The man's laugher filled the hallway.

"Snap-snap-snapping. Gonna chew 'em up."

Double doors, straight ahead. Austin quickened his pace to a sprint, and Christy matched his stride. As they moved his eyes scanned for video cameras, but he hadn't seen any.

They were going to make it.

His hand slammed down on the lever and they pushed through.

The stark clinical lights of the psych ward faded as the doors closed behind them. They pulled up in a warmly lit room. A reception area of some sort. To the far right, an unmarked metal door. Ahead, another door with the word EXIT glowing in green letters above it. To the immediate right, a small receiving area enclosed in Plexiglas. It reminded Austin of the reception area at a family physician's office. To the right of it, another door no doubt opened to the office area behind the glass.

"There's no one in there," Christy said. "Let's go."

She rushed forward and pushed the release lever on the exit door, but it wouldn't budge. She tried again. Locked.

Austin walked to the receptionist's window. Empty. Lunch time? "It's a secure door, probably an electronic lock. There's got to be a button they use to buzz people in and out."

He pressed his face close to the glass. A plastic box of paperclips and a pen sat on the countertop. Beyond it and to the right was a small green button. Out of reach.

"We have to hurry, Austin!"

The paper clips drew his attention. He grabbed the box and pulled it out. Walked to the office door and dumped them on the floor. Handed his file to Christy.

"What are you doing?" she asked. "We have to open this door."

"The only way we're going to do that is by pressing the button behind the glass." He scattered the clips on the floor and selected two larger ones.

"How are we going to do that?"

"Tumbler manipulation," he said, reshaping one of the clips into an L-shaped tension rod.

"Pick the lock?"

He bent another clip into a J-shape then knelt in front of the lock. Fed one clip into the lock then the other. "Simple mechanics. Opening a lock is easy if you know how they work."

After another twist, the lock disengaged and the handle turned. He pushed it open and went through.

"Go to the door," he said.

Christy ran to the door. An electronic lock clicked the moment he punched the button on the counter.

"It's open!"

He hurried to the exit, took the file from her, and stepped through. "Follow me. Hurry."

A dimly lit hallway stretched in front of them. Recessed lights in the ceiling created puddles of light on the linoleum floor every twenty feet. No doors that he could see and no exit signs. It ran for another hundred feet before disappearing around a corner.

"Where's the exit?" Christy said.

"It's gotta be ahead. Just keep running."

They ran to the end of the hall where it turned left.

"Did we miss a turn somewhere?"

"No." He was certain of it.

"Are you sure?"

"It's this way," he said and started walking. "It has to be. We just haven't gone far enough."

Christy followed close on his heels.

Austin knew they would eventually find a door, and that door would lead outside.

They hurried to the end, where the hall angled hard left and followed it. When they did, an identical hallway lay in front of them.

What? But there was no other way to turn. No patient rooms. No doors in the hallway like the ones in the psych ward. Just smooth, white cinderblock walls. New construction?

He said nothing. Kept them moving forward.

They reached the end of that hallway, pushed through the door, and pulled up sharply. Another hall.

"What's going on?" Christy said, the panic rising in her voice. "Is this right?"

"It has to be. I haven't seen any other exits. Or doors, for that matter."

What had he missed?

He pushed the question from his mind and ran for the single door at the end of the hall they were in. "Come on!"

No alarm had sounded. Austin had the file that would incriminate Fisher. They would be out soon enough.

Austin reached the door first and slid to a halt. He cranked the knob and leaned his shoulder into it.

Christy came too fast and collided with him, pushing him through the door. He stumbled forward and pulled up hard, half expecting to see yet another long hall.

But it wasn't another hall.

They were in an office.

A sharply dressed man sat behind a desk, combing through paperwork of some sort. He glanced up casually, looking over his glasses at them. If he was surprised by their dramatic entry he didn't show it.

The door clicked shut behind them.

Christy gasped.

The man behind the desk smiled. "Hello, Alice. Nice to see you again. And so soon."

She backed to the door they'd come through.

"I can assure you. That door is now locked." He reclined in his seat. "Go on, check it if you like, but I assure you it's quite secure."

She tried, desperate to get out. It was locked.

"Those doors can be quite deceiving, can't they?" the man said. "Which one to take?"

The nameplate on the man's desk read KERN LAWSON. The administrator Christy told him about.

The man pulled his glasses off and tapped his chin with one of the earpieces. "And you brought a friend, I see. I don't believe we've met. You are?"

"Austin Hartt."

"Ah, I see. The other new arrival. Fisher told me about you." He glanced at the red folder in Austin's hand. "You brought your file."

Austin felt his pulse thrumming in his temples. His mind spun through their options. He could make his case now—accuse Fisher of foul play—but in doing so, he would only tip his hand. Lawson would take his man's word over a patient's without hesitation.

He could take more time to think through their options. Maybe telling Lawson would end up being the right course. Maybe not. He had to give it more thought.

"Please, have a seat." Lawson indicated the two stuffed chairs facing his desk. Beyond them, a wood panel door stood closed. The main entrance into the office. They'd entered through a side door.

They sat.

The administrator picked up a jar of jelly beans that sat on his desk. "Candy?"

Christy sat still, face as white as a ghost's. Austin had never liked jelly beans.

"All right. Plenty more of these in the lounge if you change your minds."

He popped one in his mouth and set the jar down.

"Now then. Let's be clear about one thing. I understand how disorienting it can be for those with your particular challenges to adjust to a new space, but I want to assure you both personally, as the administrator, that there's nothing to fear here."

He spread his hands, palms up, indicating the facility.

"We're here to help you, not hurt you. Can you accept that?"

Austin hesitated, then dipped his head once. Christy didn't move.

"Good."

"I have copies of both of your files right here." He picked up two red files from the corner of his desk and plopped them down in front of him, eyeing them over his reading glasses.

Lawson flipped open the top file.

"Alice Ringwald. Acute anxiety disorder. Psychosis. Subject to paranoid delusions with a four-year history of the same kind of behavior we've seen from you today. The rest is all here, in perfect order."

He set the file aside and opened the cover of the second.

"And one Scott Connelly. Delusions of grandeur, acute paranoia, and psychosis among other things. Evidently you have quite the mind, Scott. We're here to help you free that mind."

He closed the folder, stacked them neatly in the corner, and folded his hands in front of him.

"But we can't help you until you first accept the truth. Both of you are quite ill. Some would say mad. Insane. Bonkers. I prefer *challenged*. I need you to embrace that much if nothing else. Fair enough?"

This time Austin couldn't bring himself to react. He wasn't sure if the man had an angle here or was merely deceived by Fisher. Maybe a bit of both.

"Just how deep that challenge runs will be up to you."

The administrator pushed himself back from the desk and stood. "Either way, I can assure you that there's no way out of this ward without my authorization. And I mean no way. This is my ward, my world, my law, and no one gets out without becoming an outlaw, so to speak, which will force me to lock them up for good." Lawson let his words sink in. "That's the law."

He walked over to the door they'd entered through and placed his hand on the knob. Turned back. "Please don't try escaping again. It will only delay your progress."

He opened the door. "Now, if you don't mind, I have to step out for a few minutes."

Lawson reached into what was now a shallow closet inlaid with wood paneling, pulled a long black coat off the rack, and shrugged into it as he turned.

Austin couldn't tear his eyes from the closet. How?

He glanced at Christy, who was also staring at that closet, fried.

"Welcome to your new home, my friends," Lawson said, then closed the closet door. "I'll check in with both of you in an hour."

With that he walked to the door, nodded at two security men who were waiting patiently just outside, and strode out.

"They're all yours."

BOOK TWO
MIRRORS

CHRISTY PACED behind the table, chewing on a fingernail she'd already worn to a nub. Austin sat, nervously tapping his fingers, staring at the wall. They'd been led to the same room in which she'd been profiled by Nancy Wilkins. At the time the therapist had seemed reasonable and understanding. But wasn't it Nancy who'd concluded that she was mentally cracked?

"Do you mind sitting down?" Austin glared at her. "You're going to wear out the carpet."

Austin had remained quiet, lost in thought, which was his way when he was engrossed in something. To say he was single-minded didn't begin to describe just how cut off he could become when he put his mind to a task—anything from reading a thick textbook to watching a boring lecture, one leg bouncing, eyes fixed on the screen.

How often had she told him things in his flat only to learn that he wasn't even hearing her? Nothing short of yelling seemed to yank him out of his fixation. In this way, she'd always been invisible even to Austin, her closest friend. She'd always known that she didn't belong to anyone or anything, and Austin's preoccupation with his own inner world only reinforced that certainty.

Christy ignored his request to sit.

"We have to get out of here, Austin."

He said nothing, which only increased her anxiety. He was hearing her perfectly, and it wasn't like Austin not to have some answers. She'd never seen him quite like this.

She could understand most of the logic behind most of the events that had put them both in the psych ward. But something seemed out of balance in her mind, something that prevented her from shaking the one thought that had buried itself in her mind like a stubborn tick.

What if the administrator was right?

What if she was delusional?

"Austin?"

He offered her a halfhearted grunt.

"I'm worried."

Austin looked at her for a few seconds. Took a long breath.

"I know you are. But it's going to be okay. I've already explained that."

"Tell me again." When he hesitated, she said, "Please? Just for my reassurance."

He closed his eyes briefly and then glanced up at her.

"You stumbled into the wrong place at the wrong time. I followed you and stumbled into something no one was meant to see."

"Alice."

"Yes, Alice. Fisher needed to get rid of Alice and get rid of me. So he made you Alice, which takes care of her—"

"He killed her."

"No, we don't know that. But he got her out of the picture. Don't make things worse than they are."

"Sorry."

He continued. "He took care of me by admitting me as a patient who suffers from delusions of grandeur, given to fanciful stories. Nobody on the inside or outside is going to believe a word I say. Nor you. So now we have to figure out how to either get out or get word out before anything worse happens to us."

"What if we can't?"

"We will. It's only a matter of time. But we have to play it smart, and that means keeping our heads on straight."

Her mind stalled. *And what if my head isn't on straight?*

Austin saw her hesitation.

"How many times do I have to tell you? You're not schizophrenic or delusional, Christy." His voice was stern yet calm. And he anticipated her greatest concern without waiting for her to ask yet again.

"Everything that happened in Lawson's office has a perfectly logical explanation. Knowing that unstable patients might try to get out, they set up the reception room to fool them, like it fooled us. The door without the exit sign is the way out to the main hospital. The buzzer opened one that leads to Lawson's office."

She nodded, pacing still. "There's another buzzer or something that opens the real exit."

"Of course. But getting out that way will probably be impossible. They're too smart to let anyone out through the front door."

"And the closet is just a mechanical trick," she said.

"A false closet that slid into place at the push of a button. Enough to freak out anyone not thinking things through. Easy enough to construct. The main point is that anyone who would go to such elaborate planning has thought this through very carefully. We aren't just going to walk out of here."

To this she had no response. Her mind was stuck on what he'd just said about the closet being enough to freak out anyone not thinking properly.

Like her.

"We have to think our way out," Austin said. "Talk our way out. Scam our way out. Something they haven't thought about. Until we figure what and how, we have to play along. We can't afford to push Fisher's buttons. We don't want him thinking he needs to go further."

He'd said this much repeatedly. She got it. His repetition of the concern wasn't helping matters.

"And there's no way they could be right about us, right?"

"We aren't nuts," he said with a little too much defensiveness for her comfort. "It's absurd. I was in a lecture hall at Harvard this morning. I got a call from you. The professor asked me if I would be interested in attending full time! I can assure you there's not one loose nut in my head."

He was right, of course, although she would have put it differently. They had both always been different. And neither one of them could remember much of their childhoods.

"What about your headaches?"

He blinked several times, then spoke in a steady tone.

"Neither one of us is remotely unstable. You just remember that. Don't let them get in your head. We're going to get out. Soon. I have a doctor's appointment to get to."

The door opened and she startled. Kern Lawson walked in, shut the door behind him, and faced them, void of expression. He put on a smile that made Christy think he savored both his role and his element.

"Hello, my friends. Sorry to keep you waiting. Wait, wait, wait." He flipped a hand. "Sometimes I think all there is to life is waiting. Waiting for things to get better. Waiting for things to get worse. Waiting to find out what's going to happen or not happen. Life can be a pain."

He walked to the end of the table and pressed his fingertips on the surface, like one of those jungle trees that has roots above ground, reaching down. He was now wearing a white lab coat.

"I like to give our new arrivals a cursory orientation personally. Have a seat, Alice."

Alice.

Christy glanced at Austin, who remained calm, then slid into the chair opposite him.

"There we are." Fisher stood erect and paced slowly to one side then back before continuing.

"The first day is always the hardest for any patient, but I'm not one to throw sedatives at the first sign of resistance like most under-staffed facilities. It only masks the illness and prevents true healing. The sooner you both accept your conditions and adapt to your new environment, the sooner we'll be able to appropriate the correct ther-apy. Make sense?"

He didn't wait for a response.

"By now you already know that getting out isn't a solution. Neither is it possible. Please tell me that you understand at least this much."

Waiting for Austin to take the lead seemed natural, so Christy let him give his nod before she did.

"Now, Scott..." The man held his smile for a few seconds. "I know that your particular condition probably has you thinking through solu-tions without end. You're certain you don't belong here, and you're probably already hatching a way out, so let me help you by cutting to the chase."

His smile vanished.

"All the exits are electronically controlled, and I'm not talking about the simple push of a button. There's no cell service inside. The few lines out of the facility are monitored twenty-four hours a day and require electronic signatures to operate. We have a total of forty-seven patients on two floors. This floor is for those who present neither a flight risk, nor any threat to patients or staff. The upper level is reserved for our more challenging cases. We employ rather advanced, unconventional treatments on the upper level. Extremely effective, I might add."

Two floors? She hadn't seen any exit sign leading to another floor, but then she hadn't been looking for one.

"It can be accessed only by a secure elevator and is operable only by qualified staff. There is no other way in or out. None."

Lawson reached into his lab coat pocket and came out with a small box of toothpicks, one of which he withdrew before returning the box to his pocket. He slipped the sliver of wood into his mouth and rolled it with practiced ease as he studied Austin curiously.

"And since I'm sure you're wondering, the crawlspace Alice found in the basement has been sealed. I was admittedly quite surprised to find it. Thank you, Alice, for bringing that to our attention."

He looked at her, and then pressed when she offered no reply.

"A 'you're welcome' would be appropriate here. Let's try to be cordial, shall we?"

Play along, Austin had said.

"You're welcome," she said.

"Well, thank you for saying 'you're welcome,' Alice."

She just looked at him.

"Are you going to say 'you're welcome' for my saying thank you for saying 'you're welcome'?"

She blinked.

"No, you aren't, because that would be circular, wouldn't it? I'd keep saying thank you, and you'd keep saying you're welcome. It would be insane. And your brain is working overtime trying to convince you that you're not insane. Not even disturbed. Not even a little bit. Classic delusional behavior."

"It's also classic sane behavior," Austin said.

"True enough. Only this time we know that's not the case. Deep inside, Alice knows that. Like many in her shoes, she's so accustomed to being the way she is that she honestly thinks it's all completely normal. As is the case with you, my friend. You can see that, can't you?"

Austin thought a moment, then followed his own advice.

"Yes."

"Yes, of course. You see how much better this is than resistance. Simple acceptance is always the first step to freedom."

"Makes sense," Austin said.

"Everything I say will eventually make sense." Lawson withdrew his toothpick and pocketed it, maybe for future use.

"All the therapists conduct their cases under my strict supervision," he continued. "On occasion, I take cases on personally, which is what I've decided to do in your case, Alice. If you're agreeable, that is."

Christy wasn't sure how to take him. The man that stood before her now seemed quite different from the one she'd first met in his office. And yet quite the same. She didn't know when he was toying with her and when he was serious.

She looked at Austin, who still sat in stoic control. He offered her a slight dip of his head.

"Yes," she said.

Lawson glanced between them. "I can see that you two have formed a bond. Scott, you will remain on this floor until we develop a more thorough treatment plan. Based on your file, your illness is severe, but I see no manic behavior that concerns me."

He faced Christy.

"Fortunately for you, Alice, we have an effective treatment for patients who display the kind of extreme dissociation you've exhibited. You'll be taken up to the second floor as soon as we're done here."

"What?" The thought of being separated from Austin and placed in some secretive upper floor pushed her mind over some unseen cliff.

"I'm not a problem!" she cried, feeling her control slip. A voice somewhere told her to *play along*, but she couldn't stop herself. "I'm not some nut and I'm no worse than Scott."

"Maybe not, but make no mistake, Alice. You are a problem. You've been in here less than a day and you've already gone to great lengths to escape, once through the basement and once out the front. You injured yourself in the first attempt and took another patient with you on the second."

"That's not how it happened," she snapped, but she saw immediately how Lawson could see it differently.

"That's not how you've *convinced* yourself it happened," Lawson said. "And that's okay—you're in a manic cycle now. You just called him Scott—that's a good start."

"Because you called him Scott."

"Because his name is Scott. The truth is you are very ill, darling. So delusional, in fact, that you are completely unaware that your name is Alice. Most psychiatrists would already have you on medication. But the meds noted in your file clearly haven't produced the kind of results we like to see. You're a perfect candidate for our more progressive programs."

"I am not!" Her hands were shaking. So was her mind. Screaming objections to his accusation that she wasn't who she thought she was. Protesting the thought that he might be right, however impossible that seemed.

However much sense that actually did make.

She spun to Austin, frantic. "Tell him!" She jumped to her feet. "Don't let him do this to me."

"You see how emotional you become, Alice," Lawson said. "I think you're making my case as we speak."

"Please, Austin!" She found her hands pressed together, begging. Tears flooded her eyes as her panic swelled. "Please…"

His eyes were calm, but his fingers were trembling.

"It's going to be all right, Christy." Then again, without offering any solution. "It's going to be okay."

But she knew it wasn't.

Nothing was going to be okay.

ONE THING was certain: Austin's quick trip to the storage room to check on Christy had pulled him into a hellish scenario that reduced the threat of a brain tumor to a mere sideshow. Fact was, he was in way over his head. That much he could no longer deny.

Showing no interest in Austin's request for an extended audience with Lawson, the administrator had instructed the staff to leave Austin in his room, door locked, alone with his thoughts. Food would be brought to him. His therapy would wait a day.

He'd watched them lead Christy from the interview room, offering her assurance that everything would be okay. The pleading look in her tearful eyes had broken Austin's heart. He was in a position to keep his senses about him, but she was already drowning in her own fear and desperation.

He spent the rest of the day pacing in his room, powerless and alone. Mind obsessing over their predicament.

Over Christy's fate. Where was she? Upper floor, but where and under what conditions? Had she stabilized? Had they broken her down and given her drugs?

What now?

There was nowhere to go, no one to reason with, no connection to the world outside of his mind—nothing but the precarious balance between what he knew and what he did not know. At times, the distinction between the two blurred.

His mind refused to shut down and sleep.

The meal tray the nurse had delivered last night sat untouched at the foot of the bed. Next to it: a small paper cup that held three blue pills. Also untouched. Something to take the edge off and help him sleep, she'd said.

He wasn't interested in sleep. Anything that wasn't focused on the singular objective of escape was a waste of precious mental energy, sleep included.

Surviving this ordeal depended on his ability to outthink and outwit Lawson. Both his and Christy's lives depended on him now, and only him.

He rubbed his head gently as he walked incessantly between the room's farthest walls. A dull constant pain sank into his forehead and spread behind his eyes. Exacerbated by fatigue and stress, his migraine had worsened through the night. Then there was the high-pitched ringing in his ears, which had started during the meeting with Lawson.

He'd spent some time considering the possibility, however remote, that Lawson was right about both of them. There were a few logical threads that supported the notion that he was, in fact, suffering dissociative delusions of grandeur, but in the end, that reasoning couldn't compete with the evidence that supported his sanity.

Still, the way his world had unraveled so quickly yesterday was unnerving. And if it was unnerving for him, it must be mind-numbing for Christy.

Who could say how far they would push her? Fisher needed them both insane to cover his tracks. He would go as far as he needed.

Some people were inclined to identify with their trauma, even to the point of falling off the cliff into madness. Christy might be such a person. He'd always known she had her issues, but maybe they cut deeper than he'd guessed.

Lawson, it seemed, was either in on Fisher's plot or truly convinced that Christy was Alice. And that he was Scott. Possible? Technically. Realistic? So far from it that Austin had dismissed even the possibility of it in his mind.

They needed to get out of the psych ward, period.

Lawson said there was no way out, but there had to be. Finding it was simply a matter of outthinking the man. Austin had mentally rehearsed a dozen escape scenarios a hundred times, but like a mythical Hydra, each problem he seemed to solve sprouted two new heads, two more problems.

The facility was designed to keep its occupants in, and every eventuality had likely been taken into account. Getting out through any conventional means was almost certainly impossible. And he could think of no unconventional means except one.

Alice. Assuming she was alive.

Everything led back to Alice. More specifically, to the words he'd overheard.

I've been there. I've seen it. I know.

Finding Alice might mean finding a way out. She might know what was really happening, information that might break this place wide open. Doing that might mean getting her out too.

So find Alice, but how? Where would Fisher have put her?

Upper floor? Maybe.

Basement? Maybe.

Killed her? Maybe.

Readmitted her with a new identity? Maybe.

Without more information, Austin was at a loss. What he did know at the moment, was that Christy was on the second floor and in dire straits, suffering treatment that was likely not sanctioned.

His desire to reach her overrode his desire to find Alice. Reaching Christy first was the most important thing, if only to know that she was safe.

He taxed his mind to the point of exhaustion, working incessantly to think of a way to her. Every course of action seemed to form a twisted knot of trouble.

But even the most tangled of knots could be unraveled, couldn't it? While the rest of the world slumbered in peace, he had methodically dissected the challenge—but he could think of no feasible way to reach Christy.

His mind wasn't processing thoughts properly. There was a way, there had to be, he just wasn't thinking about it right.

"Lost in thought, Scott?"

Austin jerked his attention toward the door. Nancy Wilkins, the therapist Christy had mentioned, stood in the doorway holding a small stack of folders under her arm.

It was strange to hear her call him Scott. *Scott Connelly.* An imaginary patient Fisher had fabricated to lock Austin in this twisted world.

"Excuse me?"

"You didn't hear me opening the door." She stepped in and pulled the door shut.

"Sorry. Just… thinking."

"I can see that. Did you sleep well?"

"I never sleep well. Insomnia. Chronic, actually."

A look of genuine concern softened her face as she glanced at the still-made bed, then back at him. "Sometimes goes with the territory."

He was tempted to correct her but thought better of it. "So they say," he said.

"Well, as you grow accustomed to your new surroundings, Saint Matthew's will begin to feel like home. You'll see."

She considered him for a long beat. Austin noticed the methodical movement of her analytical gaze. In a single smooth sweep of the eyes, she had taken in him and the entire room. Question was, what did those eyes see?

"What time is it?" he said.

"Just past ten. You're free to leave your room. Maybe go to the recreation room or grab some breakfast in the cafeteria." She nodded toward the food tray. "Looks like you could use some food."

"Maybe."

She paused. "If you'd like, I can walk down with you. Show you around if that would make you feel more comfortable."

"No thanks. I'll be fine. I can find the way."

"Of course." She reached for the door, hesitated, and then turned back. "We're here to help you, Scott. This is a safe place for you. You can trust me. Okay?"

He nodded. "Sure."

She opened the door. The faint sounds of people talking drifted in from the hallway. "I'll see you later. We're scheduled for a two o'clock session in room 408. Sound good?"

"Looking forward to it," he said with a smile, trying to suppress any sarcastic edge.

"Good. We'll find you. Any questions, feel free to ask the staff."

"I will. Thank you."

She closed the door behind her as she left. Unlocked.

He was free to roam the floor. He'd been through the halls once before, but now he had enough time to inspect the rest unhurried.

An image of Christy filled his mind. Upper floor. His failure to settle on a clear course of action coaxed sweat from his pores.

He took a deep breath, opened his door, and peered out. Wilkins stopped in front of the next patient room, knocked twice, and entered. Morning rounds.

Austin exited his room, pulled the door quietly shut, and walked toward the recreation room, ahead and to the left.

Lawson had said the upper floor was accessible only by a secure elevator. Since Austin hadn't seen any stairwells or elevators he had to assume it was in a secure section of the building.

He might force his way in, or he might get killed. Regardless, he had no force. No gun, no knife. Even if he had a weapon, he didn't have the skill to use it.

What he did have was his brain. Problem was, his brain was fried.

He paused at the door marked RECREATION ROOM and peered through the long rectangle of reinforced glass set in the middle of it. Inside, about two dozen patients sat around the room in various stages of disinterest. Some stared blankly at a TV on the far wall while others rocked to a beat that played only in their heads.

He was about to step in when laughter to his left drew his attention. A man dressed in white scrubs emerged from the patient room two doors down from his own. He wheeled a gurney through the doorway and guided it into the hallway, followed by a second attendant.

On the gurney: a patient, face to the ceiling. A girl, vaguely familiar even from this distance. His heart rate quickened.

He stared, uncaring that he was in full view. It was a psych ward, after all, and he was just another patient. The details of the girl became clearer as they drew close.

Young. Dirty-blond hair. She lay beneath a white sheet that was cinched taut. Her arms lay at her sides on top of the sheet. Four straps crossed her body—one across her upper chest, one at her waist, one at her thighs, one across her ankles.

A leather mask covered the lower part of her face. His mind completed its circuit of recognition as they drew abreast.

He knew this girl. Her name was Alice.

Time crawled as his eyes met hers. The gurney's squeaking wheels and the distant sounds from the recreation room fell away as if the entire world had been plunged underwater.

The words she'd spoken in the basement loomed in his mind.

I've been there. I've seen it. I know.

94

She stared at him without expression, unblinking, neither sad nor frightened. Just... there. She seemed to be looking both at him and through him at the same time.

His eyes flitted to the wristband cinched on her left wrist as they passed. He could see it through the bedrail. MICHELE MILLER.

After admitting Christy as Alice, Fisher had readmitted Alice under a new identity.

Or had he?

Austin dismissed the thought as the attendants made their way down the hall. Just another patient to be transported.

Austin wanted to run after them and rip the mask from her face. To ask her which way was out. How he could get to Christy. How they could get their lives back. He just needed to know the way, and the simple answer was locked in that damaged mind of hers.

But he couldn't. Not now, not yet. Now he could only stare after them and wonder where they were taking her.

The question had barely formed when the answer crystallized.

The attendants pulled to a stop at the end of the corridor, in front of the double doors marked ADMISSIONS. One of the attendants waved his hand in front of a small black pad next to the door. An electronic lock. A loud buzz echoed through the narrow hall and the doors automatically yawned wide.

An anxious twitch needled every nerve in Austin's body. He could barely keep his feet from launching him into a sprint.

Wait, Austin. Just two more seconds...

The men passed through and the doors eased shut with a pneumatic hiss.

Go...

He covered the distance to the admissions doors in long strides, hoping he wasn't drawing undue attention from hidden cameras. He slowed to a stop in front of them.

Twin narrow windows were set into the doors, steel-mesh-reinforced glass. He leaned close, then stepped aside so the attendants wouldn't see him if they looked back.

The men stood in a shallow alcove to the left of what appeared to be the admissions office. In front of them: a polished steel door, inset deep in the wall.

An elevator.

They were taking Alice to the second floor.

One of the attendants waved his wrist in front of a black pad identical to the one in the hallway, then punched the elevator button.

The secure access required some form of keycard, though Austin hadn't seen the man use one. A chip in the man's skin?

The elevator doors parted and the men pushed the gurney into it. Alice was slipping away.

As the doors eased shut, something in Austin's mind shifted. It came in an instant, unbidden and unexpected, as if a fog that had hovered at the fringes of his mind now pushed deep into his thoughts.

So close. He had been so close to her that he could've reached out and touched her.

He heard the mechanical hum of the elevator as it rose. Watched the glowing red digit above the door as it changed then stopped.

Alice was gone. Right now they were wheeling her onto the upper floor, where they'd locked Christy away from the rest of the world. From him.

Austin stepped away from the door and leaned against the wall. Stared down the long hallway that stretched in front of him, lost in thought.

The fog in his mind thickened into darkness as the situation settled on him. Hope was slipping away. Every moment they spent behind these walls diminished their chances of escape. His control was beginning to slip and he felt powerless to gain any traction.

Still, his mind swept through new thoughts that had been out of sight until now and began connecting the dots methodically. The hall, the recreation room, the sight of Alice restrained, the elevator. The security measures...

Like a mirage taking shape in the distance, a thought formed. A solution. However fragile, he clung to it as if it were a lifeline.

It was bold in its simplicity, but it might work.

He stood unmoving for a full minute, lost in his thoughts, considering his options. It could work. It had to work.

Then again, it might not. And if it didn't...

Austin settled on his course of action, took a deep centering breath, faced the recreation room, and started walking, a whirlwind of objections crowding his mind. He shoved them to the edge of his consciousness and moved forward. One foot in front of the other. He knew what he would do.

He pushed into the recreation room and stood inside the door for several moments, watching. Fourteen patients all dressed in blue scrubs sat throughout the room. Most slumped in metal folding chairs on the left side of the room, staring at a cartoon playing on the flat-panel TV that hung halfway up the wall.

A nurse on the far side of the room offered a smile, then returned to her conversation with a patient. No other staff members in the room at the moment. Two sets of double doors flanked the room, the one behind him and a pair on the opposite side of the room.

To his immediate right, a young patient sat motionless in a wheelchair, staring straight ahead with vacant eyes. The boy he'd seen yesterday. His name dangled at the edge of Austin's memory. Jacob.

Austin walked past the boy and crossed the room calmly, feet padding softly on the linoleum floor. A strange sensation hatched somewhere deep inside his gut. It swelled with each step, feeding on the adrenaline that drove him forward.

The nurse glanced up when he stopped in front of her.

"Can I help you, sweetie?"

Her name was Claire, according to the name badge clipped to her pocket. She was a slight woman huddled next to a patient at a squat table, overseeing a crayon drawing of a purple dragon and a unicorn. Two cups filled with markers and pens sat in the middle.

Austin reached for a blue ballpoint pen. "Just need one of these."

"Why, sure. Help yourself."

"Thank you." He slipped the pen into his pocket, veered left, and made his way toward the TV, eyes fixed ahead.

Odd how detached his body felt. Everything seemed to move at half speed. The better part of his logic began to suggest that what he had in mind would end very badly. But it presented no reasonable alternative, so he ignored those thoughts and followed his intention.

Without breaking stride, he grabbed an empty folding chair with one hand as he passed by it. Dragged it loosely behind him as he rounded the first row and angled for the wall.

Last chance, Austin. Are you sure? A chill cascaded over his scalp.

He stopped in front of the TV and gripped the back of the chair with both hands. In one smooth motion, he lifted it and, jaw clenched, swung it with as much force as he could put behind it. The chair came forward hard and fast, and the impact shattered the TV screen.

He spun around and stared at the horrified faces. The room filled with gasps and cries as fear swept over the fragile-minded patients. A girl pressed her hands to her ears and rocked back and forth. Another pointed at the TV with a trembling hand, shouting something Austin couldn't understand. Others pulled at their hair, peace shattered by the angry man.

He screamed full-throated and flung the chair away. It ricocheted off the wall with a deafening clang and unleashed chaos. Now patients were scrambling, trying to get up. Trying to escape.

Adrenaline surged through his veins, and Austin surrendered to the surge of emotion that raged inside him. He was on a roller coaster, plunging—too late to turn back now.

He strode toward Jacob, quickly now, intent. The boy just stared at him, unaware it appeared. All the better.

The nurse rushed to the back of the room and jabbed her thumb against a red button. A security alarm.

Austin's hands trembled and his chest heaved as he picked up his pace. At the exit next to Jacob, he stepped over to the red box housed in a Plexiglas case on the wall. He flipped the safety case open, wrapped his fingers around the white lever, and tugged down.

The fire alarm's deafening scream shrilled above the din, and patients scattered, driven by the unbearable sound.

Austin crossed to Jacob, rounded the wheelchair, and gripped the handles.

"Come on, Jacob. Let's go for a ride."

The boy didn't respond.

The doors banged open as he backed into them, pulling Jacob into the hallway. He swung the chair and pushed down the hall, heading in the same direction of the ill-fated escape attempt he had taken yesterday.

Austin moved with measured steps that matched the drumbeat of his heart. For the moment he felt the thrill of perfect control. Strange how intoxicating it was.

They'd just taken the turn and sped to a quick clip before any sign of pursuit reached him—the sounds of the rec room's door crashing open, and running feet.

So… This was it.

He spun the chair around and faced four attendants all focused on one thing: stopping him before he caused any more damage—to himself or others, especially Jacob.

The fire alarm fell silent; someone had shut it down.

Austin slipped the blue pen from his pocket, gripped it tightly with his fist, and pressed the sharp point against the side of Jacob's throat.

"No farther," he said evenly.

The attendants slowed, but they didn't stop. They spread across the width of the hallway and moved steadily, arms at their sides, palms open and forward, wide stance.

"I said no farther!"

Austin grabbed a fistful of Jacob's hair and jerked his head back. Pressed the pen deeper until he felt the resistance of the windpipe against the ballpoint. The boy didn't resist. Made no sound.

"I swear. If you take another step, he'll die." Austin's voice sounded strangely distant to himself. "I'll punch him so full of holes…"

The attendants stopped, eyes locked on Austin, but none of them spoke.

His hands were shaking, and he couldn't stop them. Again, the voice of logic told him he was going too far. But another told him he hadn't gone far enough, and the second voice rode the crest of his adrenaline.

He jerked the pen away and gripped the wheelchair handles with both hands. Began backing down the hall toward the exit doors at the far end. Then spun around and pushed the chair at a full run.

They gave chase, but he rounded the next turn safely and headed toward the doors that opened onto the reception room where he'd picked the lock yesterday.

Behind him, they made gains. Didn't speak, didn't attempt to restrain him.

Halfway down the hall, he spun to face them again, pen back at Jacob's neck.

"Stay back!"

They pulled up, eyes on him, still spread across the hall. Still no warning, no urging him to stop. It was almost surreal.

Austin started backward, feet shuffling across the hard floor as he pulled the wheelchair. Every few steps he'd glance over his shoulder. Except for them, the hall was empty. Why wasn't anyone trying to cut him off from the other direction?

Within seconds he'd closed the distance to the reception area's double doors.

"Come closer and I'll push it into his throat," he said.

They pulled up, ten feet away now, still unfazed by his threat. Why?

He glanced down at the boy, who stared forward unaffected except for tousled hair, which fell across his freckled face. A thin smear of blood had formed where Austin nicked the boy's pale skin.

Could he have pushed it into the boy's neck? He was playing a role, but how far would he have gone?

He pushed the thought aside and reached back for the door.

A sudden rush of jagged heat entered his body and climbed his arms the moment his hands connected with the door's cold steel handles. White-hot light exploded behind Austin's eyes. A million needles pressed against his skin as electricity coursed through his body.

He felt himself convulse. His jaw locked tight. His legs gave way beneath him and he crumpled to the hard ground.

His vision narrowed. Darkness crowded the edges of his sight.

Then the world simply disappeared.

EVERYONE HAD voices in their head, right? Thoughts were just unspoken words. If someone invented a speaker that could be hooked to the brain and give voice to every thought, the whole world would sound like a crowded auditorium before the guest of honor took the stage.

Christy remembered taking a bus downtown to city hall once to sign some emancipation forms that would give her full autonomy as a minor. She was seated two rows from a woman who kept mumbling to an imaginary person in the empty seat beside her. "I'm so glad I'm not like you. If they knew what kind of person you are, they'd lock you up." On and on.

The rest of the bus sat in an uneasy silence, staring at the oblivious woman. After getting off the bus, Christy headed into city hall, pondering what she'd just witnessed. *Poor woman has totally lost it,* she kept thinking. *I'm glad I'm not like that.*

She suddenly became aware that, instead of only thinking the last sentence, she'd said it, unaware of the others walking down the hall. She'd actually said, aloud, "I'm glad I'm not like that."

The only difference between her and the woman everyone regarded as plain crazy was that Christy kept most of her thoughts to herself, whereas the woman seemed either unable to or uninterested in doing so.

The whole world was full of incessant, often crazy, often cruel and judgmental thoughts that were rarely given voice.

The chatter whispering through Christy's mind told her that she had to get a grip or she really was going to lose it. *This is crazy. I'm not insane. I'm not Alice and I'm not fractured. This is all a mistake.*

Something was on the verge of breaking, and when it did, she would collapse into a mumbling heap of subhuman insanity.

But strapped in a wheelchair, wheeled first into the elevator and then onto the second floor, she was so acutely aware of the unspoken thoughts that she wondered if she had already lost it.

She knew it wasn't true. That her thinking was only the consequence of a tragic series of errors in an inhospitable environment. But her grip on that certainty was slipping.

The facility's second level was dimensionally similar to the first floor—wide halls in a U shape with doors on either side. But the hall floors were tiled in a glistening black-and-white checkerboard pattern. The walls were spotless, shiny white as if only freshly painted. And the doors were made of polished aluminum, giving the appearance that the whole floor was germ-free.

The wire-mesh-reinforced windows on each door were too high for Christy to see through from the wheelchair. She could only imagine the worst, but those, too, were only thoughts.

The attendant who transported her didn't say a word. She asked him where the other patients were as they rolled down the hall, but he kept silent, which only filled her with more uneasy thoughts.

He angled for a door near the end of the hall, turned her chair to face it, then stepped around her and unlocked it by passing his wrist in front of a small black pad on the wall. She looked back down the hall. The steel elevator doors at the end made her think of a vault door.

Austin might be more intelligent than most, but his mind wasn't going to break down any doors. She was on her own. More than anything, she hated herself for being alone, like she'd always been.

The attendant wheeled Christy in, freed her arms, and left without taking the wheelchair with him. The lock on the door snapped into place as the door closed.

A thick silence settled over her like a heavy blanket.

She looked around the large room, lost. Pressed white sheets covered a single bed to her right. The walls were shiny, like the walls in the hall. Same checkerboard tiled floor. Just past the bed, a door, maybe to the bathroom or a closet. One small chest of drawers topped with white Formica sat beside the bed.

To her left, the room ran twice as wide as the one downstairs. In the extra space sat a large white desk with a brushed-nickel lamp. One high-back chair behind the desk and one smaller chair facing it. A whiteboard on the wall behind the desk. A mirror on the adjacent wall. Likely unbreakable.

Christy sat in the wheelchair for several long minutes, unsure what she was meant to do. Even less sure she wanted to do anything at all.

The ceiling vents were narrow. No way out there. Nor would there be a way out anywhere. She couldn't shake the feeling that they'd built this place to house deranged psychopaths or insane sociopaths.

She finally stood up, walked to the door by the bed, and peered inside. Plain bathroom with a toilet, a shower, and a sink with a mirror above it. No vanity, no soap or shampoo, no towels.

She stepped up to the mirror and blinked at the image staring back at her. Her eyes were swollen and her cheeks had flushed a ruddy red. Lips dry and cracked. Strands of hair had come loose from her ponytail and were sticking out haphazardly, giving her the appearance of a crazed woman just out of an asylum.

She tapped the mirror. Chromed metal. Of course. Nothing would be breakable in this place.

A slow tour of the bedroom confirmed her thinking that everything was designed for permanence. The drawers on the desk were locked, the lamp had a sealed bulb and was bolted to the desk. Even the chairs were affixed to the floor, and the screws that fastened them down had no heads.

When she ventured to the narrow pane of reinforced glass set in the door and peered out, the hall was vacant. Not a soul.

Christy finally retreated to the bed and lay down, feeling deprived and lifeless. She stayed liked that, staring at the ceiling, for what felt like an hour and still no one came. Had they forgotten about her? Of course not. She didn't know what "progressive treatment" meant, but she could imagine that leaving someone to their own thoughts indefinitely might qualify.

There was no clock, no sunlight, no switches on the walls, nothing on the ceiling but the narrow vents and two banks of bright fluorescent lights. It could be the middle of night and she wouldn't know it.

Slowly her concerns began to sag into that place where meaninglessness meets hopelessness. She kept rehearsing the events of the day—her break in, her mistaken identity, Austin's attempt to free them.

The *what-ifs* swarmed her mind like angry crows.

If only she'd left home with her wallet, she would have walked out of the ward the moment she proved her identity. Lawson would have checked his patient roster, found no Christy Snow, and let her go.

If she hadn't made the call to Austin, he wouldn't have come looking for her. If he hadn't come looking, he wouldn't have stumbled upon Fisher and Alice. If he hadn't stumbled on Fisher, the man wouldn't have had any reason to cover his tracks and hide Alice. He'd have had no reason to admit Christy to replace the girl who'd gone missing on his account.

If only...

Christy paused. Somewhere in the back of her mind the *if* became an *unless*. Unless she was completely wrong about all of this. Unless she hadn't left home without her wallet because she'd actually never left her home at all. She'd never left her home because she lived here, not there.

She'd seen a documentary about a patient whose brain damage had so affected his long-term memory that he couldn't hold more than one day in his mind.

But the details of her life as Christy were too real. She had a couple dozen journals in her apartment that spelled out her last few years in great detail.

Hours slogged by and no one came. She made a dozen trips to the door to peer out and not once saw any movement. If there were other patients on the floor, they were in a different section.

What if she was alone?

Christy had drifted into a mind-numbing stupor when the sound of the lock snapping open jerked her back to the room. She caught her breath and sat up as the door swung open.

"Hello, Alice."

Kern Lawson closed the door behind him and headed for the desk. "Sit with me."

She rose and crossed to the seat facing the desk. Sat down as he sank into the chair opposite her.

For a long time he studied her as if trying to decide what to do with her. A minute went by and still he said nothing.

"This is crazy," she finally said. Her voice was thin, not the kind of convincing tone she wanted to project.

"It is. Very. Which is why we are here, darling." He opened his palms. "Plum nuts, bonkers, crazy. You'll note that up here we don't use terms like *mentally challenged*. We tend to go right for the heart of the issue. It's controversial, but we find it produces wonderful results with the right treatment."

She was at a loss.

"How do you like your treatment so far?"

"What treatment?"

He chuckled and she was surprised to find a sliver of comfort in the sound after hours of solitude.

"What treatment, indeed," he said. "The first step here is for me to help you see through your illusions, *capisce*? You have to see yourself for who you really are before we can begin to break down that false self. The delusional self."

"I'm not delusional."

"No? Truth is, you're not seeing what is real even now, as we speak. But I'll let you discover that on your own. See the illusion. Then break with it. That's all I'm asking of you, Alice."

"I'm not Alice."

"Okay, we can start with that. You don't think you're Alice. But the fact is, you don't really know who you are. Are you ugly? Are you pretty? Are you an outcast? You're broken, Alice. You aren't whole. Correction is needed. The first step is embracing that. I can fix you."

A distant, high-pitched whine sat at the back of her mind.

He leaned forward on his elbows.

"You're living in denial, Alice. You're so afraid of what you might find if you really get a good look at yourself that you've shut your eyes. Permanently. I can help you see the truth. But you have to face the truth, beginning with fundamentals, like how you really look, in the real world."

Her heart worked its way through thick beats.

"You think this"—he motioned to her—"is the real you. It's not. The real you is actually not quite this pretty. Most therapists feed their patients a load of lies, pump them full of sunshine, which helps in the short term but doesn't fundamentally change them. I prefer to help the patient see the real truth themselves. I call it *ther-I-py*. And I let you be the *ther-I-pist*. It upsets some."

He paused.

"Dive off the deep end with me, Alice. Think of me as the law, again, no pun intended. A measuring stick for what's good and what's bad about you. Let me reveal who you really are so we can make the appropriate corrections. What do you say?"

"You're saying I'm ugly?"

"Ugly? That's a matter of perspective. But your refusal to admit that you're ugly is triggering denial on a much deeper level. You're broken. Correction is needed. I can make you whole again."

"But you actually think I'm ugly?"

"Isn't that what you secretly think every time you look in the mirror? My nose is too big. My cheeks are too fat. I need to lose twenty pounds. No one loves me the way I am. I don't have any really good friends. No family. Isn't that why you secretly hate yourself?"

She felt her fingers trembling on the armrests.

"The problem, my dear, is that you're delusional about many things. Drop the illusion and you'll see who you really are. It might be a bit uncomfortable at first, but it's the only way to make you whole."

"You don't understand," she said with a little hesitation. "I don't even belong here. I may not like some things about me, but I'm not the person you're talking about."

He stared at her for a long moment, then abruptly rose.

"I'll make you a deal, Alice. You give it a good thinking tonight; there's no rush. Look at yourself in the mirror long and hard, and let's see if you can see through the illusion you've created around your cozy little life. Convince me tomorrow that you love everything about yourself, and I'll consider a different form of therapy. Maybe electric shock treatments. We'll see."

"Shock?"

"Just a little something to get the juice flowing. No pun intended." He headed for the door and she pushed herself to her feet. "Your call, Alice. Go deep or keep it shallow, the choice is yours."

He unlocked the door, opened it, and turned back.

"Get some sleep."

The door shut and the lock engaged.

"Wait!"

As if responding to her voice, the overhead lights blinked out. Darkness engulfed her. Pitch. A thin line of light peeked out from under the bathroom door but it wasn't enough to give the room any shape.

"Wait!"

If Lawson could hear her, he was paying her no mind.

She stood still, trying to let her eyes adjust to the darkness, mind spinning with the realization that she had no control of the lights.

The bed was straight ahead, next to the bathroom door.

She crossed the room, stepping carefully even though she knew there was nothing to trip on. Reached the bathroom door and pulled it open, half expecting to see Lawson leaning against the sink, waiting for her.

White light spilled past her. The bathroom was as she'd left it. Pristine. Clinical. Not even a water spot on the sink. Perfectly quiet.

Anxious and once again alone with only her thoughts, Christy walked back to the bed and sat for a while, staring into the dim, bathroom-lit room. She finally settled on her side and curled up.

It was there, staring at the outline of the desk across the room, that she began to consider Lawson's jumble of words. Any sane person could see through them. This was his progressive ther-I-py, a clever play on the word which set the focus on the self. She being the ther-I-pist.

Words, nothing but.

Unnerving words, but only that.

Unless...

And it was that *unless* that began to get to Christy. *Unless* there was some truth to what he had said. There was. It was true, for example, that she had a rather low self-image. But she didn't *hate* herself.

Unless he was right and she secretly did.

She blinked in the darkness and thought about that.

The *what-ifs* started to cycle through her mind. What if she did hate herself and had only convinced herself that she was okay as a coping mechanism? What if Lawson knew more about her than she did? What if her file contained details about her past that she'd forgotten?

What if she didn't know Christy's past because Christy was only a fabrication of her mind?

Fear washed down her back and she sat up, heart pounding.

It was true. She really did secretly hate many things about herself. Why else did she persistently withdraw from others? Why else did she keep a locket with a fake picture around her neck? Why else did she secretly want to be anyone other than who she really was?

Beautiful, put together, attracting men as she walked confidently across the floor to a stage that waited her appearance—who wouldn't want that?

But that wasn't her. She was the girl who'd been born plain. Ugly, even.

She rose unsteadily to her feet, Lawson's words ringing in her head.

Look at yourself in the mirror long and hard, and let's see if you can see through the illusion.

Christy rounded her bed and walked to the bathroom. She walked in and tentatively stepped in front of the mirror.

The plain face, so familiar to her, stared back. Christy.

Slowly, she began to relax. Christy, not Alice. There was no illusion here, only a very plain image of a girl who'd been born into obscurity. More than once, Austin had told her that he thought she was pretty. What did Austin know? But at least it was something, right?

She lifted her hand and pinched the flesh around her neck. Pulled it back to see what a thinner neck would look like.

The difference produced a stunning result. The slight shift in body mass transformed her into something far more appealing.

She squeezed her nose, which she'd always considered too fat, particularly around her nostrils. Much better. She let go and looked at herself again. Truth was, she did hate the way she looked. A few thousand dollars might fix it when she got up the nerve. But they couldn't lengthen fingers.

He's talking about your insides, Alice.

The room suddenly felt ominously quiet. She'd called herself Alice?

You hate who you are. And for the record, what can Austin know if you only made him up?

The door to the bathroom slammed shut and Christy spun, heart in her throat. Had the air come in and pulled it shut?

She was about to yank it open, but something in the corner of her eye gave her pause. The mirror was there, right in front of her, and the memory of Lawson's voice was whispering through her mind.

Look in the mirror long and hard, it said.

She turned back to the mirror and stared.

The girl looking back at her was her. Christy knew that because she looked enough like her to be her. But she was more than a few pounds heavier. Her neck was thick, nearly the width of her head. The end of her nose rose too high. There were more than a few pimples on her chin and cheeks, a couple too pronounced to cover with makeup. Her teeth weren't straight.

It was an illusion, of course. But it was strong enough to stop her cold, awash with horror.

She slowly backed from the mirror, mind stuttering. *This isn't real. This can't be real. I'm not that ugly. This is just an illusion. This isn't even an illusion—it's just a dream.*

But her face refused to change.

And then another thought edged into her mind. It had to be an illusion, of course it did, but that meant she was capable of having illusions. Ones that looked this real.

So then she was insane?

Her heart slogged thick and heavy in her chest. Chills washed down her arms. She lifted them and saw that they, too, were thick.

This was her?

She couldn't accept that!

You're delusional, Christy. And maybe this isn't the delusion.

The thought swept over her like a frigid wave from the crown of her head to the soles of her feet. She was breathing heavily, fixed and unmoving, as if her feet had been nailed to the floor.

She had to stop this! She had to get out!

Uttering a low moan, filled with horror and disgust, she tore her feet from the ground and staggered toward the door.

Grabbed the knob with thick fingers and twisted.

The door was locked.

She grabbed with both hands and tugged, twisting with all of her strength, but the door refused to budge.

Christy whirled, smothered by the realization that she was trapped alone in a small bathroom. But it wasn't a small bathroom.

It was, but the walls had changed. Instead of white paint, the walls were made of mirrors. She backed into the closed door. Bumped into it. Felt that it too was made of glass.

She was in a room of mirrors reflecting infinite images of her grotesque body. The new, ugly her, not the plain her. Hundreds of hers. Her legs began to shake.

Everywhere she looked she saw only the singular sickening image of someone she despised. Her mind began to fold in on itself.

Grunting with panic, she tried again to get the door open without even a hint of progress. Then again. She erupted into a flurry of frantic attempts to fix what was wrong, wheezing, sweating, sobbing, slamming the door with her fists.

None of it made a difference. The images were still there, mimicking and mocking her every move.

You're an ugly girl, Alice. Look at yourself. Look long and hard and see just how ugly you are, inside and out.

Christy closed her eyes, sank slowly to her seat along the bathroom door, wrapped her arms around her head, and began to rock gently.

Wake up. Wake up. Wake up. Wake up. Wake up.

AUSTIN WOKE with the tang of metal in the back of his throat. His tongue throbbed in lockstep with his pulse. He slowly moved his jaw and was rewarded with a sharp pain that stabbed down his neck.

Details of his ordeal filtered into his mind. As he'd hoped, they'd taken him. The question was, where?

He'd been nearly electrocuted by the hallway door the moment he'd made contact. This explained why the attendants had made no attempt to chase him. The voltage had immobilized him almost instantly and made short work of the attendants' security problem. His whole body still prickled with pain.

He pried his eyes open. They felt like they'd been packed with glass. A white ceiling came into focus.

Austin rolled his head to the right and looked down at his feet. He was strapped to a gurney with two thick bands that ran across his chest and waist. Each of his wrists had been lashed to the bed rails with double-loop zip ties—one cinched tightly around each arm and the other secured to the gurney's steel railings. Plastic, not the padded cuffs that had secured him earlier.

There was a little play, but not enough to slip through the restraints.

The room was cold and clinical, well lit by banks of lights in the ceiling. An air-conditioning unit hummed softly, pumping frigid air into the room.

A long stainless-steel table with a large articulating lamp used for medical exams stood in the middle of the room. Next to it, a tray of surgical instruments.

A medical exam room. But not just an exam room. Something more. The realization dawned on him as his attention settled on the trough that rimmed the table. Then his eyes went to the opposite wall and the four stainless-steel doors, each around two feet square, which stared back at him.

He was in a morgue. The table in the middle was used for autopsies. Acrid fear slipped down his spine.

Alarmed, Austin turned his head to his left and blinked at the sight that greeted him. A row of gurneys, and on the last one, a body. A girl, who was strapped down, motionless. His pulse hammered. He didn't have to see her up close to know who it was.

Alice.

He was on the second floor.

Everything snapped into place. Why he was here. Why Alice was here. And why this specific room.

Fisher's intentions were clear. Why else would they be in a morgue?

But he was reading into what he saw. There had to be another explanation. The man already had covered his tracks. It made no sense to kill them both now.

Then again, he didn't know who Fisher was or how deep this all ran. Either way, in conspiring to get himself onto the second floor, Austin may have inadvertently played right into the man's hands.

His breathing grew thick and heavy. He had to find Christy and get out of here. And he was staring at the one person who gave him any hope of doing so.

He swallowed. "Hey."

No response. Of course not. She was wearing a muzzle. But she didn't turn either.

His fear swelled to a panic that threatened to paralyze him. He had to find a way to shove everything except the problem from his mind. Just another problem to solve. Get her loose. Find Christy. Get out. Before anyone came.

How, he still had no clue, but he had to move quickly.

He jerked his arms violently and knew immediately that trying to break the plastic restraints was futile.

He snapped his head to the surgical instruments next to the exam table. Only a short distance separated him from them. No sound of approach from the hall.

Austin drew his legs up, bringing both knees toward his chest, then planted his feet squarely against the wall to his left. If he could kick the gurney away from the wall he might be able to reach the table.

He gauged the distance. There would be no second try. Push too lightly and he'd be stuck between the wall and table. Too hard and he'd likely knock the tray over.

He tested the gurney with a gentle push on the wall. The wheels budged, which meant they weren't locked.

One chance. Taking a deep breath, he tensed his legs and pushed off as hard as he could. The gurney shot away from the wall, then began to slow.

Not fast enough. He was going to come up short!

Austin jerked on the gurney, hoping to coax more momentum into the rolling. The gurney surged a little and he repeated the motion, desperate to reach the center table.

With a clang the gurney struck the metal stand, nearly toppling it and sending the tools to the floor.

Nearly.

The room quieted. He waited a few seconds, sure that someone had overheard the clashing of metals. The door remained closed.

Alice lay on her back, open eyes fixed on the ceiling, seemingly oblivious.

Working quickly, Austin slid the zip tie along the bedrail until it was as close as possible to the work tray. A scalpel teetered dangerously on the edge. His fingers grazed the tray. On the third try, his fingertip snagged the edge. He inched it toward him slowly.

Close enough for him to grab the scalpel's cool handle.

He couldn't stop thinking that Alice might not be able to help him in her current state. If not…

Austin carefully turned the scalpel in his hand until the blade rested against the zip tie that secured him to the bed. After a few tries the blade sliced through the plastic, freeing his right hand.

He made quick work of the other restraints as well as the wristband that read SCOTT CONNELLY. He slid off the gurney and onto the tile floor, which felt ice cold against his bare feet.

Scalpel gripped tightly in his hand, he circled around the autopsy table and hurried up to Alice's gurney. The doors were still closed.

She looked up at him with the same expressionless eyes he'd seen earlier. She either hadn't heard all the commotion or wasn't in a mental space to react. Drugs?

He scanned her arms for needle marks. None that he could see. They could've given her oral medications. As far as he could tell, she had no bruises or cuts or any other signs of abuse, though he knew what he could see was barely half the story. The trauma she'd likely experienced in her life undoubtedly ran much deeper than her skin.

He sawed through each of the straps that held her body down, snapping each one quickly. Only when he reached her hand restraints did he realize they were made of thick leather. Cutting through them would be difficult without injuring her. He'd have to find another way.

He set the scalpel down and leaned over her bedrail. His trembling fingers worked at the buckle and strap that held the leather muzzle to her face. It came loose easily.

He peeled it gently from her head and dropped it on the floor.

The girl he'd found in the basement stared up at him, pretty, with blond hair and a serene face. Her rainwater eyes were bright, without the deadened look that sometimes accompanied drugs.

But she made no attempt to speak.

"Alice," he whispered. "Remember me?"

No response. Her eyes stared into his, unblinking.

"I'm going to get us out of here, but I need your help. Okay?" He glanced at the door. They were okay for now.

"Can you hear me?"

She blinked once.

"Yes? You can hear me? Please tell me you can hear me!"

"Hello," she said in a simple, sweet voice.

Hope surged. "My name's Austin, I saw you in the basement. Remember? With Fisher."

He could see by her stare that she either wasn't tracking or didn't see the urgency of their situation. She might not be catatonic, but she didn't appear entirely lucid either. There was no telling what Fisher had done to her since the incident in the basement. Austin had to get through to her.

He cradled her face in his hands. Her cheeks were cool against his palms and the moment his thumb grazed her lower lip it nudged into a gentle smile.

"Listen to me, Alice. I overheard you in the basement. You said you already know the way out. 'I've been there. I've seen it. I know.' Been where? What did you see?"

"It's going to be okay," she said.

"*What's* going to be okay?"

She held her faint smile.

"What did you mean by *I've been there*? Where?"

"He knows," she said.

Austin removed his hands, relieved that she was talking, albeit in cryptic terms.

He glanced at the door again.

"Please, I need your help. You know something that Fisher doesn't want you to know. He's trying to keep you quiet. What you know may be able to save us." He hesitated, then pushed more directly. "Tell me the way out of this place."

Nothing.

"Do you know where we are?"

"We're here," she said. "I've seen it."

"Seen what!?"

No response. For all he knew, she was in a totally different zone, deluded by fanciful images that connected with a reality only privy to her. Austin felt his frustration rise. He briefly thought he might have a better chance at searching for Christy on his own.

Time was running out and he was getting nowhere.

"Alice—"

"It'll be okay," she said.

"No, you don't understand. Maybe you *can't* understand. This place is not okay. It's dangerous and we have to leave as soon as possible."

"You can see too."

"See what, Alice? What!?"

"The key. The way out. I saw the lamps."

Austin's heart lurched. "There's a key? Where? A key to what?"

She searched his eyes, apparently fascinated with him.

"Where's the key? Please, Alice. I'm begging you, just tell me where."

Her smile softened.

"In the basement," she said. "Where I was."

His mind spun. "You mean where I saw you with Fisher?"

She looked at him a moment, then spoke in a calm, reassuring voice.

"It's going to be okay, Scott. I promise."

Scott? He took a step back from the gurney.

"I'm not Scott. Who told you my name is Scott?"

"When you came in."

"But I didn't tell you my name was Scott. Fisher told you my name was Scott?"

Alice's eyes shifted to the ceiling as if something there was drawing her attention. He followed her gaze but saw only the florescent lights.

Still no one at the door, but someone could walk in at any moment.

His mind spun with Alice's words. She'd called him "Scott." But that was explained easily enough. Fisher had worked on her before readmitting her. Schizophrenics had highly suggestible minds.

Unless by *when you came in* she was referring to their being admitted at the same time, which, according to the administrator, they had been. Yesterday morning. He, Christy, and Alice, all new cases at Saint Matthew's. Him being Scott, and Christy being Alice.

Only problem was that couldn't be. He was Austin. Always had been; always would be.

"I've seen it," Alice said, smiling gently at the lights above them. "I've been there."

The hinges on the door behind them creaked and Austin went rigid. For a moment he refused to turn. He was only hearing things.

But then he turned and he saw: the door was open.

Fisher stood in the entry, considering Austin with a flint-hard face, arms loose at his sides.

He closed the door quietly behind him, then calmly removed his glasses, blew a speck of dust from them with a single puff, then returned them to his face. Without speaking a word, Fisher approached a wheelchair in the corner, his hard-soled shoes clacking against the tile.

If he was surprised by Austin's attempted escape, he didn't show it. It was as if he'd expected as much.

Fisher reached the wheelchair, bent down to unlock the wheels, swung it around, and pushed it toward them.

Austin stood unmoving, feet rooted to the hard floor. He wasn't sure whether to run away or rush the man. Neither, of course. He didn't stand a chance against Fisher, who was twice his size.

Even if he was able to get out of the room, then what? Break down every door until he found Christy? Get on the elevator and stroll out of the building? His logic had delivered him to the upper level, but it now failed him completely.

Fisher stopped three feet away, strangely calm. He looked at Alice, who wasn't paying either of them any mind. Her gaze was still on the ceiling. But Fisher had to know that she'd spoken. The implications settled into Austin's gut like a shot-put.

His attention drifted down to the wheelchair in front of him, then back up to Fisher, whose eyes were back on him.

"Sit down, Scott," he said. There was no anger in his voice. No malice, no emotion.

Austin hesitated. "My name is Austin Hartt."

"You really want to play games with me?" Fisher asked.

No, he thought. *I don't want to play games with you.*

But Austin's mind was otherwise too busy spinning through complicated thoughts to come up with a reasonable answer.

"If you want to live out this day, sit." Fisher held his gaze. "I won't ask again."

Austin did the only thing he knew he could do. He took a tentative step forward, turned around slowly, and lowered himself into the wheelchair.

CHRISTY FELT herself being pulled from a dream—one in which she was a student at the Special School for Advanced Placement, which ironically, was best known for its football team. And its cheerleaders.

As the law would have it, every student had to participate in a sport. The problem was, Christy wasn't exactly cut out for sports. And, worried about morale, the faculty had come to the conclusion that putting her on the cheerleading squad would dampen school spirit. She was too ugly, you see. The fans in the stands would spend the entire game wondering why such a prestigious school would put such an ugly mug directly in their line of sight. The fact that she often broke down in tears didn't help matters either. They couldn't very well have a weeping cheerleader.

But a solution had been identified. Christy could be of great use to the school by helping with the sports field.

"How?" she asked the board.

"Why, by watering the grass," an old board member with a crooked nose said.

"Water the field? How?"

"With your tears, of course. Every night while the rest of the world is sleeping, you will come down to the field and water the grass with your tears."

Christy opened her eyes and let the dream drain from her head. She was sitting on a floor. The bathroom floor.

As if dumped from heaven, the events of the prior night thudded into her mind. She'd seen herself in the mirror. In the bathroom, which had become a room of mirrors that she could not escape.

Her pulse quickened. White walls. Tiled floor. One mirror above the sink. Only one.

She lifted her hand and saw with great relief that her fingers, although far too stubby, weren't as thick as those she'd seen last night. Scrambling to her feet, she lurched to the mirror and stared at her face.

At Christy's face. Still one pimple, angry red, but not perched on a fat face that would scare away fans in the stands. It had been a dream then?

She twisted to the door. If so, what was she doing in the bathroom?

Because it wasn't a dream, Christy. You were awake and delusional.

Maybe.

She took several calming breaths. Maybe, but maybe just a dream.

Then why is the door locked? From the outside.

Christy hurried to the door, reached for the knob, and twisted. Locked.

Oh no... Oh no...

Knuckles rapped on the wood and she jumped back, thinking that maybe it wasn't over.

Oh no... Oh no!

Her heart was thudding in her ears as the door swung open. She stared up into the face of Kern Lawson, who was chewing on a toothpick, expressionless except for what might be slight curiosity.

He glanced at the room behind her, then fixed his eyes on her again.

"Good morning, Alice."

She blinked at him.

"You look like you could use some sleep," he said.

"I..." She wasn't sure what to say. "I'm fine."

"Better now?"

"Not really. No."

"No," he said. "Not really. But you will be. Let's go, shall we?"

"Go where?"

"You have an appointment with destiny, my dear. A little ther-I-py to help you see your way to the ugly truth."

He walked into the room and Christy followed, not sure what to make of the man. Somehow, he didn't seem as strange to her. More like the man she'd first met than the one who'd spoken to her last night.

Lawson walked to the door, waved his hand over a pad on the wall, and pulled the door open, facing her.

"Tell me, Alice. Did you see anything last night?"

She stopped in the middle of the room, at a loss. *Play along,* Austin had insisted. She had to get out, but right now she was helpless.

No games, just play along.

"I had a dream," she said.

"I see. And what did you see in this dream?"

"That I was ugly."

A smile slowly formed on his face. He withdrew his toothpick and flicked it across the room.

"Good. Progress, and so soon."

She looked at the toothpick lying in the middle of her bedroom floor. She was making progress; let him think that. The sooner she convinced him she didn't belong here, the better.

"The problem is, my dear ugly duckling," he said, grin now gone, "you still aren't making the proper distinctions between what is illusion and what isn't."

"Of course I am. I looked, didn't I? I saw the real ugliness that I secretly imagine in myself. Isn't that what you wanted?"

"Ah." Lawson wagged his finger. "But you still don't understand, sweetheart. You weren't having a hallucination in the bathroom last night. You're actually having one now. As we speak."

For a brief moment, her heart stalled.

She wanted to play along, but doing so felt ridiculous.

"Of course I'm not. You're saying this room isn't real? That you aren't real? That's not possible."

"I'm not saying this room and I aren't real, Alice. I'm saying the you that you see right now isn't the real you. You've suffered some kind of trauma that makes your mind see yourself differently than you really are. I'm guessing that you saw the real you last night."

She couldn't help but to glance down at her hands. Christy's hands.

"Your mind sees only what it can handle. But not seeing the truth is keeping you locked up in delusion." He paused. "When you walk into the bathroom, what do you see?" he asked.

"What do you mean? A plain bathroom."

"And the walls?"

What was he getting at?

"Just walls."

"Color?"

"White."

"You see? At this moment, you see this room, you see me, as we really are. Plain as day. But you see yourself as Christy, a far more palatable rendition of the true you. And when you're in your delusional state, you don't see that the bathroom is actually walled in mirrored glass, all the way around, every square inch." The administrator grinned, pleased with himself. "It's one of the things we do here—a little physical change can often trigger a change in thinking."

"That was only a delusion!"

"So you admit that you are delusional. Good. But I can assure you, the bathroom doesn't have white walls. You just see it that way because your mind can't bear to see you for who you are. It can tolerate one little mirror, maybe, but not a room full of them. It's too much. Last night you were able to emerge from your delusion long enough to see yourself for who you really are. When you woke, the real you had re-treated and the false you had reasserted itself. *Capisce?*"

The tremors took hold of her bones, deep down where no one could see them yet.

"That's impossible."

"Not at all. Entirely common in my trade." His eyes shifted in the bathroom's direction. "Now that you've heard the truth, you might even be able to take a peek and see for yourself. Maybe it's too early."

His eyes alighted on her.

"Would you like to try?"

His suggestion, that she really was the girl she'd seen last night, was screaming though her mind, stopping up her lungs, tilting the world.

Something's really wrong with you, Christy. Something is very, very wrong with you.

"It's all right, Alice. Let's take this step by step." He extended his hand, palm down. "Come with me. Let's get you to your appointment with Nancy."

She pushed back her fear. He was messing with her. He had to be. She couldn't possibly be the girl she'd seen last night and still have all the memories she had of herself as Christy. The orphanage, Austin, high school...

"Alice?"

She walked forward and took his hand.

"That'a girl."

Lawson led her from the room, turned to their right, and walked down the empty hallway. His hand was large and warm, and she felt comforted by his gentle grip.

"You remember Nancy, don't you? The kind lady who interviewed you yesterday?"

"Yes." She kept wondering if the bathroom would have mirrored walls if she took a peek now, as he'd suggested. But that was absurd.

He stopped at the fourth door on their right, released her hand, and twisted the knob.

"You're doing well, Alice. Just a little deeper now."

He opened the door and ushered Christy into a cozy room with a couch and an armchair. Tan walls with bookcases. An aquarium on a credenza, paintings... The first inviting room she'd seen since arriving.

Nancy Wilkins stood from her chair behind a wooden desk, looking as pretty as she had yesterday. Dressed in a blue blouse with a black skirt.

She smiled warmly and removed a pair of glasses from her face. "Hello, Alice. Good to see you again."

"Hi."

"Have a seat." She motioned to the sofa.

The door closed behind her. When she sat, she saw that Lawson had left them alone. His departure was more comforting than his hand. With Nancy, at least, Christy felt heard.

The psychiatrist settled into the armchair and spent a few minutes asking her about her experience so far, not once addressing Christy's concern that she didn't belong here. Naturally she didn't. Many patients felt the same way. It was par for the course in their world.

Play along. Just play along.

With Lawson's suggestion still gnawing at her mind, she took every opportunity to glance at her arms and legs, reassuring herself that he was wrong.

When Nancy asked about the night, she decided that talking about it wouldn't hurt her. She put it out there in summary, avoiding the details, focusing only on Lawson's conclusion that she was, at this very moment, delusional.

"But I know he's wrong," she said. "I mean, really... Do I look fat to you? This is me, right?"

Nancy smiled kindly. "Of course you're not fat, Alice. These are only perceptions and labels. Dr. Lawson is only trying to help you see the truth."

"But you see me. How can I be that girl I saw last night?"

The psychiatrist folded one leg over the other, elbows on the armrests, lightly tapping her fingertips together.

"I don't know who you saw last night or who you see now," she said. "But you're going to learn that the illusion is as powerful in its effect as the truth. When you have a delusion, it will feel just as real as any other perception of reality. Remember that."

Christy considered each word as she spoke them aloud.

"The illusion is as powerful in its…"

"Effect," Nancy filled in.

"As…"

"As the truth."

"As the truth," Christy repeated. "The illusion is as powerful in its effect as the truth."

"Good."

"Then how do you know which is the illusion?" she asked.

"Very few people do."

That was odd. Most people were confused? But before she could think about the matter more, Nancy redirected the session.

"I'd like to help you see into your repressed memories, Alice. Often, understanding what happened to us and why it happened helps us deal with hidden emotional blocks that imprison us."

Her pulse surged. "What memories?"

Nancy hesitated, then smiled warmly.

"Memories of your childhood."

"My childhood?" She had no memories. How much did Nancy really know? "I… How?"

"Using a tool we call hypnotic therapy, which is a fancy way of saying we calm the mind enough to allow memories to surface. You'll be entirely aware the whole time—it's not like what you see on television. You can stop it any point you like. I will only help you relax and see into yourself."

The appeal of knowing more about her childhood blossomed in her mind.

"Would you like to try?"

"Yes," she said. "Yes, I would."

THE EASE with which Nancy Wilkins methodically and gently led Christy away from her current concerns and into a place of deep peace felt at once strangely beautiful and surprising.

No swinging pendulum, no bright lights, no crystal balls.

She'd only asked Christy to enter a room with gentle music playing, then led her down a flight of steps that led to a door which opened to a beautiful garden, where they spent some time around a pool.

Then down another concrete staircase, even deeper under the ground into a magical place with doors. It was through those doors that Nancy asked her to see her childhood.

"Open the door, Alice. Can you do that?"

"Yes."

She put her hand on the round metal knob and turned it. The door slowly swung open on creaking hinges.

"Tell me what you see."

"I... I can't see anything."

"Is it dark?"

"Yes."

"Can you step inside for me?"

She hesitated. "It's dark."

"It's okay, Alice. Nothing will hurt you. Just put one foot in front of the other and step inside. I'm right here behind you."

Christy took a tentative step over the threshold. Then another, and another before stopping three feet in.

"I can't see anything."

"Can you see your feet?"

She looked. "Yes."

"What does the floor look like?"

"It's hard. Concrete or maybe cut stone."

Nancy paused for a moment, then spoke again, tone light and low. "Good. Now look around and tell me if you can see anything."

Slowly her eyes adjusted to the darkness. Walls took shape.

"I'm in a basement with concrete walls. It's dark." She could feel her heart rate begin to rise, a steady, dull thumping sound faintly echoing off the walls.

"Take a deep breath, Alice. It's all going to be okay. I'm right here. Can you do that for me?"

"Yes."

"It's important that you stay calm, because you know that I'm right here, and we can leave any time we want to. Okay?"

"Okay."

"Now I want you to walk forward and tell me if you can see anything else that might help you understand where you are."

Christy slowly walked forward.

"It's dark ahead. I can't see anything ahead of me, only on the sides. The sides are stone or concrete. They're wet."

"Is it warm or cold?"

"Cold."

"Good. That's good. You're doing well, sweetheart. Just keep walking forward."

She did, one tentative foot in front of the other. She knew that she was under hypnosis, only looking into the deepest parts of her mind, but it felt so real. Almost as if she were there.

"I can't see anything ahead of me…"

"Look back at the door that you came through, Alice. Can you do that?"

She twisted and looked back. The door was there, gray. Metal, she thought.

"Yes."

"You see, it's right there."

Christy swung back around and peered into the darkness.

"Yes."

"Keep walking forward."

She'd taken two more steps when a faint outline emerged from the darkness. She stopped.

"I see something."

"Tell me what you see."

"I…" She took another step. "It's… it's bars."

"You see bars on the wall?"

"No. The bars are the wall. I… I think I'm in a prison cell."

"Are you sure it's a prison?"

The bars come into clearer focus. Beyond them was a dark hallway made from the same kind of concrete as the walls in the room she was in.

"Yes," she said. "Yes, I'm in a prison somewhere."

"I want you to ask yourself where you are, because you do know. Just ask yourself where you are."

Christy thought about it and immediately had an answer. She felt her hands begin to tremble.

"I'm underground, in a room. I can't leave this place. I'm… I'm stuck here."

"Take a deep breath, Alice. Try to stay calm. Remember, the door is right behind you. We can leave anytime we want to. Okay?"

She looked back again and took comfort in the door, gray against the darker walls.

"Now tell me again, where are you right now?"

"I'm in a big house. In the basement. I can't leave."

"Why can't you leave? Is someone making you stay?"

"Those are the rules. I can't leave."

"What will happen if you do leave?"

"I… I don't know. Something horrible. I don't want to think about it."

"It frightens you?"

"Yes."

"But you don't need to be frightened now, Alice. We're just remembering. It's very safe."

Christy tried to calm herself and managed to do so, thinking about Nancy sitting close by.

"Okay."

"Good. Now I want you to walk up to the bars and touch them."

"I can't."

"I think you can. They aren't real. It's important that you touch them so that you know they can't hurt you."

They were just bars. Just iron bars running from the ceiling to the floor.

Christy edged forward, lifted her hand, and placed her fingers on the cold steel. Nothing happened.

"I'm touching the bar."

"Good. See, it's going to be all right. Can you see anything else?"

She looked down a long, dark hall that reached into darkness in both directions.

"No. It's just a dark hall. Like a tunnel."

"You're in the basement of a big house that has passageways and a room with bars. Is that right?"

"Yes."

"Can you tell me who owns the house?"

She thought. And she knew.

"A man."

"Do you know his name?"

Her father, she thought. This was her father's house.

Immediately gentle words came to her, like a thought. A man's voice, spoken from a very great distance.

Don't be afraid by what you see here, Christy. He isn't your true father.

"I hear something!"

Come to me. Remember me and I'll show you the way out.

"What do you hear?" That was Nancy. But who was the other one? The man with the gentle voice that filled her with courage. Was it Lawson? It had to be. She couldn't tell by the voice, but still, it had to be.

Then it came again.

They call me Outlaw. I'll show you the way, but you have to take the journey yourself.

"What do you hear?" Nancy asked again. "Tell me, Christy."

"A man's voice."

"Is it your father?"

"I think... I think it might be Lawson..."

A tiny giggle ran through the darkness. A little girl's voice from ahead and to her right that immediately chased away any comfort.

"I hear another voice!"

"It's okay, Christy," Nancy said. "I'm right here."

The girl stopped giggling and began to sing, thin and innocent, just above a whisper.

"Oh, be careful little eyes what you see."

Another sweet giggle sent a chill through Christy's bones. This was her as a child?

134

"Be careful little eyes what you see."

Now Christy could hardly breathe.

"For the Father up above is looking down in love, so be careful little eyes what you see."

The little girl's voice suddenly morphed into a low, guttural, accusing tone on the heels of the song, and Christy immediately knew this was her father.

"Ugly girl. Still too ugly to be seen. Just as ugly as the day you got on your knees and begged for mercy."

The fear that welled up in Christy's chest plunged her into a raw panic. She spun, screaming, running for the door, chased by a low chuckle.

Beyond her scream, she could hear Nancy's voice, just barely: "It's okay, Alice. It's okay, just take a deep breath. You can come out. It's okay."

Christy reached the door and grabbed the knob, knowing that it would be locked. She twisted it anyway, awash in dread.

The knob refused to budge.

Fear had closed off her throat and she had to push hard to get words out.

"I'm trapped! I'm trapped!"

"Open the door, Alice. Just open the door."

"I can't!" It refused to move. She had the horrible realization that she would be caught in this hellhole forever, and it made her want to rip the skin from her face so that she wouldn't be so ugly.

"I can't!"

Something slapped her face. "Wake up, Alice." Again. "The door's open, wake up."

She suddenly became aware that she was back in the office, bent over her knees, sobbing and retching. Nancy was gently stroking her back, comforting her.

"Shh, shh, shh. It's okay, sweetheart. You're safe. You're here with me. It's okay."

Christy caught her breath and forced herself to calm down. A steely resolve slowly began to replace the terrible emotions that had thrown her into hysteria.

"It's okay, sweetheart. Let it out. Everything is going to be okay."

Anger more than resolve. Bitterness.

"That's better. You see? It's all okay."

But Christy wasn't hearing anything that comforted her, because she now knew some things about herself.

She knew that the room she'd seen was real; she'd been there in the dark days, before she'd turned thirteen. She'd been a victim with a tragic past.

She knew that she really was ugly, inside and out.

And she knew just how deeply she despised herself.

Beyond that, she didn't know too much.

ON HIS fifteenth birthday, July 10, Austin traded his childhood for whatever freedom his modest trust fund stipend could buy. He was free, and he had an official court document that said as much. No longer a ward of any state, person, or organization.

Paul Matheson, the orphanage headmaster where Austin lived, had insisted on going to the courthouse with him, but after a long discussion, Austin convinced him that he should go alone. Figure it out.

He was an adult now, after all.

The bus trip across town was short. He'd navigated the courthouse halls without getting lost and, dressed in dungarees and a button-down shirt, stood before a judge who was quite taken with the articulate teenager.

All told, the proceeding took precisely fifteen minutes. Fitting.

On the way out, a portly woman in a loud flower-print dress snapped a photo of him that she promised to e-mail as soon as she got home. Just her way of paying it forward, she'd said. "It's a sad shame that no one had the decency to be here on your special occasion."

She told him with great enthusiasm how she and her rail-thin husband were there to finalize the adoption of the blue-eyed five-year-old who clung to the man. Sweet Bethany, their angel from God. The kind of child every family wanted to adopt.

The e-mail never came, of course. He didn't expect it to.

Austin thanked her for the photo and wished her well, suddenly overwhelmed. What family did he have? None. Never had, never would. Sweet Bethany didn't know how good she had it.

He'd sat on the courthouse steps for a long time, fingering the embossed seal on his document, staring at the world as it flitted by—people coming and going, rushing about like mice in a field. How many of them sensed the meaninglessness of their lives—here today, gone tomorrow, forgotten the day after that? The boredom of such an existence might kill him.

And yet, they all belonged. To someone, somewhere.

In that moment, in every way that counted, Austin had felt strangely lost. Lost to his past. Lost to the world. Lost in thought. He was free, but he wasn't sure what that really meant.

For a brief moment he considered turning east and just walking until he hit the ocean. Then taking a boat to the far side of the world and walking some more, all the way around in search of nothing, or something. Sooner or later, though, he knew that if he walked long enough he'd end up exactly here again, in the same place he'd started.

Here.

Here, where he was no longer a child but not yet old enough to be considered an adult. Living in two worlds but belonging in neither.

That thought boiled his emotions until hot tears welled up in his eyes. He'd wiped them with his sleeve before anyone could see and left the courthouse steps chiding himself for breaking down so easily.

Allowing emotions to control him was ridiculous. Irrational. How many times had he explained this to Christy during one of her many emotional tailspins? They were dangerous. Master your thoughts, he'd told her, time and again, and the emotions will follow.

That was then.

Here he was now, drowning in emotion, unable to hold it at bay. Smothered by his own weakness and totally lost to the world, he was without friends or family to even know he was in terrible trouble.

Trouble so deep that he was unsure he could survive it.

Fisher had secured him to the wheelchair with straps and wheeled him down a vacant hall with checkerboard floors to the room adjacent to the morgue, which he'd accessed by pressing his right wrist against a security pad. He'd checked Austin's restraints and left him without explanation.

Austin found himself in a stark white operating room. Why would a psychiatric ward have a surgical space? Lawson had said they employed progressive therapy, but by invasive means?

Medical equipment on mobile stands lined the far wall. Heart monitors and ventilators. Something like a dentist's chair sat in the corner behind a state-of-the-art operating table, which was surrounded by clusters of light stands.

A door on the room's far side suddenly swung open and Fisher entered, pushing another wheelchair.

At first the operating table blocked Austin's view. He couldn't see who was in the wheelchair, only that it wasn't empty. But when Fisher rounded the operating table in three long strides, the wheelchair came to a halt directly in front of him, six feet away. The solitary figure sat motionless, hands cupped almost prayerfully in his lap.

Jacob.

The boy's pale face was neither surprised nor perturbed. His slight frame and slumped shoulders made him look weak. Jacob was oblivious to the world around him.

Fisher engaged the wheel brake and walked toward a cabinet across the room.

Austin tried to steady his trembling hands, but they weren't obeying so well. The air conditioner hissed too loudly in the cavernous room.

Fisher returned, a pair of blue surgical gloves dangling from his hand. He stopped and gazed down at Austin.

"You should know that no patient has ever escaped from the

facility. Like you, several have tried, of course."

Austin didn't reply.

"I can assure you, you won't succeed. Still, I appreciate your initiative. It's"—he paused—"enlightening."

Fisher considered him for a moment, stone-cold, void of expression. "Curious, isn't it? At first glance, you appear complicated. Not all people do, so please take that as a compliment. You relish the fact that people see you as complex. It's your mask. It's what makes you different from those around you, but the truth is you're really quite simple."

"You don't know me."

"Oh? I think I can read you like a book, Scott. It's not that hard, really. Despite what most people believe, hiding behind our own skin is impossible. Every day, we betray ourselves in a thousand ways without realizing it. The true self always claws its way to the ugly surface."

He shoved his chin at Austin and glanced at his hands.

"Take your mannerisms, for instance. Even a moderately observant person could deduce that yours is an obsessive mind, always thinking, thinking, thinking. That nervous tick you have with your hands is a manifestation of such angst."

Austin realized he had been mindlessly touching his fingertips. He stopped abruptly and balled his hand into a fist.

Fisher continued. "If you have an obsessive mind, you also probably suffer from a bit of insomnia, the bane of a brain that won't shut off. I suspect yours is quite severe. I can only imagine how many nights you've suffered in an endless loop of data, questions, and reasoning as you stare at your ceiling in the dark, lost in thought." He paused. "How am I doing so far?"

Austin shifted his weight in the seat.

"You're an avid reader, I presume," Fisher said, pacing now, eyes on the walls as if only half interested. "Most obsessive thinkers are. You likely devour a wide variety of subjects, doggedly in search of pieces to the puzzle in your mind that never quite seems to come together. That driven nature is what makes you special, but it's also what drives you from others. And that's lonely for you, isn't it? Have many friends?"

"Enough."

"And yet you and I both know you'd choose a book over a friend any day."

Austin sat quietly. Heat spread across his neck.

"So you could say that, yes, I do know you. I would guess that you have a deeply rooted addiction to your mind. You find your identity in your intellect. Knowledge is your drug and without it you're afraid you'll die. At the very least, your life would feel meaningless."

"An arrogant diagnosis informed by only a few observations," Austin said.

"Is it?"

"Everyone thinks. It's what humans do. Our ability to think separates us from the animals. Everyone pursues knowledge."

"A romantic notion, but let's be honest, shall we? You ride high enough on your horse to think that most people traipse mindlessly through life without asking a single meaningful question. Tell me I'm wrong."

A beat.

"Unlike most people," Fisher said, "questions are what make you tick. *Knowing* is what gives you a reason to roll out of bed in the morning, because you're not just in search of knowledge. Facts are never enough. You're after something else, something more fundamental. You're after the truth."

Fisher stopped his pacing and regarded Austin directly. "But the problem with believing you can think your way to the truth is that you can't know the unknowable."

"All things are knowable."

"Is that so?"

"With enough time, yes."

"Then tell me, where did you come from? In the very beginning."

The question caught in Austin's mind.

"It's a simple question," Fisher said. "Surely you know the answer."

The question turned over in his mind. "No one knows."

"Of course not. Just as you can't know with certainty the other questions that drive you to the brink of madness. Is life eternal and if so, where were you before you were born? Does God exist? Do you even matter in this great big universe of ours?"

"Esoteric questions," Austin said, wondering why Fisher was taking the time to give him a philosophy lesson.

"But those are the ones that will eventually drive you crazy. Our minds ask questions we can't know the answers to with certainty. Our answers depend on when and where we were born, which myths and legends we were taught to believe, our perceptions that mold our very small realities. A few hundred years ago, you would've believed the world was flat and sickness could be cured by leeching the blood from your body. And you would've been right as far as you knew. Which of your beliefs today will turn out to be obviously false tomorrow?"

The blue surgical gloves in Fisher's hand were starting to concern Austin.

"You're obsessed with figuring out the truth, but you can't. It's unknowable, a mystery sunken so deep in the universal ocean that the only way to reach it is to die. You're going to spend the rest of your life chasing illusions of certainty, but you will never find peace. You see, it's not what you know that matters, it's how you *are*. And you, Scott, are ill."

A thick silence passed between them.

"You say I'm ill," Austin said, "but where's your data? In the file you fabricated, of course."

"Fabricated? Tell me, how are your headaches?"

"What?"

Fisher lifted his index finger to his left brow. "They radiate from here, don't they? Is it a throbbing pain or more like a jagged ice pick?"

Austin could hear his own pulse in his temple. How could Fisher know about his headaches? From his file? Scott's file.

No. He could have found Austin's medication in his jeans pocket. It wasn't too much of a stretch.

"Frontal lobe lesions are quite common in patients who suffer from delusional maladies, particularly those of a grandiose or schizophrenic nature. Severe headaches are quite common among patients like you."

"You keep saying I'm delusional."

"Like you, I follow the data wherever it leads. But rest assured, I'm here to help you. I want to help you find peace."

Fisher crossed to Jacob. Stepped next to the boy and placed a hand on his shoulder. "What do you think Jacob knows? Hmm?"

"He doesn't know what's going on around him," Austin said. "He's in his own little world."

"And yet he is quite happy." He turned to Jacob. "Tell us, Jacob. Are you afraid?"

The boy blinked. Slowly shook his head.

"No, of course not. Is anything upsetting you at all right now, Jacob?"

A slow response again, but a definite shake of his head. This time Austin was sure that Jacob smiled, although his lips didn't move per se.

"You see."

"He's practically a vegetable," Austin said.

"Or so you say. And even if that were the case, is that so bad? Look at him. Jacob enjoys an enviable state of being, peace that you can only dream of. You may have read about it in your books, but Jacob… Jacob experiences it."

"He's unaware of any danger; of course he isn't worried!"

"He's very aware, just not of any danger. If he is aware of danger, he doesn't care, because he sees no threat to his life or his well-being. Survival isn't a concern to him. He's practically a Zen master, and yet you see him as a vegetable."

The comparison gave Austin some pause, but his mind was still on those blue gloves, which Fisher periodically slapped against his palm.

"Haven't you ever watched a bird on a sunny afternoon and wondered what it would be like to live completely free, to have no concern for anything? Or a cat who must accept life only as it is in the moment—no worries, no problems to be solved, nowhere to get to. What must that feel like? Welcome to Jacob's world. He's at complete peace."

"You can't know that. You're not in his mind."

"That's where you're wrong. Emotions are simply chemical responses to thought patterns, the physical manifestation of which can be accurately measured in the body with the proper instruments. I've helped Jacob for quite a while, and I can tell you with absolute certainty that he's at perfect peace. You, on the other hand, are looking at the gloves in my hand, and, filled with knowledge of what they might mean, are filled with anxiety."

The simple truth of it hit Austin. Needled him.

"So tell me, who is better off? You… or Jacob?"

Austin looked across at the boy. His serene eyes were void of any concern, any confusion, any anxiety. There was a gentle air of peace about him, but what Austin really saw behind those eyes was a detached human with a broken mind.

"He's not all there," Austin said.

"Not fully human, is that it?" Fisher said.

"Not really, no."

"You think a body part, like a leg, makes you more human than someone who doesn't have it? If I were to remove your leg, you would be less than you are now?"

The gloves loomed large in Austin's mind. With them, a saw.

"No," he said.

"No. Are you your hands? Your face? Your brain? Or are you something else?"

"I'm my mind."

Fisher regarded him for a while, staring directly into his eyes.

"So then Jacob, with less of a mind, is somehow less human? I don't think he would appreciate your opinion, frankly."

"He can't even process my opinion."

"Maybe not. Which perhaps gives him an advantage over you. He's at peace."

Fisher began to pull on the surgical gloves.

"Let me ask you a very important question, Scott." Fisher's eyes drilled him. "Given the choice, would you rather be in perfect peace, or would you rather be right?"

Austin's mind spun. He did want peace. In fact, being right gave him peace.

Or did it? Actually, in all honesty, the need to know answers with absolute certainty kept him in a constant state of low anxiety.

"There are two ways we can do this," Fisher said, pulling on the second glove. "I can sedate you and treat you while you're unconscious, but I think it would be far more effective if you face your fears now. My data sets indicate that a willing entry into therapy has a markedly positive influence on patient outcomes." He released the tight elastic latex glove and let it snap loudly on his arm.

"Your choice."

Austin's heart rate was at a full gallop, and he seemed powerless to calm himself. He realized that his knees were bouncing nervously, but he no longer cared about appearances. He only wanted out of this chair, out of this madness. The idea of being sedated terrified him. Images of catatonic patients filled his mind. No mind, no self.

His anxiety raged unchecked. Part of Fisher's argument made some absurd kind of sense, which only pushed Austin deeper into fear. The man wanted him out of the way. Fisher wasn't going to kill his body, he was going to kill his mind, which was worse.

"Nothing? So be it," Fisher said. He removed a vial and syringe from his lab coat pocket. Uncapped the syringe and carefully drew a clear liquid into it. Tapped the side to remove the air bubbles.

"Please…"

Fisher looked at him. "Please? Please what?"

"Please don't do this."

"No sedation?"

His mind didn't seem to be processing his choices properly. He knew that he was already giving himself over to fear, but he couldn't stop it.

"No," he said.

The man nodded lightly. "An excellent choice." The edge of his mouth nudged into a faint smile as he capped the syringe.

"Let's help you find perfect peace, shall we?"

Fisher walked behind his wheelchair and rolled him toward the corner, where a dental chair waited. No, not a dental chair. This one had a circular head restraint with bolts above it.

Austin saw the contraption and knew immediately what Fisher intended. He was going to secure Austin's head in that device and surgically fix his brain. Permanently.

Terror unlike Austin had ever felt swept down his body in sudden, unrelenting waves. His arms were fastened to the chair, but that didn't stop the tremor in his hands.

"You're going to lobotomize me?" His voice was high and it cracked.

"Far too rudimentary," Fisher said, wheeling him. "We'll use an advanced procedure—a single small-gauge needle through your right nostril up into the brain. The chemicals I inject will kill the appropriate matter. Clean."

Austin's mind stuttered as his grip on his own awareness began to dissolve. The tremor spread up his arms and consumed his entire body. Swallowed him whole.

A high-pitched ringing screamed in his ears as Fisher's voice faded to a muffled drone. His chest heaved uncontrollably, sucked at the thick air in long draws. He was going to die.

In the sliver of the space between two breaths, the world around him slowed as his mind collapsed. Austin saw himself as though he stood outside himself. The room. Fisher. Jacob. The pulsing of his heart hung in the air like the sound of a distant drum that came from nowhere and everywhere at once.

He blinked.

Unbidden, a swell of rage rose from somewhere deep inside and shook him. He screamed, ragged and full-throated. Every fiber in his body strained, stretched taut to the breaking point.

Driven by a primal instinct to survive, Austin violently threw his head back, then pitched his weight up and backward with only one thought in mind.

No.

No, he would not die.

No, he *could* not die.

There was no calculation in his movement, only raw impulse, but that basic drive to live followed a logic of its own, previously unknown to Austin.

The momentum carried Austin up off the seat and over. The ceiling came into view, then Fisher's body.

The movement was so sudden, so forceful, so unexpected that it caught Fisher flatfooted. Before he could move, Austin's knee slammed into his face, crushing his nose with a loud crack.

With a grunt, Fisher dropped to the ground.

Austin's trajectory carried him over, then stalled. He crashed to the tile floor, facedown, arms still strapped to the wheelchair, which was now above him.

He gasped in pain. He was on his knees with the wheelchair on his back and Fisher was behind him, momentarily stunned, but the large man would quickly recover and crush him.

Then kill him.

Austin jerked one leg under his torso and shoved up. He staggered to his feet. But he could hear Fisher's heavy breathing, wheezing, another grunt. The man was getting up!

Blinded by rage, Austin whirled, taking the wheelchair with him. He roared, as if by the sound of his voice alone, great strength would flood his body.

He was halfway through his turn when he saw Fisher, just pushing up from the floor, blood streaming from his broken nose. The man's hand was at his face, feeling the flow of blood.

Only then did it occur to Austin that he actually had a weapon in his hands. At his back.

The wheelchair.

It was metal. It was heavy. It was already swinging around behind him, strapped to his arms.

Austin threw all of his weight into his turn and spun through and around.

The wheelchair connected with a jarring thud, jerking Austin to an abrupt halt. He couldn't see what impact the contact had made behind him, and he had no desire to twist and look. He only wanted to get away.

But when he tried to run, he found that the wheelchair was snagged.

He twisted viciously, pulled it free, and staggered forward. Only when he'd taken three full strides did he glance over his shoulder and see the damage he'd caused.

Fisher was on his knees, staring at him with wide, disbelieving eyes.

Blood ran from a gaping hole near his right temple. He didn't seem capable of moving.

Austin caught his breath and spun back to face the man, stunned. For a moment they remained fixed, staring at each other. Something about the man's eyes sent a chill down Austin's spine. Why wasn't he pursuing?

Fisher's body tilted forward and then fell face-first onto the hard floor with a sickening thump. Blood seeped from the wound in his temple and began to pool around his head.

Unconscious?

Austin twisted his head around and looked at the wheelchair strapped to his arms. At the right wheel, the protruding chrome brake-lever was slick with blood.

His heart plowed through three heavy beats.

And then he knew. He knew as much as he'd ever known anything in all of his life.

Heaving with exertion and panic, Austin slowly faced the director of admission's prone, unmoving form on the floor.

He had killed Fisher.

BOOK THREE
UNSEEN

HOW LONG Christy had been alone, pacing in her room, she no longer knew. Time seemed to have shifted into a new paradigm that cycled back on itself every few minutes as the memory of what had happened spun through her mind.

What had happened? She'd seen some things. For the first time she could recall, she'd broken the barrier that blotted out her childhood. It's what she had always wanted.

It was the stuff of nightmares.

She was a nightmare.

One that walked on two legs, with blood pumping through her veins, and a mind to record each dreadful step. If there was a hell worse than the one she'd been thrown into, she pitied the followers of the god who'd made it.

Her left index finger was bleeding at the nail, which she'd long ago chewed down to nothing. She'd seen her ugly self last night and, truth be told, she hated both of her selves—the ugly one and the uglier one.

Which one she really was didn't matter as much as what she'd learned about her childhood. Her delusional state, now all but certain, was the clear result of inhuman treatment. An abusive adult had held her captive in a prison. Her mind had shut off the horror of it all as a means of coping.

She paced back and forth on the tile floor in her bedroom, crushed by the memory. How could anyone do that to a child? How old had she been? Twelve. And younger, because while in that basement room she had the distinct sense that she'd been there a long time. Maybe her whole life.

The thought sickened her. But there was more than deep self-pity flowing through her veins now. Bitterness and rage screamed through her mind, demanding some kind of justice.

Nancy had comforted her with soothing words for half an hour, and had then led her back to her room with the promise that, however painful, this was all part of her healing. She would give her an hour to gather herself before meeting again.

Healing? How could anyone heal from being born ugly to abandonment and abuse?

She couldn't get the song she'd heard under hypnosis out of her mind.

Be careful little eyes what you see... Why? Because the father up above was looking down in love, of course. Her father.

Evidently, she hadn't been careful enough. Not good enough, not pretty enough. Thoughts of what kind of father hers might be made her cringe.

What had she done? That's what she couldn't figure out. What could any little girl have possibly done to deserve such a terrible warning?

Something. And the truth was, she hated herself for doing whatever she had done to become what she'd become. And the only way out was through Lawson, who, in her mind's eye, was called Outlaw. Assuming that's who the other voice belonged to—and she was quite sure it had to be.

Christy glanced at the bathroom door again. She had to pee, but the thought of going inside was too much. What if she opened the door and found the walls mirrored? Or, worse, saw the uglier Christy staring back at her? She was ugly either way, but coming face-to-face with the image she'd seen last night would be too much. That's what they wanted, she knew that. But she wasn't ready, not for that.

She would rather pee in her pants.

The thought made her stop and stare at the door. *You're being pathetic, Christy. This is insane.*

Wasn't that the point? She was insane. But insane enough to stand here and pee in her pants?

There was no reason to think that when she opened that door she would actually find a room of mirrors. She was evidently a master of delusions. She would simply maintain the delusion—assuming it really was one—walk right in, go pee, flush, and walk out.

Christy headed for the door before she had time to reconsider. She'd covered half the distance before time slowed enough for her to think twice, and in thinking again, her pace slowed.

Another three steps, not six feet from the bathroom, the room began to grow fuzzy in her mind's eye. What was she doing? She couldn't face this!

You don't know what you'll face, Christy. Keep moving. Just open the door, go to the toilet, pee, and run out.

She pushed her feet forward, one after the other, if for no other reason than to prove to herself that she wasn't who she feared she might be. They were messing with her head. There was no way she could be as jacked up as they were suggesting.

No?

She reached the door, lungs working like billows, long and deep. Placed her hand on the knob. Twisted.

Oh be careful little eyes what you see…

Christy closed her eyes and pushed the door open, half expecting to hear the little girl's voice singing the song inside. But there was no song.

Open your eyes, Christy. It's going to be okay.

She snapped them open, saw immediately that the walls were

covered in mirrors, and, before she could slam the door shut, stared straight at the image of herself reflected back from the opposite wall.

Her neck was thick, her nose flat and wide, her thighs massive, her face puffy and covered in pimples. Not just ugly: in her eyes, hideous.

She tried to close the door but her muscles weren't obeying.

"Don't like what you see?"

Christy jumped at the sound of Lawson's voice. She slammed the bathroom door shut with a loud bang and spun to her right.

He stood in the doorway with one hand in his pocket, twirling a toothpick between the fingers of his other hand.

She glanced down at her own fingers, sure they would be thick and stubby. But they weren't. Not as thick and stubby as they really were.

"It's a delusion, Alice," Lawson said. "Nancy gave me the good news. She said you had a real breakthrough. That we might be unraveling the events that initially triggered your disassociation with reality."

"Tell me what you see," she demanded, pulse still racing.

He smiled at her, then stepped in and shut the door.

"The truth?"

"Yes. Just tell me who you see standing in front of you right now."

"I see Alice. Someone who's broken, inside and out. A girl who was born into a world so threatening that she now pretends to be someone else named Christy."

"What do I look like?"

He hesitated.

"Tell me!" she snapped marching toward him. "Just tell me! Just how ugly am I?"

His pause more than his tone sealed the authenticity of his judgment.

"Ugly," he said. "Inside and out. Broken. But I'm here to make the appropriate corrections, once and for all. You just have to be patient and walk through the fire. I'll be here every step of the way. I promise."

She lifted her hands to her head, dug her fingers into her hair, and paced, unable to hold back tears.

"Not all would agree with my methods, my darling, but I get done in days what psychiatrists all over the world only dream about achieving in a lifetime. If ever."

"Achieve what?" she cried, spinning to him with her fists balled at her sides. "What?" She jabbed her forefinger at her head. "This? Proving that I'm a basket case?"

He lifted the toothpick and slowly inserted it into his smiling mug. "For starters, yes. But it doesn't stop there, my dear. I've only just begun. The real shift will come when you begin to trust me completely. That could be three hours from now, three weeks from now, or three years from now. Just depends on how quickly you want to be you. The real you, the beautiful you."

"I'm ready now! Now!"

"Truth is, you hate yourself. You don't feel like you belong. You don't think you're good enough for anyone, including yourself. You're locked in a prison of your own making. The first step toward freedom is trusting me completely."

His words worked deep. She wasn't good enough. She hated herself. She always had, deep down where no one knew or cared, because she had no one to know or care.

"I said I'm ready."

Lawson chuckled. "A bit hasty, don't you think? Patience, my dear. Patience. You've only just discovered who the ugly you is."

"I'm not this!" she cried, stepping toward him. "You hear me? I'm not this!"

Lawson tsked. "You see? Still all wrapped up in denial." He turned toward the door as if to leave, and the thought of being left alone with herself frightened Christy more than she was prepared for. "I was just checking on you. I can see our work is cut out—"

"Wait!" She hurried forward. "Wait."

Lawson twisted back. "Wait for what?"

"You said that I don't have to be like this. That you can help me be beautiful. What did you mean? How? Not in three years but now. Anything... Just tell me how."

He turned and regarded her somberly. "I don't think you're ready."

"For what? Ready for what?"

"For a jump-start," he said.

"A jump-start? What's a jump-start?"

"Something not so different from hypnosis, or placing mirrors on the walls of the bathrooms. There's no magic in it. They're just shifts on the physical plane that can sometimes help us make mental shifts. Juice you up, so to speak, to get the healthy part of the brain running."

"Do it!" She snapped. And then, with some curiosity, "What kind of physical shift?"

He eyed her over. "Well... you seem to be quite concerned with appearances. Quite natural, mind you. You weren't exactly born to make the beauty pageant circuits. Fixing you up a bit might help you see things differently."

"Fix me up? How?"

"In your case, fix you up means cut you up. And frankly I don't think you're ready for that."

Cut her up? She balked.

He saw her expression and offered an explanation.

"Cut you up," he said, drawing his finger over his face. "Make some minor cosmetic changes to your face." His eyes dropped to her midsection. "Your body."

Cosmetic surgery. The idea made her cringe.

"It's amazing what we can do with a surgery or two these days," he said.

"What could you do?"

He shrugged. "Your face. Nose. Give you a thinner neck. Stomach."

"What about fingers?"

He looked at her with steady eyes, dead serious.

"If that's what'll fix your brain, that's what we'll do."

Silence passed between them.

What was she thinking? She glanced at the bathroom door. Beyond it, there were mirrors, and the images she saw in those mirrors were of a girl who'd been victimized in the worst possible way. Christy didn't think she could live with that girl.

"But like I said—"

"I want to talk to Austin," she said.

"Austin?"

"Scott. I mean, I want to talk to Scott."

Lawson cocked his right brow. "You're thinking he might help you break free from your delusions."

"I'm thinking I need to think, and Austin helps me think."

He frowned. "An intelligent boy. You do realize that he's as delusional as you are."

"The illusion is as powerful in its effect as the truth," she said. "Isn't that the way it goes?"

"Impressive."

"What does it matter if he's delusional? I don't see him that way. I just want out of this"—she waved her hand at her head—"whatever this is."

Lawson rolled the toothpick in his mouth and grinned. "That's my girl. Maybe you're further along than I thought."

He dipped his head as if to take a bow.

"I'll talk to Nancy."

DEAD. THE stone-cold reality seeped into Austin as he stood near Douglas Fisher's motionless body. The man lay facedown in a pool of blood that seeped slowly across the floor, his eyes pried wide open by death's cold fingers.

Austin stood there, strangely detached from his body. The room seemed airless. He could not breathe.

A part of him wanted Fisher to rise to his feet, walk up to him, and pound his skull in. At least then this nightmare would end with a well-placed blow to his head. But the other part knew Fisher had to die, that there was no other way, and that this man on the ground would never hurt anyone again.

Not him.

Not Christy.

Not Jacob, not Alice. He had to believe that.

Hold it together, Austin...

The wheelchair still hung awkwardly behind him, its thick leather straps gnawing at his wrists. Mind reeling from the turn of events, he hunched under the chair to alleviate the pressure on his arms.

He had to get out, but now, doing so seemed absurd. He had just killed a man! There would be an investigation. That might be good, but it might also seal his fate. No witnesses. No one to...

Austin spun to his right. Jacob sat in his wheelchair, gentle eyes fixed on him. The boy had witnessed it all.

The boy who had half a brain and could not speak.

"Jacob." The name caught in his throat.

He slowly walked toward the boy, dragging the wheelchair, side-stepping Fisher's body. Glanced at the doors to his right. Still closed, but for how long? The commotion had surely drawn someone's attention. The building had too many electronic eyes and ears for something like a murder to go unnoticed. At any moment, a security detail would storm through that door. They would see Fisher, put the pieces together, and know what he'd done.

Keep it together.

"Look at me," he said, turning back to Jacob.

Jacob was lost in his head. Did he know what had just happened? He had to, but how would a mind like his process something like this?

Austin stopped directly in front of him and sank into the wheelchair at his back.

"I know you can hear me."

Jacob just looked at him.

"I need your help." He nodded toward his hands. "See these restraints? They're tight and I can't free myself. I need you to help me get them off. Can you do that?"

Jacob blinked slowly.

"Please." A thick knot of desperation rose in Austin's throat. "I won't hurt you. I promise. What you just saw... I didn't mean to kill him. I swear, Jacob." He looked over his shoulder at the door again. "I need you to help me. Please."

The boy's chest steadily rose and fell. If he heard Austin, there was no external sign of it.

"I can't do this alone, Jacob. I need you to unbuckle these straps."

He stared into the boy's soft, unmoving eyes, keenly aware that no amount of encouragement would likely get him to move. He wasn't even sure the boy *could* move.

He closed his eyes. *Think. Think!* But what was there to think? There was no way to undo what he'd done, no way to free himself that came to him.

He suddenly envied Jacob's oblivion. The boy was at peace because of his ignorance. The thought of it now seemed like bliss. Ignorance was bliss. It had to be better than the hopelessness that shredded Austin from the inside out. What now?

Soft fingers grazed his hand and he opened his eyes wide in surprise.

Jacob reached toward him and drew his slender hands across the restraint that cinched Austin's right arm. His fingers lingered. Then slowly, as if remembering the solution to a difficult puzzle, the boy worked the strap through the buckle, folded it back, and after several tries released it.

"Good boy," Austin breathed. "Good boy."

The pressure from the leather band eased and he carefully slipped his arm out. Working with trembling fingers, Austin quickly freed his left arm and stood.

"Thank you." He leaned forward and kissed the top of Jacob's head. "Thank you."

Jacob's head angled down, eyes staring blankly at the floor once again.

Okay… Okay, one step at a time.

Pushing the wheelchair aside, Austin stumbled toward a stack of surgical towels on a work stand next to the operating table. He had to clean up the blood and move Fisher's body before they were discovered.

The door was still closed. He still had time.

Just one step at a time.

He grabbed an armful of the blue rags, ran to Fisher's prone body, and dumped them on the floor. Working feverishly, he spread them out in a patchwork that quickly soaked through with blood.

The metallic scent was too strong to ignore, but he pushed the thought aside and mopped as fast as he could. So much blood. So much...

By the clock on the wall, it took him nearly five minutes to get the floor clean, a task that required him to roll the director's body over so he could wipe up under the head.

Good enough. He dumped the rags, grabbed one of two gurneys along the far wall, and wheeled it next to Fisher's body. Getting him onto the gurney wouldn't be easy. It was all taking too long—way too long. And he still had to dispose of the body. He couldn't shake the voice in his head telling him that it didn't matter, he was a goner. The only thing that kept him going was that key Alice had spoken of.

That key, located where she'd been, which could only be where he'd first seen her. He didn't know what door it unlocked, but whatever it was, she'd been there.

After lowering the gurney as far as it would go, he leaned over Fisher and grabbed the dead man's belt. The guy weighed two hundred pounds if he weighed one. Too heavy to lift like this. Austin had to get him up piecemeal, first his feet, then his legs, but when Austin tugged on the man's head, his feet fell off the mattress.

It took him several tries to wrestle the limp form fully onto the gurney, and by then his arms and shirt were matted with blood. There was no way he would make it through the halls searching for Christy or down to the basement looking like this.

No shirts in the operating room that he could see. Better to go shirtless until he could find one. He'd just say he'd taken it off because it was scratchy. If he was capable of taking a pen to Jacob's neck, he was capable of anything. After all, he was a nutcase, right? So then he could just play the part.

He pulled off his shirt and stuffed it under Fisher's body, then ran to a wide stainless-steel sink at the end of the room. After opening the faucet all the way, he furiously scrubbed his hands and slid his forearms under the water, desperate to get the evidence off his skin. Fisher's blood stained the undersides of Austin's fingernails, and it took some doing to get it out.

A crimson swirl disappeared down the drain. There was so much blood.

He stopped and gripped the sink with both hands. Nausea swept through his gut and he tried to swallow it back. But he couldn't. He leaned forward and retched into the sink. Then again.

Get it together, Austin.

He coughed and wiped his mouth. Turned off the water.

Austin pulled upright and looked into the mirror. Exhausted eyes etched with red veins stared back. Only yesterday he'd been in a classroom, mixing it up with grad students. Today he was just a skinny kid who had finally bitten off more than he could chew. Way more.

His head still throbbed. Brain lesions in his frontal lobe, Fisher had said. What if it was true?

He took a few steadying breaths and tried to gather his nerves. Christy was in a room somewhere on this floor. He knew what he had to do; he just had to do it—one step at a time. If he didn't make it, he didn't make it, but he'd gone way too far to give up now.

Now or never.

He ran for the gurney and wheeled it toward the door, aware of the harsh soap scent that lingered on his skin. They'd smell that. No they wouldn't, because no one was going to be watching when the skinny, shirtless kid wheeled the gurney with the dead guy down the hall. That's what he told himself.

"You're okay, Jacob." *Maybe better off than me.*

Too true at the moment.

He stuck his head into the hall, saw that the way was clear, then quickly pushed the gurney through the doors and wheeled it back toward the morgue at a run. Slid to a stop next to the wide double doors.

Unlocked. Finally, a break. He banged through with his back and pulled the gurney all the way in. With a whoosh, the doors swept closed.

The room was quiet. He looked to the far corner where Alice had been earlier.

Gone.

Urged forward by fear and adrenaline, Austin pushed the gurney next to one of the refrigeration units in the wall and tugged. The long tray slid out on rails. A cool draft spilled over his arms.

He dragged Fisher's body onto the metal slab and carefully pushed it back into the wall. Latched the door. The large steel handle engaged with a hollow click.

Austin stepped back. His shirt was under Fisher's body, but it hardly mattered. The evidence would show that he'd killed the man. He simply had to live with that now. It was self-defense. He hoped Jacob could confirm that somehow.

Okay… Okay… He had to think. First things first. A shirt.

He ran to a rack against the far wall and pulled off a blue shirt that looked about his size. Slipped into it. Good enough.

Okay… Good… This was good. He ran his hands through his hair, clicking through the thoughts crowding his mind. He was on the second floor. Fisher was out of the way. He was alive. Christy had to be somewhere near.

Good, good, all good. Right? He was actually in a good place.

He had to find Christy, and the only way to do that was to check every room, rule each one out individually. Problem was, the rooms were secure, accessible only with a biometric chip.

Austin caught his breath, an audible gasp that sounded throughout the room.

Fisher's chip!

He whirled around and ran to the scattered instruments on the surgical tray. He grabbed a scalpel and rushed back to the refrigerators.

The drawer that held Fisher's body slid out at his first tug. Right arm. He could do this. For the first time since waking on the second floor, he actually felt the all too familiar rush that came with solving a challenging problem.

Next to mopping up blood and disposing of a dead body, cutting a microchip out of a man's arm felt like a summit of victory. Why?

Because with this chip, Austin would have access not only to whatever door separated him from Christy, but to the elevator.

To the front door.

He turned Fisher's hand and ran his finger along the forearm until he found the chip's hard shape embedded beneath the flesh, one inch above his wrist.

He pressed the scalpel's razor edge against the skin and sliced cleanly with only slight pressure. The flesh parted easily, and Austin peeled the skin back and worked the blood-coated cylinder to the surface. He wiped it clean on the sheet before returning Fisher's body to the cooler.

This small silver chip would be their savior.

He palmed the chip and headed for the door. He just hoped it wasn't too late.

Austin entered the hall and began his search at the elevator. The first five rooms along the northern wall were empty. The sixth housed an old man who sat on the corner of the bed and grinned at Austin with two teeth.

"Sorry."

He pulled the door shut and noticed that a small green light just above the entry pad was lit. The others had all showed red. Green for occupied, red for empty. Set by a motion sensor inside the room?

Christy had to be in one of these, and he now knew how to search.

Unless she wasn't in any of these rooms. Unless Lawson had her locked up tight in a special place far away, where he could probe her mind with far more progressive measures.

Austin hurried forward, glancing at the lights on each pad. Red, red, red. All red.

He was well past the operating room, nearing the end of the first corridor where it turned sharply left, when the sound of someone walking stopped him in his tracks. Hollow footfalls echoed ahead. High-heeled shoes. Whoever it was would round the corner within seconds.

A single thought crashed through his mind: They'd found him!

He rushed to the next room and lifted the microchip to the access pad. But before he could use it, the chip slipped from his fingers and fell to the floor.

The sound of the clacking feet was closing. If they found him with the chip...

He snatched it up and frantically waved the transmitter in front of the security pad. This time the door clicked open. He barged in and eased the door shut behind him, breath still, praying he'd made it without being seen.

But there was another problem, wasn't there? The light. If he was right about the motion detector, it would shine green.

The room he'd entered was larger than the others and contained more furniture—a desk framed by a whiteboard that hung on the wall behind it, a bed, a dresser, and just past the bed, a bathroom.

He padded across the hard floor, slipped into the bathroom, and eased the door closed. With any luck, whatever sensor indicated occupancy wasn't active in the bathroom.

Austin turned his back to the door and looked around. Mirrored walls. Every wall. He tilted his eyes up. The ceiling, too, was covered in mirrors.

For what purpose, he neither knew nor cared. His mind was on the footsteps in that hall, willing them to pass. *Just keep going.* He had the chip, he had the way out. They couldn't find him now. *Not now, please not now.*

Knuckles rapped on the bathroom door and Austin startled.

Okay… So it was now.

"Hello?" A woman.

Thoughts tumbled through his mind. Thoughts like taking the curtain rod from the shower and beating the woman on the head. Thoughts like curling up and hiding under the sink. Absurd thoughts.

He stepped away from the door and turned as it swung open.

Nancy Wilkins, the psychiatrist who'd interviewed him and Christy, stood in the doorway.

"Scott? What are you doing here? I thought they were putting you in a different room."

Stay calm. Nothing to hide. Play along.

He shrugged. "I don't know. They put me in this room."

"Huh. Not that it matters." She regarded him for a moment. "Are you okay? You seem upset."

A thin bead of sweat slipped along the edge of Austin's face. He smeared it with his hand. "Just not feeling very well. That's all."

"The headaches?"

He nodded. "They can be pretty bad."

"Hmm. I'll get something for that, okay?"

"Thank you."

"I was just coming to get you."

"Get me? What for?"

"It's what we do here, Scott. We call it therapy."

He stared at her, aware of the chip in his palm.

"Actually, our first appointment isn't scheduled until later this afternoon, but I think that you might be able to help us out now."

"How?"

"Alice has hit a rough patch. You two seem to have a bond. Sometimes having a familiar face in the room can help a breakthrough happen in two days instead of twenty."

Alice. But to Nancy, Alice was Christy.

Christy.

"Sure."

"Perfect. Let's say…" She checked her watch. "Ten minutes?"

"Where is she now?"

"With the administrator. Dr. Lawson. My office is down the hall and to the left. You can't miss it. I'll open your room remotely a few minutes before."

"Remotely? How do you do that?"

"All of the locks are on a central system that the therapists and staff can access remotely from certain computers." She cocked her head and smiled. "Ten minutes then?"

Austin nodded. "Okay… yeah. Ten minutes. I'll be there."

"Good. I think this will be a turning point for her. And maybe you, too, Scott."

He forced a smile and nodded. "I hope you're right."

15

IT WAS an odd reunion, a mix of great relief and terrible trepidation at once.

Great relief because seeing Austin again after being on her own for a day returned Christy to a place of familiarity and security. He was real, in the flesh, the same person who'd spoken reason to her a thousand times since they'd become friends in the orphanage four years earlier.

This was Austin, the one who had his head screwed on straight. The one who always had the answer no matter the question. The one who could solve any problem given enough time and thought.

And great trepidation, because her own thoughts now told her that he might not be real at all. At least not the Austin she thought she knew. If she'd fooled herself about herself, she could have easily tricked herself about him.

Lawson had taken Christy to Nancy's office a few minutes early and stepped out with the psychiatrist for thirty seconds—presumably to discuss her case—before ushering Nancy back in.

"I have a speaking engagement outside the hospital at one o'clock," he said. "But if you need anything, Nancy knows how to reach me. Fair enough?"

Nancy had smiled.

Christy had nodded.

Austin had knocked on the door a couple of minutes later, stepped in looking a little shell-shocked, and quickly put on his brave face. She'd rushed to him and thrown her arms around his neck, unable to stem the flood of tears that his arrival brought to the surface.

"It's okay, Christy," he said, rubbing her back. "It's going to be okay."

And for several minutes it was.

For starters, they'd admitted him to the second floor, which came as a relief. If they were going to find a way out together, they had to be together. The closer, the better.

More importantly, seeing him seated on the couch next to her, she was able to think that she might not be delusional at all. Or at the very least to hope that her delusion was Alice, not Christy. She was letting the suggestive powers of being in a psychiatric hospital get to her. Once outside, she would be just Christy—the same one she'd always known herself to be.

At least the one she'd known the last four years.

But as Nancy led them through some general small talk to break the ice, so to speak, Christy began to notice the change in Austin's demeanor.

Nancy was talking about the history of the psychiatric hospital and Dr. Lawson's rise to his current position here at Saint Matthew's. His earlier papers on progressive therapy had been received with skepticism, she said, but the results of his sometimes unorthodox methods couldn't be ignored. The medical community didn't know what to do with him, nor he with them.

He'd found a home at Saint Matthew's, which gave him some autonomy and allowed him to treat patients in a manner consistent with his better judgment. His success rate over the last five years was astounding.

"How do we know your information's reliable?" Austin asked.

Nancy crossed her legs and leaned back in her chair. "Well, Scott, let's talk about that, shall we? Is it fair to say that you can't really be sure that anything I say is, in fact, true?"

Austin, Christy thought. *His name is Austin.*

Or was it?

"You tell me," Austin said, crossing his arms. He shifted his eyes from her and glanced at her neatly organized desk: a stack of files, two wooden receptacles—one with highlighters, one with ballpoint pens and pencils. A Green Bay Packers coffee cup on a white ceramic coaster. Two thick leather-bound journals of psychiatry stood next to her iMac, which cycled through nature scenes.

Austin continued without looking her in the eye.

"I'm evidently suffering from delusions of grandeur, which afford me all the answers. If you're right, I can't know what is true and what is delusional."

"That's true."

He finally returned her gaze. "If I can't be sure that this isn't a delusion, how am I to know if anything you say is true?"

"That's right, Scott. You can't. And we're here to help you differentiate the two so that you can know, with absolute certainty, what is true. I'm assuming you want to know, Scott. Am I right?"

His eyes were shifting more than usual, like someone trying hard to hide something.

"Yes," he finally said. But Christy couldn't help thinking that he was only playing along with Nancy. That was smart, wasn't it? That was what Austin would do. Gain their confidence so he could do what he needed to do to get them out.

But it was smart only if they really needed to get out.

"You're extremely intelligent, Scott," Nancy said. "In fact, you've perfected your delusion to the point that you've become it. Most psychiatrists would look at you and conclude that you're nothing more than an eccentric genius even though we know the truth. Can you see how that would be possible?"

He nodded. Again, there was that slight shift in his eyes. It was something that only she, knowing him so well, might notice.

"Good. I want you to play that role for me. Can you do that?"

"What role?"

"I want you to explain to Alice the logic that supports her delusions. Play the psychiatrist for me. You can probably do it better than most real doctors."

He averted his stare again, clearly uncomfortable with the idea.

"I'm not sure how I can help," he finally said.

Nancy slowly dipped her head. "Well, let's leave that judgment to me for the moment."

"I thought you wanted me to play the psychiatrist. As the psychiatrist, my judgment is that I'm not sure that's a good thing for me to do."

"Then humor me."

Christy knew that he was vacillating, think, think, thinking, the way he always did. Why wasn't he playing along?

"It's okay, Austin," she said. "Something's off in me; I know that now. In fact, I've always known something was wrong with me. You're the smart one... just tell me."

"Tell you that you're delusional?"

"Just explain why I'm seeing things in mirrors."

He flinched. "Seeing what?"

Her mind filled with the image of herself, the uglier one, and with that single, fully formed memory, her pulse began to surge.

Nancy redirected the conversation.

"Scott, why don't you tell us how delusions are formed in the mind."

Austin stared hard at Christy for a few seconds, then faced the psychiatrist.

"There are a number of possibilities," he said. "But delusional disorders usually present themselves as non-bizarre illusions triggered by chemical imbalances affecting the neurotransmitters in the brain. They are thought to be either hereditary or the result of environmental influence. Sometimes they result from trauma. More severe delusions are present in cases of schizophrenia and dissociative identity disorder. Again, the causes are often genetic but can also be triggered by trauma."

He stopped.

"Good. Now tell Alice how she might have become delusional."

"I already know," Christy said.

"It's okay, Alice," Nancy said. "I want Scott to explain."

"You know?"

He didn't know what she'd learned about her childhood.

"We've made some real progress with Alice," Nancy said. "Just tell her, based on what you know of her, what might have triggered her delusional disorder."

He took a deep breath. Began to count his fingertips with his thumb, as he was prone to. Nodded.

"You don't have any memory of your childhood that I'm aware of. It's possible that you suffered some form of trauma severe enough to trigger disassociation with that former identity."

"Go on…"

The speed of his tapping fingers increased, timed to some invisible meter in his head. Christy typically found his compulsive behavior endearing. At the moment it was getting on her nerves.

"Depending on how severe that trauma was, you may have shut out the real world in favor of a fictional one that is more tenable. After prolonged abuse, the pain of the trauma may have become too intense to bear. But the mind cannot live in a vacuum; it needs content. Over time, a new identity was formed. Eventually it became you. All memories of what previously existed have been repressed. It's very rare, but possible."

"Very good. Now we're making some progress."

He'd just described her to a T. The last shreds of Christy's doubt slipped away. Tears welled in her eyes. She wanted to hug him, to cry on his shoulder, to tell him thank you, thank you, because he'd helped her see the truth, however ugly that truth was. Knowing was better than not knowing; at least in knowing, they could fix it.

"Thank you, Scott," she said.

He blinked. And with that blink his demeanor shifted.

"We both know that's not what happened to you, though," he said rather forcefully.

She flinched. "How do you know?"

"Because we both know that you're not delusional. And if you are, then this"—he flung his arm out—"is the delusion. And my name isn't Scott!"

"How do you know?" she snapped.

The sudden anger coursing through Christy took her off guard. But how could he just sit there and in one fell swoop dismiss her suffering as a child?

"Because I know!" he said.

"Is that so? And did you also know that my father kept me in the basement and refused to let me out because he was a monster?"

Austin went perfectly still. His eyes glared, angry.

"How dare you!" she cried.

"Take a breath, Alice," Nancy said.

"No! No, I won't just take it easy." She slapped the cushion with her hand. "I'm sick and tired of taking it easy. Calm down, Christy," she mimicked. "Think, Christy. Take a deep breath, go to sleep, quit being so emotional, things will look differently in the morning. Well, you know what? Things don't look better in the morning. They never look better. You know why? Because I'm thinking your way too much!"

"Christy…"

"Don't *Christy* me!" She wasn't sure she'd ever talked to Austin this way, but then again she wasn't sure she'd ever talked to Austin. She'd probably been talking to Scott all along. Or not at all.

The thought cut a deep rut through her mind.

Austin's face turned red.

"You haven't suffered like I have. You spend thirteen years locked in a dungeon with bars, knowing you're too ugly to see the light of day, and then you can *Christy* me! Until then, keep your thoughts to yourself. They never did me any good before and they aren't helping now."

"What are you talking about?" he said. "They're filling your head full of psychobabble!"

"They're not doing anything to me! If I look in a mirror and see something, that's *me* doing it, not them. If I go into hypnosis and see where I grew up, that's *me*, not them."

"You're seeing what they want you to see," Austin snapped.

He'd dropped whatever walls he'd erected to protect himself, and for some reason that felt good to Christy. If she could see herself for who she was, he could too, never mind that he was Mr. Brain.

"Is that right? By what, putting mirrors in my bathroom? By asking me what I remember from my childhood. I was a victim. I was horribly mistreated and that's why I'm screwed up. Don't you dare try to gloss over thirteen years of suffering just so you can feel good about your little theories."

She was breathing hard now. Shaking. It was all bubbling over, she knew that, but she let it spill because it felt good, like the draining of a boil full of pus.

"And the only way out is to break this… this cycle of the way things are, to become a better me. I have to go outlaw."

"Outlaw?" Nancy said.

"That's right. That's what he said. Outlaw."

Her brow arched. "Who said?"

"Lawson. When you hypnotized me. Anyway, it may just be my mind playing tricks on me, but I can't keep living this way!"

Austin wasn't liking it, but that was his problem, not hers. He was as delusional as she was. He had to be.

Christy shoved out her hand. "Tell me what you see."

He glanced at her trembling fingers. "What do you mean? Your hand."

"Stubby fingers," she snapped. "And my face. How many times have you told me I look pretty? But I'm not. I'm fat and thick and gross. But you can't see that, can you?"

"You're not fat—"

"No, because you're as delusional as I am." She withdrew her hand. "Have you ever thought, just for one second in that brilliant skull of yours, that maybe they're right about you too? Have you ever wondered why you can't remember your childhood? Why all the evidence here points to you being a patient named Scott, not Austin?"

Christy let it sit for a moment, aware that she'd struck a chord.

She jabbed a finger at her head. "You think I'm the only one who's whacked out?"

"I didn't say that. We all have our issues."

"Oh great. We all have our issues. Too bad mine are the kind that makes everyone cringe every time I walk into the room. *I* can hardly look at myself."

"Stop this!" he shouted.

She felt slapped. He'd never yelled at her.

"You're losing it!"

His words reached deep into her mind and flipped a little switch of awareness that wanted desperately to be flipped.

How she suddenly knew, she didn't know, but she did. Austin or Scott or whoever he was could do what he wanted. She wanted only one thing.

To be free. At any cost, for any reason, to whatever end. She wasn't going to live with her old self anymore. Not even one more day.

Christy, flushed with anger from head to toe, turned to Nancy.

"I want to talk to Dr. Lawson."

Nancy was the perfect picture of control, but her face was a shade lighter.

"I don't think we're done—"

"Yes, we are. We're done. Call him!"

The psychiatrist made no move for the phone on her desk.

"You're in an agitated state, Alice. I think you should take a deep breath and—"

"Call him!" she shouted, shoving a finger at the phone. "Now!"

Nancy grew very still.

"Are you sure you want to do this?"

"Call him!"

Nancy nodded, stepped to her desk, lifted the black phone, and punched three digits into the base.

"She wants to talk to you," she said. Then nodded and held the phone out.

Still drowning in self-hatred and anger, Christy rose from the couch, snatched the phone from Nancy's hand, and spoke into the receiver without any preliminaries.

"I want to do it," she snapped. "I want to do it now."

16

AUSTIN'S UNSTEADY fingers raked through his hair, as if doing so would calm the angry swarm of thoughts that hummed inside his head. Now back in his room, he stood in the spill of light coming from the bathroom.

It was all unraveling. Everything. The bitter notion burrowed into his psyche, sinking deeper with each passing moment. It wasn't simply a notion, though. It was a hard fact, judging by what he'd just witnessed.

Christy, the Christy he knew, was slipping away. Whatever they'd done to her had sent her careening off the thin rails of her mind. He'd heard it in her voice. Seen it in her eyes.

Lawson had force-fed her an illusion, and she was choking on it.

Christy was gone. Even worse, she believed he was too.

Have you ever wondered why you can't remember your childhood?

Austin shoved the thought aside, but it doubled back and sank its hooks into his mind.

He wasn't delusional. He didn't believe that. He couldn't believe that. Stressed? Yes. Traumatized? Likely. Suffering from a tumor in his brain? Likely. All together, it was enough to split more fragile minds wide open. If anything, it was his rational grasp of the situation that kept him from crumbling like Christy had.

Have you ever thought, just for one second in that brilliant skull of yours, that maybe they're right about you too?

What if Christy was right?

No, she wasn't right. She couldn't be.

He circled the room once before he realized he was pacing again. Lost in thought, turning the problem over in his mind.

If there was any hope of getting out of this place, he had to go now. Escaping with Christy was no longer an option. If anything, she was now a liability.

There was no other choice that he could see. No other path.

He had to go alone and he had to do it now. Soon, they would reach a point from which there was no return. No rescue. No escape. There was a dead body with a hole in its head and a sliced wrist where a security chip had once been.

The security chip that was now his ticket out of the hospital.

It was now or not at all.

Crossing to the door, Austin shoved a hand into his pocket and fingered the microchip. The door unlocked with a wave of his hand. He cracked it open and peered into the hall.

Vacant.

Now, Austin. One step at a time. Go now.

Moving at an even pace, he retraced his steps to the elevator at the far end of the hall. His mind seemed strangely untethered, as if his body were moving on its own, animated by an unseen hand.

He rode the hum in his mind all the way to the brushed-steel elevator doors. With a push of a button, they opened and he stepped in. Felt it shudder and begin to drop.

His plan was simple: Get to the front door and use Fisher's chip to get out. If that didn't work, he would resort to plan B.

He wouldn't run. He wouldn't panic. The last thing he needed was to draw attention to himself.

One step at a time, Austin.

The minute he made it out, he would alert the authorities. Before the sun set on Saint Matthew's, it would be crawling with federal agents.

Lawson would be arrested and, most importantly, Christy would be free. They would get their lives back and everything would return to normal, whatever that meant now.

That's what he had to tell himself, because he knew that if he couldn't get out, something very wrong was going to happen.

The elevator doors opened and he tentatively pushed through them. No guards, no alarm, no sign of any threat.

Walk, just walk, as if nothing is wrong. He could barely feel his feet.

He entered the hall and turned down the corridor.

An attendant pushing a patient in a wheelchair was walking toward him, talking to a woman who rocked back and forth. The attendant's lips were moving, but Austin heard only the thrumming drone in his head, low and heavy.

One step at a time. Just one step at a time.

He walked as if in a dream, aware of distant voices and doors and walls on either side, but only as moving scenery. They had no bearing on his objective, which was ahead, then down the long hall to the main entrance.

The corner came within ten seconds, and Austin veered to his left, pulse quickening. No pursuit. He'd told himself that there would be none. Even if they were monitoring the chip, they would only see that Fisher was walking down the hall. But he was still surprised he'd made it this far without even a questioning glance.

But that was good.

He could see the main doors at the end of the hall, like a glowing light at the end of a tunnel.

One step at a time. Just walk, Austin. Keep walking.

So he did. Past the doors on either side. Past two more patients who saw him and quickly retreated into their rooms with worried looks. They'd been in the recreation hall when he'd taken Jacob captive. That was okay. They hadn't cried out, right?

Just walk.

He walked.

And then he was there, standing directly in front of the double doors that led into the reception area. He tried the door to see if it was unlocked as it had been before, knowing it wouldn't be—Lawson had made that much clear.

The door was locked.

Which was why he had the chip.

He lifted it to the security pad. Waited for the clack of metal as it unlocked.

Nothing happened.

He swiped it a second time. A small red light blinked in the corner of the black square. Once. Twice.

His chest tightened. A signal.

Okay... That was okay. He couldn't panic, not now. He simply had to switch to plan B. He'd known this might be the case.

One step at a time, Austin. Don't think about the fact that the chip didn't work. Just go.

He dropped the small chip to the floor and retraced his steps, pulse now pounding in his ears. His thoughts thundered like massive toppling dominoes. Someone had discovered Fisher's body upstairs and deactivated his chip.

They would've immediately begun tracking the chip's electronic signature. A quick search would verify that it had been in his room and that he was now missing from it. They would have known exactly where he had been. Where he was now.

Over the din of his mind, a single voice arose. Alice's.

Where I was... I've seen it.

Lawson had already sealed off the passageway in the boiler room. He'd said so and Austin believed it to be true. It was a loose end, and Lawson was the type to tie up loose ends.

It's okay, Austin. One foot in front of the other.

But he no longer resisted the booming voice in his mind that demanded he run.

Run, Austin. Run!

He ran.

Not in a sprint, but in fast jog, rolling his feet so that they wouldn't slap on the tile floors. As fast as he could without looking like a patient who'd gone berserk.

To the corner. Down the western hall, which was now empty. Past the admissions wing, where the elevator was located, doors still shut.

All the way to the stairwell that led to the basement where he and Christy had first entered the hospital. Dead ahead, the administrator's office was shut.

Breathing hard, Austin pulled up at the door into the stairwell and glanced back down the hall from where he'd come. The recreation room, the patient rooms, the admissions offices—closed. All of them. He could hear the distant voices of two patients arguing in the recreation room, but he'd managed to navigate the halls without raising any alarm.

And with Fisher's chip no longer in his possession, they could not track him.

He tested the door. Unlocked. Shoved through, ran to the staircase, and took the steps two at a time. The sound of his feet slapping the cold floor echoed off the cinderblock walls. A loud click chased him as the stairwell door closed.

When he reached the basement entrance, he banged through the door and sprinted to the supply room.

Where I was, she'd said. There was only one place that made any sense to him.

A few strides carried him to the supply room door. Moving with reckless abandon, he bolted into the darkened room. Snapped the light on.

Images of his first glimpse of Alice with mouth taped shut filled his mind.

He swept aside the curtain that divided the room.

He pushed forward and spun into the space, panting. The stretcher he had seen Alice on that first day was gone. White walls hemmed in the narrow space. A squat metal desk sat against the back wall. A swiveling chair with peeling paint and torn vinyl upholstery was shoved under it.

He was looking for a key. What door that key opened was still a mystery, but if Alice had found a way out, so could he. Maybe it was labeled. Opened a door to an old passage that led to the surface. A coal chute or something. He was grasping for straws, but straws were all he had left.

There was no sign of any such door here, but he hadn't expected any. This was where the key was, she said. Assuming that when she'd said "where I was" she meant here.

Austin went to the desk and pulled out the chair. Sent it sliding across the floor on clattering wheels. Except for an old Underwood typewriter covered in a skin of dust, the desktop was clear.

He dropped to one knee next to the three narrow stacked drawers and jerked the bottom one out. It was empty.

The next one had some newspaper clippings and what appeared to be old paperwork, which he rifled through and tossed to the floor. Nothing beneath them.

Heart banging against his ribcage, Austin tugged the handle of the last drawer. It caught and he pulled harder until it slid out.

The contents looked typical: a plastic tray with small compartments filled with paperclips, pencils, pens, some thumbtacks, pads of Post-it notes, a green ruler, staples, and a stapler. One roll of gray duct tape.

In the compartment closest to the handle lay three keys held together by a piece of wire that had been formed into a rudimentary ring.

Small keys. Not door keys.

Austin scooped them up and stared at them in his palm. The simple truth quickly became all too apparent to him. Alice had seen the keys in the drawer, probably when Fisher had opened it to withdraw the same duct tape he'd placed over her mouth. Her fragile mind had embraced a fantasy that these keys were some magical way out of her predicament.

But they weren't. They were just simple office keys, likely for this very desk.

Which left him with what? With nothing. Nothing at all.

"Find anything interesting?"

Austin bolted upright. The words reached into his world like icy fingers. Not because he'd actually heard them, but because they had sounded so real, as if actually, audibly spoken, which was impossible, because he knew that voice.

It belonged to a man who was dead. Which, in turn, meant that he was hearing things.

Not Christy, or Alice, but *him*.

"There's nothing to find, Scott."

This time the voice was so real that Austin cried out, spinning with his fingers folded over the keys.

Douglas Fisher stepped into the light, arms hanging loose at his sides.

Austin stared, dumbfounded.

Fisher pushed the chair to the side and took a step forward. "You're quite the persistent one, aren't you?"

Austin backpedaled. Bumped against the desk.

"I killed you."

Fisher offered a shallow smile. "Is that what you believe? Just like you believe that your name is Austin? And that you're not delusional? Tell me, do I look dead to you?"

The room began to blur.

"I can assure you that I'm quite alive," Fisher said. "I personally transported you to your room after discovering that you'd managed to break out of your restraints in the morgue. You don't remember that?"

"I... I killed you in the operating room."

"The operating room? You weren't in the operating room."

"Then..." His mind was stalling. "Then how do I know about it?"

"Because you've been there before."

His eyes met Fisher's. There he stood, not six feet away, without a scratch. The hum in Austin's head swallowed him whole.

Fisher walked up and placed a hand on Austin's shoulder. "You're ill. The problem is, you don't know that. You're trapped in your mind, Austin."

Austin? Fisher had just called him Austin.

"Austin?"

Fisher removed his hand and offered him a plastic grin.

"See, now you have me confused."

The man was here, in the flesh. Alive. So even if Austin was Austin, he had to be delusional, because he clearly remembered killing this man.

Unless this was the delusion and Fisher was really dead.

Austin's mind began to shut down.

"We're trying to make progress, Scott, but ultimately, only you can control your mind. If you let us in, we can help you. Would you like that?"

"I don't know." His eyes searched the ground.

"We'll take the first step together. Just one. Okay?"

One step at a time.

He saw no other choice. His mind was too exhausted to consider any other argument.

Austin nodded, just once.

"Good. The administrator wants to see you."

Fisher led him out of the room and down the hall. Austin didn't remember climbing the stairs to the first floor or entering the administration wing or walking into Lawson's office, yet that's where he found himself. Staggered. Dazed.

Lawson sat on the other side of the desk, watching Austin over steepled fingers. He removed his reading glasses and pinched the bridge of his nose.

"Dr. Fisher tells me we've reached a roadblock in your treatment, Scott."

Austin said nothing.

He smiled. "But where some see an impasse, I see a gateway to the next level. Nothing really begins until the time is ripe. Some things cannot be rushed, you see." He leaned back. "I think the time for more aggressive therapy is upon us, wouldn't you say? Alice is making such progress and yet you're only just beginning. A late bloomer, just now discovering that you have some pimples in your head that need attention, among other things."

He grinned, clearly pleased with his analogy.

"I'm going to heal you, if you'll let me. I'm already in there, so to speak, just let me do what I do, and I'll show you how to solve all of your problems. Deal?"

Something was wrong, but Austin couldn't put his finger on it.

The administrator rose to his feet and stepped toward the closet door through which Austin and Christy had entered only yesterday.

"Time to lock and load, Scotty boy. I'm gonna lock, you're gonna load. Deal or no deal."

Lawson opened the closet.

Only it wasn't a closet. Nor a hallway. The space beyond the door was dark, like the gaping throat of a monster.

"Take a walk with me. I want to show you something."

Austin stood slowly, then followed the administrator into a very dark hall, about ten paces in before stopping in front of a riveted black door with a narrow window at eye level.

Lawson opened the door. "Step inside."

Austin stared into the darkened room. "In there?"

"In there."

He stepped forward cautiously and entered the room.

"I've always said that humanity's great malady is quite simple to summarize: *lost in thought*," Lawson said behind him. "I would say that describes you succinctly, wouldn't you?"

Austin looked around him. Every inch of the six-by-six-foot room was painted black. He teetered on his feet. Blinked into the dark. He tried to move, but his feet were rooted to the ground as if they'd been sunk in concrete, anchored by raw fear.

"Consider this the first step to your liberation. I'm going to lock this door and let you load up on your thoughts for a while. I think a week should do it. Fair enough?"

"I…" Austin's voice echoed in the small room.

The door slammed with a heavy boom that reverberated through the cell. The force of it thumped Austin's chest.

His world was plunged into thick darkness and he thought, *I'm going to break.*

For a long time he couldn't move, because there was nowhere to go. He simply stood on his feet, swimming in disorienting darkness as waves of pain washed through his head.

He had to sort things out. So he began to sort. But with that sorting came fear, because he knew that he couldn't sort things out.

It wasn't just any ordinary fear, but a kind of debilitating fear that Austin had never before encountered.

The trembling began then.

17

CHRISTY HAD spent two days sequestered in her room, and on each day she'd been visited by Lawson three times—once at ten, once at three, and once at six. Preparations were being made, he said. There was only one surgeon he trusted for the job; one who understood the full nature of the objective. In this case, to transform her into a walking picture of beauty without having to endure taxing procedures that might take months.

The surgeon's name was Paul Bigoti and he lived in New York. Wednesday night was the soonest he could make the trip, but the wait would be well worth it. The man could work magic with a blade, a pump, and a few sutures.

Christy spent the days embracing her true self. Her uglier self. The one who stared back at her in the mirrors most of the time now.

Every time she began to doubt her resolve to go through with the procedure, she would creep into the bathroom and take a good look at herself. Thirty seconds was enough to plunge her into a pit of self-hatred and pity, fueled by her growing rage over her own victimization.

It was critical that she fully embrace her true self. Lawson helped her understand that with absolute clarity during each session. In fact, that was his primary thrust.

Hate the person you are so that you can love the person you will be.

Accept just how terrible your life has been. Sit in your oppression and realize just how unfairly you have been treated. Just how awful it is to be trapped in such an unjust situation.

There was no use pretending that things were better than they appeared to be. Putting a bit of makeup on an ugly mug was pointless, because the makeup would only wear off and expose that bulldog face once again. The only way to fix it was to actually change things once and for all.

Strong language, yes, but it was for her own good. He was accomplishing what no one else had. Things were going to get better for her because of him. She was finally going to be able to love herself.

She'd asked about Austin only once and was told that he was working through his own issues. Not to worry, Lawson said. Scott would soon realize that he was as messed up as she was.

For the most part, she put him from her mind. It was time she thought only of herself for once. And she was in a horrible, horrible place because she'd suffered a dreadful, dreadful past.

By the time they rolled the gurney into her room on Wednesday night she was so entrenched in her own misery that not a whisper of doubt crossed her mind. Or perhaps the mental storm raged too loudly for her to hear it.

They rolled her down halls for a long way, and the whole time she kept her eyes on the ceiling lights, passing like a countdown to mercy.

Lawson stood by the operating table to offer her an encouraging smile and a gentle squeeze.

"These corrections are so exciting, my dear. You're going to be a very happy girl. This is the first step to becoming whole. A whole new you."

"Thank you," she managed. And she meant it.

She still hadn't met the surgeon, but that didn't matter. His assistant, a nurse named Charlene, had flown in early and spent an hour explaining exactly what to expect. Their procedure was particularly noninvasive and they utilized lasers that minimized recuperation time considerably. Charlene had carefully drawn lines on her neck, her face, and her belly, went out of her way to make sure Christy was emotionally ready to proceed with the surgery, then left.

The fingers would have to come later, Lawson had told her. They would just get her main parts looking stunning, then worry about the rest.

A technician made some adjustments to a machine behind her, placed an oxygen mask over her nose and mouth, and asked her to count down backward from ten.

"Ten. Nine. Eight. Seven. Six. Fi…"

Vacancy swallowed her mind and left her in a state of nothingness. Peace. If nothing was peace. For how long, she didn't know.

What she did know was that when she suddenly regained awareness, such as it was, she was looking down at the room from above. It was all there right below her—the large silver bowl lights, the stack of monitors tracking her vitals, the blue-smocked doctor working with gloved hands, Charlene assisting him, and the anesthesiologist. All looking down at the operation table with interest.

At the body on the operating table.

At the very bloody, gashed up, lumpy, naked form.

At her.

The sight of her neck, peeled open like a banana, was so distasteful that she gasped loudly. Was she dead?

The heart monitor's steady beep echoed through the room. So, not dead. Of course not. This was how they got rid of all that ugly fat. That was all.

She looked around the room, stunned by her vantage point. It was like she was really here, lying on the ceiling, staring down at the operation. She could see them, hear them, smell them, probably touch them if she reached down far enough.

"Hello?"

They continued without reacting to her call. But she could hear herself.

"Can you hear me?" she asked, louder now.

The surgeon held out his hand palm up. "Cannula."

His assistant placed a long, thin cylindrical instrument into his hand, oblivious to her presence above their heads.

Surprisingly, she felt no anxiety. Maybe because she was here, on the ceiling, and her body was there, on the table.

In some ways, she was like a driver looking down at her car. If the body needed some work done—into the garage it goes, up comes the hood, out comes the old oil. Replace some parts and put it back together. Simple. That wasn't her down there; it was only her body.

The surgeon shoved the thin silver tube under the skin he'd folded back from her neck.

"Suction."

A whining, sucking sound filled the room as the clear tube connected to it shook violently. Christy watched with swelling horror as thick, yellowish fluid filled the tube.

They were vacuuming her fat out. If this was noninvasive, she hated to think what invasive looked like.

But then she remembered that this was just her car, so to speak. Whatever got rid of the old fat was worth it. This was just Lawson's garage, and it was time for an oil change.

Thoughts of the room fell into the background as a question suddenly filled her mind. If she wasn't that body, then who was she? Not her mind, because she was quite sure that her brain was still under that hood down there, not floating on the ceiling.

"Prep her thighs," the surgeon said.

Her thighs? She didn't remember talking about her thighs. But as long as she was in for service, might as well fix it all.

Suck it all out, fellas. Every last drop of fat.

With that thought she suddenly felt herself falling toward her body. Then she was inside a dark space.

And then back into vacancy.

CHRISTY'S NEXT conscious thought entered her mind slowly, like mud sliding down a piece of tin. Or shaving foam slowly filling a hand. At first she thought she was waking from a dream, snugged under covers at home.

She tried to open her eyes but couldn't. Yes, of course. Because she wasn't at home under her blanket. She was in Saint Matthew's psychiatric ward, and her face was wrapped in bandages.

A monitor beeped steadily to her left. They'd finished, she thought. She was alive. Excitement sparked in her mind.

She was a new creation.

And then the beeping faded and she slipped into a beautiful dream.

It was Christmas morning. She was standing in a large garage, which looked somewhat similar to an operating room, staring at a brand-new, sleek red car with a bow on top. Her father dangled the key in front of her.

"Merry Christmas, darling. She's a beauty. You'll be the envy of all your friends now. You can finally be proud."

She jumped for joy, squealing with delight. "Thank you, Daddy!"

The keys were blocking her view of his head, and when her fingers grabbed the keys from his hand, she was too excited to be bothered by the fact that he had no face.

"What about my old car?" she asked, walking up to the shiny red car.

"It's in the dump where it belongs," he said. "Never could stand the sight of that hunk of junk. You're a new girl now. Brand-spanking, beautiful new."

It isn't just a car, she thought. *It's my body.*

It's me.

She woke again later, disoriented, clueless as to the passage of time. This time she woke enough to feel the raging pain slicing into her skin. Not just sections of her skin, but over her whole body.

She moaned and turned her head slowly. She tried to stretch her fingers but her hand was wrapped up thick. So were her feet and legs.

She was bound in bandages, she realized. From head to foot. Swaddled up like a mummy.

"There you are," a soothing voice Christy recognized as Nancy's said to her left. "Welcome back. Everything is just fine."

Her mouth was bound so she couldn't speak, but the woman's reassuring tone calmed her.

How do I look? she wanted to ask. *Did it go well? Am I beautiful?*

"The doctor said you did so well, Alice. We are so proud of you. Can you hear me?"

She slowly nodded.

"Good. That's good. He said you would be in pain for a while, but your body's reacting very well to the healing agents injected into your skin. It's only been three days."

Three days? She couldn't remember more than a few hours, if that.

"Barring any unforeseen changes to your recovery, they should be able to take the bandages off at the end of the week."

Three days and they'd felt like a few hours. Only three or four more and they would unwrap her.

Merry Christmas, darling. She's a beauty.

She could hardly wait. All of these years in a cage and now, finally, she was going to walk out, a free, beautiful woman that her father would proudly show the world.

You're a new girl now. Brand-spanking, beautiful new.

Like that car.

Or better, like a beautiful butterfly emerging from its cocoon. That's what she would be. An ugly slug of a caterpillar turned into a stunning butterfly free to escape its tomb. Reborn.

"Try to rest, darling. You'll feel some discomfort, but the drugs will take the edge off and help you sleep."

Nancy gave her bandaged hand a gentle squeeze that hurt only a little. She didn't really care about the pain. It was a small price to pay for her rebirth.

A gorgeous butterfly with red and yellow wings would unfold on the stage as the world watched with rapt attention. And when she turned the key and took flight, a gasp would fill the skies, because no one had ever seen such exquisite splendor.

The days slipped by in a drug-induced fog, spinning with dreams that kept evolving. The car dream became an elaborate butterfly dream, which morphed into a dream of a royal mummy walking out of her grave. Such beauty was beheld when they unwrapped her that they pronounced her queen again.

You're a queen, my darling. The cell in the basement was only your tomb. Now you get to come out and show the world just how beautiful you are, because Daddy is dead.

Dead?

Yes, dead. And that gave her even more comfort. She would surely be a queen when they removed her grave wrappings, but even then she would never forgive her father for making her ugly to start with. Nor for keeping her in that grave so long.

THEY CAME for her on the seventh day. Some people claimed that it took seven days to make the world, and Christy didn't know if that was true or not. But she did know that it took seven days to remake Alice.

And now Alice was about to become the queen in her new wonderland.

"Well, then," Lawson's voice boomed. "Here we are."

"Here we are," Nancy said.

They were still in the recovery room and Christy's head was still wrapped up in bandages, so she didn't know who else was watching, but that didn't matter. Her mind was full of what she would see when she looked in the mirror for the first time.

"How's the pain, Alice?" Nancy asked.

She nodded, brimming with excitement.

"Pain, or no pain?"

She shook her head this time.

"Good," Lawson said. "Sit her up and let's take off her facial bandages so she can talk, shall we? Is that okay with you, Alice? I want you to keep your eyes closed until all the dressings are removed, but we're going to free your face first so that you can talk."

Again, she nodded.

There was still a little pain, mainly in her joints, but most of it was gone. Either way, she didn't care. She only wanted to feel the new air on her new body as her eyes fluttered open like those butterfly wings.

Hands began to unravel the bandages. Cool air whispered over her exposed lips.

A tremor of anticipation spread through her bones.

"Ah... There it is. So beautiful. I can't tell you how excited we are to show you what the doctor was able to make of you, my dear," Lawson said, carefully peeling the long swaths of gauze from around her head.

He unwound another loop, this one from her forehead.

"We were able to see your progress when we replaced your bandages. Twice, while you were in a drug-induced sleep. I can assure you, you're going to be very happy."

The revelation came as a surprise.

"Can you tell us how you feel?"

Christy opened her mouth, felt only a tinge of pain on her cheeks, then spoke for the first time in a week.

"I'm fine," she said.

"Only fine?"

"I feel good. I feel very good."

"I'm so happy to hear that. Isn't that good news, Nancy?"

"It's very good news. We're very proud of you, Alice."

Air cooled her skin as the bandages came off, from her neck down to her waist. Despite her eagerness to take a look, even just one, she held her eyes closed as he'd suggested.

"Can you swing your legs off the bed for us? Let's get you on your feet."

"Yes."

She felt some discomfort in her stomach and buttocks as she eased her legs off the bed, but not as much as she had anticipated.

"Can you stand for us? We're right here, don't worry."

Christy scooted off the bed, placed her feet on the floor, and slowly stood with their help.

"Good. That's good, darling."

The rest of the bandages came off quickly. Fresh air spread down her legs like a cool cream.

"Beautiful," Nancy said. "It's hard to believe such a simple procedure can produce such stunning results."

By the time the last dressing slipped off her left foot, Christy's breathing had quickened with such anticipation that she thought she might pass out.

"There we go. There we go." Lawson made no attempt to hide his enthusiasm, which only increased her own.

She heard him step back.

"Alice? We've placed a full-length mirror five feet in front of you. Now remember, there will still be some swelling, and you'll see the sutures, but those will go away soon. This is it. This is the new you."

A beat.

"Open your eyes, Alice."

She let her eyes flutter open, squinted once as light filled her vision, then focused on the image in the mirror directly in front of her.

Her impression came all at once, as if dumped over her head from a bucket. She gasped.

Blinked once, to make sure she was seeing what she thought she was seeing.

She was.

Yes, there was some redness around the sutures and a little swelling, but she could easily see past that to the remolded beauty beyond.

Christy felt tears of gratitude pool in her eyes.

She was a queen.

She was such a beautiful queen!

FOR THE first several hours after Lawson had put Austin into the black room, which Austin came to think of as his mind, he could do nothing but stare wide-eyed into the bottomless dark. It was as though the slamming steel door had severed his connection to the world. The deep shadows swirled and pooled around him, so thick and black that it didn't matter if his eyes were open or closed.

He'd been abandoned to his thoughts.

He had to stay calm, he knew that. Had to keep his mind focused, but resisting did nothing more than feed the fear and panic welling up inside of him.

Slowly, the stakes grounding him began to pull out of the eroding sands of his mind—he began to lose his hold on himself.

He couldn't allow that to happen, yet he felt powerless to stop it.

Drenched with sweat and frantic to anchor his body to something, anything, Austin had finally crawled across the cell and huddled in the corner with his back pressed against the hard wall.

There, he trembled uncontrollably as the cyclone in his mind swallowed everything and began to uproot the deepest parts of his being. He was powerless. It was happening *to* him because he no longer possessed his mind. It possessed him. Dragged him into the depths as it spun relentlessly.

No matter how he tried, Austin couldn't shut his mind down. If only he could rein it in, bring his thoughts into submission like he always had, then he would be fine. But, with each passing moment, the buzz in his head grew defiantly louder. The rush of thoughts caught in an endless loop wouldn't relent.

Thoughts about how he had killed Fisher. Watched him bleed out and moved his lifeless body.

Thoughts about how he had come face-to-face with the same man, now inexplicably alive.

Thoughts about the only conclusion that made sense: His mind was shattered. He was delusional. He had eliminated all other explanations, from the impossible to the improbable, and faced only this truth. It was the most rational explanation. The only explanation.

His senses couldn't be trusted. His mind couldn't be trusted.

Over and over his thoughts turned until they circled endlessly, a cacophony of madness.

Time slipped by, each second agonizingly slow, like a snail along the razor's edge of his mind. And his mind was no longer so sharp. It, like the snail, had been severed layer by layer, until only a puddle of goop remained, twitching on the floor.

The door was opened at intervals, once each day, he assumed. The first few times he'd started to rise, thinking the ordeal was finally over, but the attendant only changed out a jug of fresh water and a toilet bowl before leaving without having spoken a word.

After the third time, he hadn't bothered to get up. After the fifth, he hadn't even opened his eyes.

There, alone in the thin gap that separated insanity and truth, he was forced to pick through the wreckage of his mind, trying to salvage what he could. Not because he wanted to, but because he couldn't stop thinking.

Each time he considered the events of the past few days, the conclusion became more obvious and convincing. The winding halls, the shape-shifting closet in Lawson's office, Fisher, Alice—all of it pointed to the fact that he had imagined it all.

They were right. Christy was right. He was Scott. Scott was Austin. Austin was Scott. Nothing else could make sense. Nothing else could possibly explain it.

Yet it couldn't be true. He couldn't allow it to be true, because giving life to the idea meant the death of everything that made him who he was—his mind, his personality, his very being. The existence of Scott meant the death of Austin.

And yet, what if it was true? His mind had never failed him before... *Failed.*

If his mind had failed him in this one regard, how else had it failed him? How could he trust anything he'd ever known to be true? How could he even know who he was?

Who am I?

I am I.

I am.

Am I?

And herein was the single greatest problem he had ever faced: his *I* was broken and therefore unreliable.

At first, the notion had felt like falling. There was nothing to grasp, nothing to stop his descent, no way to escape. Then the falling sensation gave way to one of being suffocated, as the crushing weight of his own mind buried him. But that, too, gave way to a third sensation, the most horrific one.

Oblivion. Utter meaninglessness.

It came upon him in a rush that stole his breath and pressed so heavily upon him that the dread sank bone deep. The first time it settled on him, Austin tried to scream, but he couldn't.

Who am I?

I am my thoughts.

I think, therefore I am.

I am, therefore I think.

I am mind. I am body. I am soul. I am my beliefs.

But with this came the undeniable awareness that he couldn't know if his beliefs were true. They were informed by an unreliable mind. Did a reliable mind even exist?

I have a problem. I can't know that what I believe is true.

I am broken. I am lost.

I am trapped.

Like worms methodically devouring a corpse, the thoughts consumed his mind, inside and out. Little by little, his resolve faltered until it was replaced by a void so absolute that he wished for death.

I can't know who I am; therefore I am nothing.

I am terrified.

His terror would begin to ease; then it would cycle again and again in an endless loop. Each time he relived this descent into madness, each time he lost a little bit more of himself, until eventually his body could go no farther.

Who... am... I?

He did not know. He could not know.

Time and time again, Austin collapsed, exhausted, facedown on the cold floor, and wept. And each time the threads holding his mind together frayed. Then snapped.

In his mind's eye, he saw himself lying on a beach. He was a fish that had washed up on shore—gills flaring, moments from agonizing death. All he needed was just a puddle of the vast sea of knowledge that had sustained him for so long.

And yet, there was no sea.

There never had been. It was, like him, a delusion.

And even that might be a delusion.

Austin lay curled up in the corner, trembling, eternally trapped in hell.

WHITE-HOT LIGHT angled across the cell floor. A voice called out, drawing Austin from the thick fog that hung over him. He turned his head and shielded his eyes with his hand. Blinked.

The cell door lay open. A silhouette stood in the brilliant rectangle of light on the far side of the room.

"Hello, Scott."

This was the thick voice of Kern Lawson.

Can I know that?

The man took two steps into the cell. "It's time."

The words drifted across Austin's consciousness. He'd heard them. Or had he?

He knew what they meant, but they filtered through him like bits of a dream. An ember of hope was fanned deep inside him.

It's time. He was leaving this place?

Lawson stepped aside as a man rolled a wheelchair into the cell and stopped in the middle of the room.

"I trust the time to yourself was enlightening," Lawson said. "The path to truth is narrow and difficult, to be sure. That's why so few actually take it. It's much easier to believe a truth someone else has lived, but I find hearsay to be a shoddy foundation upon which to build a life. Don't you?"

Austin raised his head and squinted at the man. Swallowed hard. He tried to speak, but nothing came out.

"I usually only prescribe three days, but yours is a particularly resilient delusional state." Lawson paused. "Tell me, boy, who are you?"

Austin stared dumbly at the man. His tongue felt thick in his mouth.

"You simply can't let go of your old mind, can you?" A pause. "It doesn't have to be like this, Scott."

Austin cleared a hole in his swollen throat. "My name is Austin.

Austin Hartt."

Lawson pulled a toothpick from his pocket and lifted it to his lips. "Defiant even in the face of evidence. I appreciate your tenacity, but clinging to a lie doesn't make it true. Your problem isn't that you think; it's that you do not think the right things."

Lawson motioned to the attendant, who looped his arms under Austin and pulled him to his feet. Helped him into the seat.

Weakened by seven days with no food, his head slumped forward.

Lawson leaned close and brushed the back of his hand softly across Austin's cheek. "Being left to your thoughts is quite unnerving. The truth gets all jumbled up in there. Until you accept your true self, you'll suffer. And your true self is Scott, flesh and bone. It's a plain and simple fact, like one and one equals two. Truth."

He bent lower until his mouth was by Austin's ear. "You're still blind, Scott. I'm going to help you see. I'm going to set you free and give you back to yourself."

He stood upright, turned, and crossed the room to the door.

"Clean him up, then bring him to the second floor in one hour. It's time for Scott to see with his own eyes."

THE SIGHTS and sounds of the hospital ground into Austin's senses like bits of glass. He watched the world through slits of eyes as the attendant pushed him to the elevator, then onto the second floor.

He'd been wheeled from the dark room to the showers, where he'd been stripped, washed down like a hog, and dressed in new scrubs, all without a single word.

Then they took a trip to the cafeteria, where he'd been fed broth and some toast. Slowly, his strength had returned, but he didn't have the strength to look the other patients in the eye. Doing so might require more thinking, and Austin was too dead up there to consider much more than simple body mechanics.

Per Lawson's instruction, the attendant had wheeled him all the way around the halls to the far side. Where? He didn't know. He didn't really care.

The attendant opened a door near the end of the third hall, wheeled him into a patient room with a desk, nodded at Lawson, who sat behind the desk peering at him over his glasses, and left.

From his wheelchair at the end of the bed, Austin looked dumbly about the room. This was his new home? And what about Christy? There was no sign of her.

Lawson stood and rounded the desk. "There, isn't that better? All cleaned and fed, mind bright and snappy once again. Yes?"

Austin cleared his throat, still raw. "Yes," he said, thinking *no*.

"That's good. We have something very special to show you, my boy. Something to make your day brighter. Are you ready?"

Austin just stared at him, mind numb.

"Speak up, boy."

"Yes," he said.

"Yes. Of course you are." Then toward the bathroom door, louder: "Alice? It's time. You can come out now."

Her muffled voice reached him from beyond the door. "Now?"

Austin shifted in his seat. So Christy was okay after all. His pulse surged. And she sounded strong. Even upbeat. How many hours had he thought about her in that dark pit?

"Yes, now, my dear."

The bathroom door opened slowly and Austin pushed to his feet. He didn't want Christy to see him sitting in a wheelchair. Not now.

Christy stepped into the room, dressed in a white halter top and a yellow skirt, complete with black shoes, white socks, and yellow ribbons in two pigtails. She wore rouge on her cheeks and glossy red lipstick on a grin that might have split her face if she smiled any brighter.

"There we are, my darling," Lawson said. "Such a beautiful girl." He faced Austin, beaming. "What do you say, Scott? Isn't she quite the looker?"

Austin took her in at a glance and felt the blood drain from his face. The girl standing across the room wasn't the Christy he knew, but a shell of her. A virtual stranger who was just a shadow of the girl he had once known.

High cheekbones jutted from a once rounded face. Her nose was hard and angular, unnaturally thin. Black stitches zigzagged along both sides of her neck where they'd pulled the skin taut, revealing the ridges of her windpipe.

His eyes drifted down. He could count her ribs, see the outline of her skeleton beneath her pale flesh. Her body was little more than bones wrapped in a thin layer of skin. They had sucked all of the fat out of her body, leaving a brittle girl behind.

And yet Christy seemed delighted with the result.

She beamed at him like an excited little girl showing off her new Christmas dress. She nervously curtsied, eager for his approval.

"Well? Do you like it?"

He blinked, unable to speak.

"Of course he does, my dear." Lawson chuckled. "He's seeing reality, maybe for the first time. He's overwhelmed. Isn't that right, Scott?"

Lawson flashed a grin at Austin, then crossed to Christy, lifted her hand, and placed a kiss on her knuckles.

"I'll leave you two to digest some truth for a change." He strode for the door and turned before exiting. "We are making such promising progress. I'm very proud of you both."

And then he was gone, leaving Austin and Christy alone to stare at each other.

"Aren't you going to say anything?" Christy asked.

A look of mild apprehension had replaced her smile. She crossed to the mirror on the wall and stared at herself, turning this way and that to offer herself better angles of her body. "I mean, it's much better, right? The doctor says the swelling will do down in a couple days, and I get my stitches out in a week. But most of the ugly fat is gone."

Austin didn't know what to say. She looked appalling, but he couldn't bring himself to say it.

Christy cast him a nervous glance. "You don't like it? He says that if I'm still not happy, they can take more out."

More? There *was* no more to take out.

She continued, speaking in a brittle voice that sounded like it might crack as easily as her bones. "Do you like it? I mean... It's so much better!" Gazing at her reflection, she pursed her lips, straightened her skirt. "Do you like it?"

Austin was about to offer his support, at a loss. But then he saw the tremble in her hands. The slight quiver in her upper lip. She was struggling.

"You're thinner," he said.

"Much thinner," she said. "I'm so much thinner, and this is so much better. It's the beginning of a whole new me. Amazing what a few corrections can make."

But she was saying it more to herself than to him, he realized. She was desperate to convince herself that this ghastly body was actually what she'd always wanted.

With that simple realization, Austin felt his deep dread return. His time in the black box had left him numb, which was its own kind of resigned peace. But staring at Christy now, he remembered their predicament, and his heart began to free fall once again.

"I'm not sure I like the skirt," she was saying. "Not really my style. Maybe—"

"Christy…"

"Maybe jeans. What do you think? And I'm not crazy about make-up, but Nancy says it suits me. I think maybe a different color…"

"Christy."

"I love my nose." Her fingers were on her face but they were shaking. Her whole body was trembling. "They say that I can get my fingers lengthened…"

"Christy!"

"What?" she snapped, glaring at him. "What, Austin? I'm thin! I'm perfect!"

The hopelessness that had swallowed him in the dark room sucked at him again.

"What have they done to us?" he asked in a thin voice.

Christy stared at him.

"They've sucked my mind dry," he said. "And they've sucked you dry."

Tears began to well in her eyes.

"They're destroying us," he whispered.

Her sob came suddenly. She dropped her head into her hands and coughed up deep hiccupping sobs that shook her shoulders.

He went to her and lifted his hand to her shoulder, wanting to offer comfort but too broken himself to feel he could.

"What have I done?" she moaned. "What did I do?"

"It's okay, Christy…"

"I hate myself," she rasped. "I hate myself!"

She was shaking so violently that he thought she might crumple. He put his arms around her and she lowered her head into his right shoulder.

He had to find some strength, if not for his sake then for hers. The problem was, he didn't know where to find it.

So he just said, "It's okay, Christy. It's going to be okay."

But it didn't feel okay at all. It felt like they were both standing in hell, and there was no way out.

"What are we going to do, Austin?" she wept. "What are we going to do?"

"Come here."

He led her to the bed and eased her to her seat. Then he sat next to her with one arm around her bony shoulders, at a loss. How could it have come this far? An hour ago in the dark hole, his world had felt upside down. Now he was no longer sure he even had a world.

Slowly her sobs began to ease. She sniffed and wiped her tears away. For a long time, neither of them spoke. There was nothing to say. There was no way out, there was no way in, there was no way. And that was all.

But he felt obliged to put up a strong front for her sake.

"We have to find a way out," he finally said. "If not, we're going to end up dead."

She held her hands in her lap, staring at the floor with a distant look in her eyes.

"I know," she said, as if she was already accepting death as a foregone conclusion.

"I don't think I can live through another round of this."

"What did they do to you?" she asked.

"They put me in a black room," he said.

She nodded but didn't ask for any elaboration. That was fine by him.

"When we were in with Nancy you said that you didn't see me as fat," she said. "Was that true?"

"You looked the same as you always do. Not fat, no."

"Are you delusional?" she asked.

He hesitated. "I think so."

"So you could be wrong."

He nodded. "Maybe."

She looked at the wall, away from him. "Did you find Alice?"

"Yes."

"Was she any help?"

He shook his head, still feeling dazed and lost. "No. I found some keys but they're no good."

"Keys to what?"

He remembered that they were in his pocket. He'd noticed them while in the dark room. He didn't remember putting them in his pocket after Fisher had found him—he was in too much shock. When he'd taken a shower earlier, he'd found them again and palmed them until he could slip them into his fresh pants.

He reached into his pocket and pulled out the three keys on the wire. Held them in his palm.

"Desk keys," he said.

She looked at them, hardly interested.

"There's a desk in here."

Nothing more, just that. Not said with any hope or eagerness. It was just an observation. But with no other options apparent, Austin stood up, walked across the room, and rounded the desk.

Three metal drawers ran up one side. Without much thought, he slipped the key into the bottom drawer and twisted it.

The key turned without a fuss.

"It fits," he said.

Christy pushed herself up and crossed the room. "It does?"

He pulled the drawer open as Christy rounded the desk.

The inside of the drawer was lined with velvet the color of a rich wine, more purple than red. An old wooden box sat in the middle. Someone had scratched the word *Lamps* onto its lid with a knife or a nail.

"What is it?" Christy asked.

"A box," he said.

His pulse surged as he pulled it from the drawer and set it on the desktop.

For a moment, they both stared at the strange box, which looked ancient now in the light. The keys Alice had led him to delivered this box to them. This is what she'd seen? Not a way out, but something they wanted to remain hidden?

"Are you going to open it?" Christy asked.

Austin unlatched the small brass clasp that held it shut. The box opened to reveal two pairs of wire-frame spectacles on a velvet lining identical to the drawer's.

"Glasses?" Christy said.

Austin lifted a pair gently from the box. They felt insubstantial in his hands. He passed them to Christy, then took the other pair out and set them on the desk. Surely there was something else, maybe hidden inside the box.

But there wasn't.

"Alice mentioned something about lamps," he said. "This is what she meant. Glasses. Just glasses." He sighed and glanced at the desk. "Maybe there's something else in one of the other drawers."

Christy rounded the desk and held the glasses to the light. "They're just old, smudged glasses," she said as she lifted them to her face. "Nothing..."

She gasped, mouth gaping.

Austin followed her stare and saw that she was looking at the mirror. But he saw nothing unusual—just a full-length mirror fixed to the wall.

She, on the other hand, stood rooted to the floor, staring with such shock that he wondered if she was having some kind of attack. One glance at her emaciated frame, and anyone could see a heart attack wasn't out of the question.

"Austin!"

"What is it?"

She didn't seem able to respond.

The second pair of glasses lay waiting on the desk. He reached down and picked them up. Glanced at Christy again.

"This... This isn't possible," she said, face white.

A knot of fear twisted in his stomach as he brought the glasses to his face. He took a breath, faced the mirror, and slipped them on.

BOOK FOUR
SEER

"IS IT just me?"

Austin wasn't answering.

Christy tore her eyes from her reflection, jerked her head around, and saw that he'd put on the other pair of glasses. He stared at the mirror, ashen.

A single glance around the room told her that nothing else had changed. Only what she saw in the mirror.

She turned back to her reflection. She was still dressed in the yellow skirt—still had yellow ribbons in her pigtails, still had on the makeup and black shoes—but that's where the similarities ended.

The Christy returning her gaze now wasn't the gaunt bag of bones who'd had all her fat sucked out, not the ugly pig she'd seen in the bathroom mirrors. She in fact looked identical to the Christy who'd first found her way into the psych ward by way of the old storage room.

But that wasn't entirely true, either. Whereas she had thought of that old Christy as too thick, too pimply, too stubby in parts, the Christy looking back at her in the mirror was identical, but she wasn't too any-thing.

Christy blinked.

Austin, on the other hand, looked like plain old Austin, blue duds and all. He hadn't changed.

"Do you see me, Austin?"

"I see you," he said, voice full of wonder.

"You see yourself?"

He hesitated. "I haven't changed."

"But I have, right?"

"You... Yes, you've changed. Back to the old you."

"The ugly one?"

"You never were ugly."

"But not the fat one."

"You never were fat."

She glanced at him. Saw him lift his glasses and peer at the mirror, eyes round. Then quickly lower them back onto the bridge of his nose.

Christy looked down at her hands. Normal. So were her belly and her legs. So the change wasn't only in the mirror. Everything about herself had changed.

And without the spectacles?

Christy lifted her hand to her glasses.

"Don't!" His hand grabbed her wrist and jerked it away from her face. "Leave them on."

"Why?"

"Because... trust me." He quickly scanned the room. "Leave them on."

The dejected, rail-thin Austin who'd been wheeled into her bedroom was dejected no longer. He looked the same, she thought, but he wasn't quite as thin. Or was that her imagination?

"What's happening?"

"I'm not sure," he said. "Nothing else has changed." He glanced back at her image in the mirror, as if to make sure it was unchanged. "But I have a feeling that we're looking at reality somehow. Through these glasses."

"So... my fat hasn't been sucked out?"

"Maybe not. No. And that's what we're going to believe. Which might mean that the problems we see here aren't problems."

"What problems?"

"*All* the problems! Lawson. Fisher. The locked doors…"

She followed his logic immediately.

"You're saying that these glasses are helping us see things the way they really are."

"Something like that," he said in wonder, gazing around.

"So then the room is real, but not the way I see myself in this room."

"Maybe."

"What do you mean, maybe? How does that help us?"

He faced her, urgent. "I don't know! I don't know squat, but I'm going with it, okay?"

She blinked at the eruption of emotion. It made her wonder what they'd done to him.

"Fine," she said.

He faced the door and stared hard.

"We're going to get out."

She stepped up beside him. Nothing about the room had changed. "How?"

"Just keep your glasses on. Promise me."

Her heart was pounding. If he was right…Really? Could they just walk out? But that seemed impossible. The guards, the doors… Lawson.

"Promise me," he repeated.

"I won't take them off."

"Let's go."

He started for the door.

"Just go?"

"Just go." The authority in his voice sent a chill down her spine. "Now, Christy. I can't go back into that hole."

He placed his hand on the doorknob and hesitated while she

hurried up to him. If he was right, the handle would turn. If he was wrong, they were still locked in. She could hear his heavy breathing, matching her own.

"Turn it," she said.

He turned it.

The handle rotated without resistance.

He pulled the door wide and stepped back. The black-and-white checkerboard hall waited beyond the opened door.

Open!

Austin took her hand and they walked into the hall, then turned to the left without speaking.

Goosebumps prickled her skin and chilled her flesh. Her skin. Her flesh. The real her.

"Keep walking," he said.

Christy matched his stride down the middle of the hall, half expecting to see Lawson or Nancy round the corner ahead. Instead, they walked, without encountering a soul.

Down the next hall and around the last corner.

Then toward the elevator.

"Just keep walking," Austin said. "No matter what, just keep walking."

They passed the operating room, like two ghosts gliding unseen. But that was because there was no one to see them. As soon as someone saw them, it would be over.

No... No, the door had been open. They were seeing differently now. And now there was no problem.

They reached the elevator and Austin pressed the call button. It shone bright. The car was coming up, responding without needing a keycard.

Christy exchanged a look with Austin, who stared stoically as if afraid any display of emotion might pop this dream.

The metal elevator doors opened. Empty.

They stepped in, Austin pressed the down button, and the elevator ground slowly to the first floor. The door slid open.

"There is no problem," Austin said. "Just keep walking. Right to the front."

He reached for her hand and they left the elevator.

When they entered the main hall they saw Linda to their left, talking to one of the patients about medication. She cast them a glance and went right on as if there was no problem.

And there wasn't.

A warm glow spread down Christy's body. She was walking down the hall beside Austin, head up and stride strong, and nothing was stopping her. Nothing could, right?

This was the way out. Alice had been right. Somehow, the glasses she called lamps were the way out. What it all meant, Christy didn't know or care at the moment.

They passed several attendants and four other patients without so much as a worried glance or a question. They reached the main door that led into the main reception area. It was almost as if they didn't exist. They did, of course, because people obviously saw them, but no one seemed to care.

Nor did anyone make any attempt to stop them when they pushed through the door into the reception area.

Austin pulled up, hand sweaty in hers. Two doors—the one straight ahead that had led back to Lawson's office, and the one to their right, which led into the main hospital.

Or did it?

Then she saw the sign above the second door. OUT, it read, with an arrow pointing the way. *Out,* as in *Outlaw,* not *Exit.* So this had to be it!

"The right one," she said. "Outlaw . . ."

"Outlaw?"

"Hurry!"

When Austin started forward this time, he went fast with long strides, ignoring the watchful eye of a receptionist behind the glassed-in receiving counter. They were going to get out. The exit was right there and through that exit, freedom. Christy could feel it in her bones.

Real bones. Hers.

Austin banged through the door's crash bar with her close on his heels.

They flew down a short corridor that ended at double doors marked OUT. This was it. They were getting out!

Fresh air filled her nostrils as she slapped through the doors.

Bright sunlight.

Christy could not remember feeling the kind of relief and gratitude that swept through her body as she tore after Austin. Away from the hospital, never mind that he was dressed as a patient. The nightmare was behind them.

She'd taken only five or six long strides when he came to a skidding stop, forcing her to veer sharply to avoid crashing into him. And only then did she notice that the ground under her feet wasn't made of asphalt or concrete as it should have been.

It was made of sand. Sand and rocks and boulders that stretched out fifty yards or so before ending at the base of a cliff.

She gasped and jerked back, heart stuffed into her throat.

Austin half crouched, panting, arms spread out as if to steady himself.

She blinked. Jerked her head to her right.

They were in a canyon with vertical walls opened onto a serene mountainscape a few hundred yards ahead. The sky on the horizon was colored in rich reds, streaming with golden sunrays—a breathtaking sunset.

Her lungs were working hard, trying to supply enough oxygen to her confused mind. A mind that was telling her she was dead. They had done surgery on her and she'd died during the operation. This was the in between. Unless this was the no between, a place where only the insane live.

Christy whipped her head back to Austin, who had turned and was staring back toward the hospital.

She turned with him and stared at a cliff, which rose where Saint Matthew's had stood.

Twin ancient, weather-worn doors with rusted handles had replaced the glass doors through which they had escaped.

Christy stared, unbelieving and yet, strangely, believing. In what, she didn't know, but the thinnest thought whispered through her mind.

You've been here before, it said.

"What's...?"

She couldn't find the words to express what she wanted to ask. Didn't even know what she wanted to ask.

"It's gone," Austin said. "That can't be."

True. And yet it was.

"How...?" He looked at her and blinked. "Is this real?"

Christy looked at the ground. Sand. She bent down and raked her fingers through it. Warm. Lifted a handful and let it spill through her fingers. A hot breeze caught the finer dust and blew it away.

Austin turned a full circle, gazing up. He cautiously stepped away from the cliff toward the middle of the canyon. Looked both ways. Then up again.

He was slowly lifting his hand toward his face, going for his glasses, Christy thought, when she heard the distant sound of boots crunching in the sand.

The world seemed to stutter around her, then slow to half time. A quarter time.

Austin, with his fingers on his glasses.

She, turning her head slowly toward the sound.

The mirage-distorted image of a tall man approached. He was dressed in a wind-whipped black trench coat, striding toward them in slow motion, like an outlaw who'd stepped off the screen of a high-budget western and forgotten slow motion only happened on the screen.

The man pulled a splinter of wood he'd been chewing on from between his lips and flicked it casually to the side, still caught in quarter time. She watched the stick tumble through the air as the man came to a stop, ten feet from them.

"Leave the glasses on," he said.

20

THE WORLD around Christy stalled completely. The wind forgot to blow, the pounding of her heart faded, the canyon stilled as if it were a painting. There was Austin to her right, thumb and forefinger on the wire-frame spectacles that had shown them a way out; there was the man in the trench coat standing ten feet to her left, strong hands loose by his sides; there was her. Frozen in time.

Immobilized, because something told her that she might know this man. And then the world restarted, and she blinked.

"Hello, Christy." The man dipped his head. Shifted his eyes past her. "Austin."

And evidently this man knew her. Knew both of them.

"Been a heck of a day, I'm guessing."

There was something about his soft voice that bathed Christy in enduring calm.

The man stood about six feet tall, worn blue jeans and a white shirt under his coat. Black boots, those worn by bikers, not cowboys. No hat. His hair was dark and his jaw was strong, the kind that had seen its share of harsh weather and was no worse for the wear. How old, she couldn't tell, but he stood with the ease and self-assurance of someone who'd circled the world a dozen times on foot and lived to tell of it.

For several seconds the man looked at her with kind blue eyes that seemed to hold her in a place of unquestioned safety, gentle and powerful at once. Her mind didn't know where he had come from or why he'd come, but her heart seemed to bond with him in way that made her want to cry.

With one glance, this man had given her more love than she'd felt in her entire life. Or maybe she felt so emotional because she'd just been through hell to find him.

And yet, looking at him now, she didn't feel like she'd been through hell. In fact, she felt no distress at all.

Not about where she'd come from or why. Not about what she looked like or didn't. Not about what she had done in the past or would do in the future.

The wind toyed with the man's hair and lifted the tails of his coat.

"You can call me Outlaw," he said.

Christy felt her knees go weak. She immediately connected his voice to the one she'd heard in Nancy's office.

"Outlaw," Austin said.

Christy saw the circular stone pendant that hung on a leather cord over the man's breastbone. A large *O* with tribal markings and a single, embossed word inside the *O* that she didn't know.

O for Outlaw.

"Out," the man said, walking up to Christy. "The narrow way that few follow. Beyond the laws bent on death, where the burden is light and the yoke is easy. And yet oh so hard to find." He lifted his hand and drew Christy's hair behind her ear. Brushed her cheek with his thumb. She could smell the faint scent of fresh earth on his skin.

"Which is actually in," he said, placing his hand flush against her heart. "Where you're already perfect."

He was speaking with words using his mouth, but she might have guessed that his meaning came from his hand, because with that touch, she felt warmth wash through her torso. An overwhelming urge to weep rose through her chest and throat.

"I've been searching for you for a very long time," he said. "I've come to call you home, Christy… To the place you belong. You're so beautiful." Outlaw leaned forward and placed a tender kiss on her forehead. "So very beautiful."

"Home?"

"To that place where you're whole. Perfect. Complete. And so very, very beautiful."

"I am?" The words came out choked. A tear slipped down her right cheek.

"More than you can possibly see. But you will."

He stepped past her to Austin, who looked utterly lost. Gently placed a large, strong hand on the side of Austin's head. Austin looked as if he might melt.

Outlaw pulled Austin forward and kissed the crown of his head.

"I know it hurts in there, Austin. It's not your fault. With every gift comes a curse." He placed his hand on Austin's chest, as he had hers. "And so it begins."

He dipped his head and then turned to face them both.

"We don't have much time, so please listen carefully. It's very simple, really, but until you use your minds as they were meant to be used, it will sound a bit overwhelming. If you're not very careful, you're likely to forget what I say altogether."

He searched both of their eyes as if looking for a response. But Christy was too busy searching her own mind, wondering why she felt such an overwhelming connection to him. And what begins?

"You're wondering who I am," Outlaw said. "But the real question is, who are you willing to be?"

"I'm not using my mind as it was meant to be used?" Austin said, stuck back on what the man had said earlier. He stared up at the man with wide eyes as if he was seeing a ghost from an unknown past.

"To be honest," Outlaw said kindly, "you're not using your mind at all. It's using you." And then he added, with a casual look at the cliff wall behind them, "But then, that's true of almost everyone."

"Is this real?" she asked, facing him again.

His eyes locked on hers. "Is it? Depends on your perspective. If you step out of a boat and try to walk on the water, can you? Or do you have a problem?"

She knew he was leading her, but she wanted nothing more than to be led right now.

"A problem." she said.

"Yes. You have a problem, but only if you know you have a problem. Just like the place that has you trapped right now. Your darkness. No way out, only because your lamps are turned off."

"Lamps?" Austin said.

"The eye is the lamp of the body. Turn it on, and you'll see that you have no problem. That you're full of light. That the dark sea below you can't swallow you at all. But take your eyes off the light and you'll drown in the darkness you see."

"These glasses…"

"Lamps. Which is why you shouldn't take them off. Not until you realize that we all have lamps. Only question is, are they on or off? If you see your beauty, they are on. If you see your suffering, they're off."

"So…" Confusion swarmed Christy's mind. "So we're seeing what's real right now?"

"Is it? You can decide. Think of the glasses as a life ring tossed out to keep you from sinking into the darkness. A gift to help you see the narrow way out of darkness. You once learned this from the master you followed, but you've forgotten. And so you suffer."

The words swelled in her mind and gave her goosebumps. This was real. She was seeing the light. And in the light, she felt strangely and perfectly connected to this man, Outlaw. He was showing them the way.

"Where did you come from?" she asked.

His mouth slowly turned upward, and he looked at her with wise eyes that had seen many lifetimes.

"From a jungle on the other side of the world. But that's a story for another time. I've come for you. That's all that matters right now."

"What did you mean, the master we once followed?"

He hesitated, then squatted on one heel, plucked a stalk from a dried tuft of grass near his foot, and absently stuck it in the corner of his mouth, eyes on her as he straightened.

"I'm guessing neither of you have much recall of your childhood. That about right?"

She exchanged a glance with Austin.

"All in good time. Truth is, although you're both quite special, any who choose to see the light are Outlaws. All of those who are willing to step beyond the law of darkness and death and see. I've come to call them all home, where we all belong. This will be our tribe."

Stillness lingered.

"I saw myself in a dungeon..." Christy said. "My father..."

The memory of that dark cage wove a thread of fear through her mind.

Outlaw turned his head and looked directly into her eyes.

"It was so real," she said.

He slowly stood. "It was real. Not your actual father, no, but the one who tells you that you're not good enough. That you don't belong. The one we all secretly fear when the lights are off. The one that religion has turned into a god made in their own image, capable of hatred."

His words struck a chord deep in her, and she felt the fear rise.

Outlaw saw her visceral reaction and stepped forward. The world seemed to slow again. He put his hand on her shoulder and tilted his head down so that his forehead was only inches from hers. When he spoke, his words were soft, like a warm sun rising in her heart.

"Listen to me, Christy. I need you to remember what I'm about to tell you. You hate yourself because you fear that your Father is capable of disapproval and rage. All of your fears come from this single image. The truth is you are treasured."

His voice came like honey to her tongue.

"You are perfect even as your Father is perfect. Made whole and blameless a long time ago."

Like warm bread to the famished; like cool water to a parched throat.

"Beautiful. As you are, without a single further change to the real you. Atoned. Made right. No condemnation possible, no further correction needed. Your only problem now is the one you make for yourself when you are blinded to just how beautiful you are right now."

"Beautiful?" she said.

"A new creature. As you always will be. I'm calling you home, Christy. To this reality, with those who see it as you now do. We are one."

She could barely speak.

"He told me I needed correction. That I was broken. That I don't belong. I... I don't understand."

"That's Lawson's way. He confuses and accuses. The truth is, you're whole already."

He brushed a tear from her cheek.

"You cannot love anything or anyone more than you love yourself and you can't truly love yourself unless you see yourself whole. If you secretly disapprove of any part of yourself, you will secretly hate part of the One who made you. Can you understand that?"

"Yes," she whispered.

"The good news is, you can love yourself because you, too, are now love, dead to anything but love. Everything else is of your own making: a lie you believe; a story from an accuser that ravages you and keeps you locked in that cage. Love yourself, Christy, as he who made you loves you and has made you whole, without any further blame or fault. See with new eyes. Then you will know just how beautiful your world is now. All of it. Every scar, every bruise, every tear, every joy. Beautiful."

Christy began to cry, not with sorrow, but from a place of overwhelming relief and joy. It bubbled up through her chest and spilled out of her like a river.

"See, Christy. See."

And then it all became too much for her, and she lunged forward into his warm, musky clothing and chest, wrapping her arms around him as if he were love itself.

"I see," she sobbed.

Her head was under his chin, and he cupped it with his hand and stroked her hair, accepting her tears. "You are loved. You are love itself. This is your family. You are home."

And in that moment, she knew that she was. Nothing bad had ever actually happened to her, and if it had, it was only because she'd mistaken it as bad. How could anything bad have brought her here, to this man who held her like his own child?

She was home.

She stepped back from him and stared up into his face, trembling with wonder.

"Thank you," she said.

He dipped his head, held her eyes with his own for a moment longer, then turned to Austin, who was staring as if struck by a star.

Outlaw reached into his coat and pulled out a dark brown leatherbound book, pages curled from use. He stepped up to a large boulder on Austin's left and studied the volume's worn, soft cover, as if taken in by some deep secret buried in the pages of that singular book.

"What do you see, Austin?"

Austin was staring at the journal. "A book," he said in a thin voice.

Christy edged to the other side so that she could see what they were looking at.

"It's more than just a book," Outlaw said. "It's my mother's story. My story. We all have our stories, but in the end they all come back to one word."

The leather cover was embossed with the same markings that were on the pendant around Outlaw's neck. A large *O* with a word embossed inside of it.

DEDITIO.

"Do you know this word, Austin?"

"*Deditio.*"

"And its meaning?"

"It's Latin for 'unconditional surrender,'" Austin said. "The demand of the Roman Empire when it conquered its subjects."

"The same Romans sometimes exacted that total surrender using a cross." Outlaw faced Austin. "But in the end, it is surrender that conquers."

He put his hand on Austin's shoulder and spoke in a soft tone.

"Surrender, Austin. Surrender who you think you are to who you truly are. Surrender what you think you know. Surrender even the need to know anything more than who you are. Do not lean on your own understanding."

Austin's eyes skittered from side to side, searching Outlaw's.

"Our greatest challenge in life is remembering who we really are. Life is a cycle of remembering and forgetting. Do you know who you are?"

Austin blinked.

"You are not your mind. You are not your body. You are not even your beliefs—these are only of this world, mere flesh and blood and a few electrochemical reactions. You, my friend, are far greater than this. Be still and know, not with your mind, but with that which is beyond your mind. Are these words true to you?"

Austin hesitated, then offered a shallow nod.

"There are no longer any problems to solve. If there are no longer any problems to solve, there's no longer any need for correction. If there's no need for correction, then there's no need for law. Live in the grace of that which is now perfect, as it is. *Be* perfect, don't try to *become* perfect. You already are, you just don't know it yet. Be still and know. You must surrender your old perception and see with the lamps on and there you will find that the light is bright."

Slowly, Austin's face twisted into a knot. Tears filled his eyes, and Christy thought, *He sees too. He's saved from this insanity too!*

Outlaw lingered for a moment, then picked up his book and shoved it into a pocket sewn inside his coat. He walked several steps away, as if his work was done and it was time to leave. His strides were sure, like a man who knew where he was going but had nowhere to be.

When he turned around his coat rose with the wind.

"See, my friends. With eyes wide open. Don't forget. You don't have to understand everything right now, but you are going to have to decide if you trust me, or trust Lawson. The choice is yours. Keep your eyes open."

I will! Christy was thinking. She'd never felt so elevated and sure of that fact than any she'd ever known. She was beautiful, perfect, loved, love. As she was. She'd been seeing herself without the lights on and in that shadow, she'd imagined that she was ugly, at terrible fault, and deserving of punishment. But the good news was that she wasn't. Not any more. Not one more minute.

She was thinking that in a long rush of exhilaration, but those thoughts were suddenly darkened by a shadow across her face.

Like a crow coming in from the sky, the shadow covered her vision and she caught her breath.

Not a shadow, but fingers. Fingers that grasped the glasses and jerked them from her face.

Christy gasped.

In the space of one blink, her vision of the canyon vanished.

Replaced with the face of Kern Lawson. He was grinning and her glasses were in his hand.

They were in her room.

"Are we courting our delusions again, Alice?" He opened his fingers and let her glasses fall. They landed on the floor with a metallic clink. Then he lifted his boot, and, without looking down, crushed them under his heel.

"Fairy tales are for children, my dear."

"No..." She felt gut-punched. Visions of Outlaw swirled in her mind.

And yet... And yet she was here. In her room. Standing exactly where she'd been standing when she first put the glasses on. And the image in the mirror showed her plain as day.

She looked like she'd just stepped out of a prison camp.

"No?" Lawson said. He stepped over to Austin, who was still lost in his own world, ripped the glasses from his face, and smashed them under his foot.

"Playtime's over, children."

21

WITH A twist of his heel, Lawson ground the last remaining bits of glass into the floor. Slowly, he bent and picked up the twisted frames. Turned them as if inspecting a butterfly with broken wings.

"I'm disappointed," he said without looking at them. "And this after so much progress."

Austin took in the room with a glance. He was back in the hospital with Christy, but it was the skeletal Christy—skin drawn tight on a brittle frame, stitched up, and looking like a coat rack. Gone was the girl he'd just seen in the canyon.

He was having a hard time getting oxygen into his lungs. There was no explanation for any of this—the glasses, the man in the canyon, the brilliant sunset. They'd left the hospital, yet here they were again.

Both couldn't be true—either they'd left the room and the canyon was real, or they hadn't and everything was an illusion. He felt like he'd just awakened from a distant dream.

Remember what I've said, Austin. Remember every word.

Austin stared at Christy, whose wide eyes searched the room as if looking for the man. Outlaw.

"I expected more, honestly," Lawson said as he let the glasses slip from his hand.

Christy's fingers began to twitch. Her anxiety fed Austin's own and caused the fear in his own mind to swell.

"We need to go deep now, while the door to your mind is still open," Lawson said. He walked to Austin and took him by the elbow. Austin tried to jerk his arm away, but the man's grip clamped down like a vise.

He shoved a finger at the wheelchair. "Sit."

Austin sat.

His mind spun like bald tires on hard packed dirt, unable to bite into the ground. Because there was no ground at all. It had been jerked out from under him.

Deditio… Surrender, Austin.

The thought was sparked in the corner of his consciousness as Lawson turned the wheelchair toward the door. Surrender, but to what? To this reality or to the other, which was no longer present?

"No, wait." Christy took a step forward.

The man glared at her. "Reacquaint yourself with reality, my dear. I'll be back when we're ready."

Christy stood there trembling. "Ready for what?"

Lawson smiled. "Why, ready for some correction, obviously." He shifted his stare down to Austin. "Beginning with you."

Without another word, he wheeled Austin to the door. Opened it with a swipe of his wrist.

"Remember, Austin!" Christy cried. "We have to remember!"

Lawson wheeled him through the door and turned down the hall. He had already taken several long strides before the door slammed shut behind them, sealing Christy in and him out.

Life is a cycle of remembering and forgetting.

Already the episode with Outlaw felt unreal. Like a dream he couldn't quite put his finger on. His head began to throb—the pain was back like a pounding fist.

"Where are we going?" Austin asked.

Lawson didn't respond.

Spikes of fear sank into Austin as the stark image of the pitch-black cell materialized in his mind. He couldn't go back to the cell. He wasn't strong enough. Not anymore. His mind was too fragile, untrustworthy.

Don't forget who you really are.

The long hallway stretched in front of him like the throat of a terrible monster. He clenched his eyes shut. Slowly opened them.

Who am I?

Lawson's voice jerked him back to awareness. "Your problem is that you're stuck."

There's only a problem if you say there is.

"Even after a week in that hole. Stuck, stuck, stuck, my boy. Like a pig that can't see beyond its pathetic little mud hole, you're hopelessly mired in a persistent delusion—blind to the fact that you need correction. Well, Scotty, I'm going to help you see. With those two little orbs floating in your skull."

The man's words flared in Austin's mind, sparking a wildfire of fear. Something had changed in Lawson. Austin had to convince Lawson that he was okay, that he wasn't delusional. It was the only way to stay out of the cell and hold onto whatever tattered pieces of himself remained.

"You're right," Austin said. "I'm already beginning to see. There's no problem."

"No problem?" The man chuckled. "You and I both know that's not true, don't we? You're still blind."

"Blind to what?"

"To the truth, of course. You're being sucked into a lie that's rooted deep inside."

Remember the truth, Austin.

Hold on to the truth.

"What truth?" he asked, voicing the thought circling his mind.

"The truth that this is reality. Everything you see around us—all of it is absolute, verifiable, concrete reality. Not the mirages you've conjured in your cracked little mind. You can't accept that because you're still trapped in your delusion."

They passed under the cold, harsh lights that illuminated the corridor as they made their way to the elevator at the far end. The world was beginning to slow.

"There are laws that govern the universe," Lawson said. "Laws that cannot be broken or violated without consequence. You've fooled yourself into believing you can live outside those laws. Problem is, those laws *are* reality. You can imagine until the cows come home; you're still bound by them."

Lawson jerked the wheelchair up and dumped him forward, out of the wheelchair. His mind registered what was happening as his knees slammed against the hard floor.

Palms slapping the hard tile, Austin scrambled to keep upright. He managed to push to all fours, breathing hard.

Before he could react, Lawson planted a foot on Austin's backside and shoved him off balance. The force knocked him forward, and he slammed facedown against the cold floor.

There was only time to blink once before the heel of Lawson's boot darkened the edge of his vision. It pressed against his temple, pinning his head to the ground. Unbearable agony flared through his skull as the man leaned his weight into his boot.

Austin grunted.

"Sometimes we just need a change of perspective." Lawson's voice was calm and flat. "Tell me, what do you feel?"

Austin sucked a ragged breath. Swirling specks of light formed on the air.

Lawson pressed harder. "Does this feel like a delusion to you?"

"No," he managed through short breaths. "No."

"No, what?"

Darkness crept into his vision. "No, it's not a delusion."

"See, that's not so hard. If it's not a delusion, then what does that make it?"

"I... I don't know." The ache in his skull worked into his neck and pulsed down his spine.

"Of course you do. It's very simple. Think. What does that make it?"

"Real." The word came slow and drawn out.

"Good boy. The laws of reality are at work. Laws you can trust to be infallible. You fell out of the chair because the law of gravity is real. You feel pain in your body right now due to physiological laws. My boot is stimulating nerve endings, which in turn are sending impulses to your brain. Do you think your brain is lying to you, Scott?"

His consciousness began to slip, like the last layer of sand through a sieve. He wanted to scream, but there was no one to hear. No one to come to his side and tell him it would be okay.

"Speak up! Is your brain lying to you?"

A beat. "No."

Lawson held his boot down a few moments longer, then lifted his foot, grabbed him by the collar, and jerked him to his feet.

"Follow me."

Austin wavered on his feet as the sound of Lawson's hollow footfalls ricocheted off the cinderblock walls. His vision pulsed with the pounding of his heart.

He walked after the man, concentrating with each step so he wouldn't stumble. With each step, the world drifted slowly back into focus.

Lawson pushed a door open on the right side of the hall and watched him with unflinching eyes.

Austin paused at the door. Another patient room.

"Inside," Lawson said. He jutted his chin toward the room.

Austin reluctantly entered, then stopped cold. Jacob sat slumped in his wheelchair near the center of the room, perfectly still, face expressionless. He gazed at the floor as if contemplating a riddle that had been etched into it.

Lawson stepped past Austin and stopped by Jacob's wheelchair. He retrieved a black leather pocketbook from inside his jacket. He unzipped it, splayed it open like a book, and slipped out a silver scalpel.

"Cut him," the man said, holding out the sharp instrument.

He held the man's gaze.

"If none of this is real, then Jacob is an illusion. If Jacob is an illusion, then the logic follows that you can't really harm him." He paused. "So *cut him.*"

Austin's heart pounded. Surely, the man didn't mean it.

"No? All right then." Lawson turned to Jacob. He palmed the blade and, using his index finger to guide it, drew the blade across the boy's porcelain cheek.

Jacob flinched but didn't cry out. A crimson wound formed beneath his eye and began to seep blood.

Lawson reached down, smeared the wound with his index finger, and shoved it toward Austin. "Taste it."

Austin's stomach twisted. His eyes flitted between Jacob and the man. More blood welled up and dripped down the boy's face.

"Do it," Lawson said. His voice was flat, void of emotion. "Now."

Austin hesitated. He couldn't. He wouldn't.

"No?" Lawson regarded him with stone eyes. "Fine."

Lawson reached down and drew the scalpel across Jacob's left cheek. The blade sliced deeper than the first, and the boy shuddered.

Austin's world tipped crazily. This couldn't be happening…

"Why are you doing this?"

"To set you free from the delusion, Scott. Part of you believes that Jacob is nothing more than a figment in your head. If that's true, then I could carve him up like a pumpkin. But you know that's not true, don't you?"

Austin stared at Jacob's trembling form, pleading eyes locked on his. Real...

"Trust your senses, Scott. Taste and see." He stepped up and brought his bloodied finger to Austin's lips. "Open your mouth or I'll cut him again."

Austin's heart thrummed louder. Jacob sat, unmoving. Screaming inside.

"I'm waiting," Lawson said.

Austin parted his lips. Lawson shoved his finger into Austin's mouth. A metallic tang assaulted his tongue and slid to the back of his throat.

He jerked back and spit to the side. A glob of blood-tinged spittle smacked the floor.

"You see? Real," Lawson said. "All of this—real. Isn't it?"

He wiped his arm across his lips and choked back a gathering wave of nausea. Nodded slightly. "Yes."

"Good." Lawson replaced the scalpel and slipped the leather case into his jacket. Walked to the wall, punched a red button, and leaned close to an intercom.

"Edna?"

A thin voice answered through the speaker. "Yes, Dr. Lawson?"

"Please see to Jacob immediately." He looked toward the boy. "It appears he's acted out again and cut himself."

"Right away, sir."

"Thank you."

Lawson opened the door. "Let's go."

With a parting glance at Jacob, who had settled somewhat, Austin stepped cautiously past Lawson and into the hall. The administrator led him toward the elevator.

Thoughts crowded Austin's mind, a hundred voices all vying for attention.

Deditio…

The single thought sliced through the maelstrom, silencing it for an instant. It came a second time, lower and distant. *Surrender.* He knew that's what it meant: surrender. But to what?

Austin stepped into the elevator and the machine hummed, low and thick, as they descended to the hospital's main level. He listened intently, concentrating on the deep pulsing of his mind as loud thoughts cluttered it again.

Surrender what you think you know… even the need to know. Don't lean on your own understanding.

The doctor looked at his reflection in the elevator's polished steel interior. Straightened his tie and smoothed his lapel. His gaze shifted toward Austin.

"Think of me as the law around here, Scott. I'm as sure and reliable as gravity itself. Until you're healthy, I'm your connection to reality. You'll come to trust that in time. How soon is up to you."

The doors slid open and Lawson led him into the main hallway.

"All that you see now is real. Your mind may still be questioning that fact, but I assure you that this is not a delusion. Take a look around."

He did. Patients shuffled through the hallway, some led by attendants while others moved on their own. Ahead, four men in white coats gathered in front of the administration office. Fisher stood among them, motioning as the others listened intently.

Lawson nodded in their direction. "They're visiting from the Mayo Clinic. Word about our remarkable successes here at Saint Matthew's is getting out. The gentleman on the right is one of most prominent neurologists in the world."

The air crackled with vitality as Austin walked through the hall with Lawson. With each step, the fog in his mind began to burn away. The world before him was utterly real—the ground beneath his feet, the people walking through the halls, the faint scent of bleach that hung on the air.

Look with eyes wide open, Austin.

"Good afternoon, Doctor," Fisher said as he passed by with the men in tow. He nodded at Austin. "Hello, Scott. Good to see you again."

Something lurched inside of him. His attention was drawn to the side of the man's head where his wound had been, but there was nothing. Of course there was nothing. The man hadn't died.

Lawson led him into the administration office. The small space swirled with the busy sounds of normal life—a ringing phone, the whirr of a printer, the low drone of a radio somewhere in the room.

The receptionist at a desk greeted them. "I have a few things for you to sign, sir."

Lawson flipped through several forms, pausing only long enough to scrawl his signature on each, and then passed them back. "Has the report from Dr. Bishop come yet?"

Dr. Bishop? His doctor, Austin realized.

Beverly slid an oversized yellow envelope across the countertop. "A few minutes ago," she said. "Interoffice courier just dropped it off."

"I hope you don't mind," he said to Austin as they stepped into his office. "I had your file sent over after my conversation with Dr. Bishop yesterday."

"You know Dr. Bishop?"

"Roland and I go back to our premed days. I've tried to lure him into our program for quite some time, but he's got his sights set on other goals. I requested a consult because your medical records indicated him as your attending neurologist. I would've brought you in for that discussion, but you were indisposed."

Lawson opened the file and withdrew a stack of images as he crossed the room, Austin by his side. Black-and-white cross sections of a human skull. MRI images.

His MRI.

"We had a long talk about your symptoms and diagnosis."

Austin's breath thickened. The low-level buzz in his head built to a deafening crescendo.

Lawson stopped by the closet, then turned and flipped the image around so Austin could see it clearly. He pointed to an irregular mass of white that appeared on the frontal lobe.

"A small tumor. Operable."

"A tumor. I have cancer?"

The room began to blur. Austin stared at the image of the seed growing in his head. It was true then. His mind was rotting from the inside out.

"Cancer? No, but it's undoubtedly contributing to the severity of your delusions." He dropped the file on his desk. "Either way, the root of your problem is your refusal to accept that you've been delusional for a very long time, long before the presentation of this tumor."

Austin stared at Lawson blankly. Nodded.

"Good." A faint smile nudged Lawson's lips as he put a hand on Austin's shoulder. "Everything is going to be just fine. And now it's time to get back to work."

Austin's heart quickened as the man placed a hand on the doorknob to his left. The door that led to the black cell. He wanted to run, but there was nothing from which to escape. The enemy was growing in his head. There was nowhere to go.

"In there?"

"Yes, in there. In, until you accept the fact that you're broken."

Lawson swung the door open and led Austin into the cell by the hand. The man had said something else to him, but Austin was already drifting into the borderlands of his mind. It wasn't until the world went black that he realized Lawson was no longer at his side.

Crushed by emotion, Austin groped his way to the corner, crumpled to the ground, drew his knees to his chest, and began to shake. He really was delusional.

Delusional, which meant that he could not know what was real and what was not.

He knew that he was supposed to remember something, and part of him did. Something about never forgetting, about stepping beyond his mind. But none of it was connecting, because he didn't know how to step anywhere except into his mind.

Without his knowledge he was nothing. Without his beliefs, a mere skeleton.

Who am I?

I am my thoughts.

I think, therefore I am.

I am, therefore I think.

He saw himself in his mind's eye, sitting alone in a room, staring blankly at the wall. Not him, but a shell of what he used to be.

My mind is dying, therefore I am dying.

If I should die before I wake…

Who… am… I?

I am terrified.

REMEMBER, OUTLAW had said. And Christy had. She'd even told Austin to remember, so vivid was that memory.

More vivid than the memory of the canyon and Outlaw was the memory of the love that had roared through her. It was like a lion making an irrefutable claim to dominance. Love had tenderly whispered her name, like a lost lover come to wake her from a deep slumber. Love had washed over her like a waterfall, cleansing her of any other memory besides love itself.

She had known the love more than felt it.

Life is a cycle of remembering and forgetting...

The words echoed through her mind as she paced the room with one arm around her skinny midriff, propping up the other to give her access to her nails, which she was chewing on. There was nothing left of them, but her teeth didn't seem to know.

Life is a cycle of remembering and forgetting...

She now understood why Outlaw had made such a point of this. Less than an hour had passed since Lawson jerked Austin from the room, and already she wasn't quite sure what she was supposed to remember.

Or which was the illusion and which wasn't. What if she had it all wrong?

The forgetting wasn't so much about the words themselves. She could remember what Outlaw had said. She was perfect as she was. She was love. There was only a problem if she believed there was.

The good news is, you can love yourself because you, too, are now love. Everything else is of your own making: a lie you believe; a story from an accuser that ravages you and keeps you locked in that cage of hell.

Sure, she could remember the words. Most of them. But she couldn't quite get the same feeling of love that she'd felt when she had those glasses on. Those lamps.

In fact, the feeling had all but gone, as if it had been caused by a drug that had worn off.

You're not your emotions, Christy.

No, but there was more. She couldn't quite connect with the meaning behind the words either. They said she was beautiful, but she couldn't get herself to think she was beautiful. And that was a problem, a real problem, never mind what Outlaw said. She didn't just say so, the mirror said so.

Christy glanced at her reflection for the hundredth time in less than an hour and saw the same thing she'd seen every time. The ghastly skeletal body that she'd convinced herself was beautiful, for a little while at least.

See with lamps on, Christy. Eyes wide open. See yourself as beautiful.

The truth of that command had lost more of its power with each trip across the cold tile floor.

She'd long ago ripped off her yellow skirt, pulled out her pigtails, and washed her makeup off, thinking that the plain blue uniform would help her see past the illusion.

It's not real, Christy. What you see in the mirror isn't you.

But it was. In fact, she could no longer even remember why it wasn't.

Life wasn't so much a cycle of remembering and forgetting, because there really was nothing to forget in the first place. She was ugly and always had been.

She knew that the Outlaw image in her mind would tell her that she'd forgotten how perfect she was, but that was wrong. She hadn't forgotten how perfect she was, because she wasn't perfect.

She was deeply flawed and she hated herself for it. And yes, she did hate whoever had made her this way. Her father.

End of story.

No, no... That's wrong.

But it no longer felt wrong.

"Are you ready, Alice?"

She spun to the door and saw him there. Lawson. Her new maker.

"Sorry to startle you." He smiled and crossed the room, arm held out, palm down. "If you're ready, we can go."

"Go? Where?"

"To see the doctor, of course. We've been watching you and decided that another slight correction is in order. It will help you accept yourself and break from the more stubborn delusions."

She lifted her hand and took his, thinking only that it was the right thing to do.

He's not real, Christy.

And yet his hand felt perfectly real.

"A correction?"

"Yes. The doctor has been studying the post-operative photographs and has suggested smoothing out some of the grooves. Judging by your reactions, we concur."

He led her toward the door. The idea blossomed in her mind.

"Smooth out? How?"

"Simple. They kept your own fat cells. They'll just put some back."

"They can do that?"

"It's done all the time. They call it an autologous fat transfer."

He opened the door and sat her in a wheelchair manned by an attendant she recognized. Something in the back of her mind was telling her to remember.

Remember, Christy. Don't put yourself back in that cage. No more lies.

"In your case, they might do more than just some," Lawson was saying. "In fact, Nancy seems to think quite a bit might be just what you need." He made a fist and gave the air a tiny punch as he walked down the hall beside her chair. "That extra push that puts you over the edge and finishes the job, so to speak."

An image of the fat Christy flashed through her mind. Fat or skinny, which was she?

Who was she?

You are beautiful, Christy. So beautiful.

Outlaw's low, tender voice rumbled through her mind like an aftershock, and she blinked with it. Why, she wasn't sure, but a snippet of that meaningful memory slipped into her veins.

Lawson was talking again, but she wasn't hearing the words.

For a brief moment, maybe two seconds, she remembered. It was what he had said to Austin. *If there's no longer any problem, there's no longer any need for correction.*

Otherwise, she thought, where do the corrections end? What is good enough? Can perfect be measured by a scale or a law of better or worse? It either is perfect or it isn't at all.

She thought it, and, in that moment, it made perfect sense.

And then she could no longer grasp the thought. What if the canyon really was just an illusion?

"… to put you under again," Lawson was saying. "Just in case we go for the whole caboodle, if you know what I mean."

"Not really."

He glanced down at her as he reached for the doors that led into the operating room. "Make you fat again, Alice. To give you some appreciation for what is." He pushed the door open and stepped in. "Don't worry, we can always take it back out."

She wasn't sure what to make of that. It sounded horrible, but she was suddenly past horrible. It was what it was. She could either accept it or resist it. And for now she was too tired to resist it.

The pungent scent of ether greeted her as she crossed the threshold and scanned the room. The same team who'd worked on her before stood by the bed, this time accompanied by Nancy, who was the only one not dressed in scrubs.

Paul Bigoti, the surgeon, white mask already in place. Charlene, his assistant, smiling warmly. The anesthesiologist, a redheaded man whose name Christy had forgotten.

See with new eyes. Turn on the lamps.

But hers were back on the bedroom floor, shattered.

Everyone has lamps.

"Let's get started then, shall we?" Lawson said. Evidently, he'd decided to stay this time.

Charlene helped Christy to her feet and led her across the room, and all the while Christy's mind was half gone.

Gone on the inevitability of it all.

Gone on what was or wasn't.

Gone on anything but shuffling one foot in front of the other and wondering if Austin was okay.

They helped her back onto the surgeon's table and prepped her, and she let them do it all without a single question. It was what it was. She felt oddly at peace.

It was while she was staring up at the bright, circular lights that the words came again, like a voice beyond her mind.

Beautiful, Outlaw said. *As you are. Without a single change. Your only problem now is the one you make for yourself by being unaware of just how beautiful you are right now, in this moment.*

She remembered the words very clearly, and their meaning sank into her bones.

Perfection needs no correction.

I am perfect. As I am.

Her heart rate surged with this single awareness. She both felt it and heard it because they'd already hooked the electrodes to her wrist and the monitor began to chirp with new urgency.

See, Christy. See.

The mask was over her face, and the anesthesiologist began to count her down.

"Ten."

"Nine."

"Eight…"

But Christy wasn't saying *ten, nine, eight*. She was whispering, just barely into the mask.

"Help."

"Me."

"See."

And then she wasn't saying anything because she surrendered to those words and faded into the white lights above her.

"OPEN YOUR eyes, Christy."

Christy heard the words far away, as if they were an echo of a voice that had not spoken. She lay still, thinking that she might be dead and had heard an angel.

She wasn't concerned about being dead, because if dead was, it was. Somehow that seemed obvious to her.

Then she remembered that she was on the operating table, and they were putting her fat back into her body. They were trying to make her beautiful even though she didn't need to be made anything.

That was interesting. It wasn't alarming or worrying, only interesting. Not even interesting, really. It was, in fact, a bit absurd.

She felt silly giggles bubble up in her chest, and she let one out, like a tiny hiccup.

Strange… She was laughing?

Christy let her eyes flutter open, half expecting to see the operating table below her, like she had once before. Instead she saw that she was standing near the door staring at the surgeon, his assistant, and the anesthesiologist huddled over her, with Kern Lawson and Nancy Wilkins looking on from either side.

They were talking in low tones, pointing, hard at work on her body. Seeing it with her own eyes, Christy felt fear begin to edge back into her mind.

With her eyes closed, she'd thought the notion preposterous.

With her eyes open, she was suddenly uncertain. Maybe even afraid.

"We have an irregular pulse," the anesthesiologist said.

The surgeon glanced at the monitor. "She's lost a lot of blood. Heart's just working to keep up."

She was losing blood? She thought they were putting fat in, not cutting her open.

"What are they doing?"

She jerked her head to the right and saw the girl who'd spoken, three feet away. A patient, staring with casual interest.

The girl looked over at her. "They're operating on you?"

Christy knew the girl. It was Alice Ringwald, the girl she'd seen Fisher take to the basement on that first day.

"Alice?"

The girl smiled. "Hi, Christy."

"Are... Are you..." Christy glanced at the operating table and saw that no one had turned to the sound of their voices. "Are you really here?"

"Sure I am. As much as you are."

"I mean really here? Why can't they hear us?"

"Because they're here too," Alice said. "The whole world is here."

"Where?"

Alice lifted her hand and tapped her head with a finger. "Where everyone dreams."

Christy's meeting with Outlaw came back in a rush. Was he only a dream too? But something had to be real. Either what Lawson said or what Outlaw said was true, not both.

"I think we're seeing now," Christy said. "Really seeing."

"Sure we are. But it's only a dream."

No. No, she couldn't accept that.

Everyone has lamps.

She was seeing with her lamps on now. She was seeing that she wasn't the girl on the table, that she was more, far more. She was seeing because she was near death, and her eyes had been opened.

But could she see, really see, when she was fully awake and out of this place? That was the real rub.

"They think I'm you," Christy said.

Alice laughed. "That's just Fisher trying to cover his tracks. They don't want you out."

"But is this place even real?"

"If you say so."

"And if not?"

"Then it's not."

There's only a problem if you say there is.

"The thing is," Alice said, looking at the operating table. "I don't think they even know they're not in control."

"We are?"

"Sure. Of what we see. It's a dream. That's why I come here. It's just a dream."

No, that's wrong, Christy thought. *Not all of it was a dream.*

She stared at her form on the table, breathing up and down, out like a light. That was the illusion. It was the problem of her own making. That body on the table was only ugly if she said so. In truth, imperfection had already been corrected. The law was dead. Out. Perfection was in. She was alive. Perfect. As she was, outside of this illusion.

And she kept forgetting that.

You don't have to understand everything right now, Outlaw had said, *but you are going to have to decide if you trust me, or trust Lawson.*

She looked at her hands and saw the same hands she'd always had, neither skinny nor fat nor anything. Just… there. Hands.

"It's an illusion," she said. "My whole life has been run by illusions."

"Then maybe you should unplug them," Alice said, as if it were an afterthought.

You're not your body. You're not your mind. You're not your emotions. You're not even your beliefs.

The meaning of all this dropped into her awareness like a star from heaven, and she suddenly knew what she would do.

Without thinking another thought, Christy stepped forward and headed across the room toward that body on the table.

It was her false self that was confused, thinking that it knew what ugly was and stewing in it, trying to be good enough when there was no such thing.

The ugliness had been corrected a long time ago through forgiveness. It was time to forgive herself and surrender to the truth.

She walked up behind the anesthesiologist. "Excuse me," she said. But he didn't move.

She tapped him on the shoulder and he turned, looked through her, and returned to his task. So he could feel her but not see her.

They had her stomach open and the doctor was chipping at her rib cage with a small chisel. Evidently he intended to remove a few of her ribs.

Ribs that weren't really a part of her any more than her ugliness was. She wasn't sure about all the logic, but she knew this plain as day, as if a light had come on to reveal the truth.

Lamps.

Everyone has them.

She felt no anger or even frustration as she looked at the five people working to fix her body and mind. They were clueless, thinking they were doing what they needed to do.

There was Lawson, just now lifting his phone to respond to a page or a call, one eye on the operation.

There was Nancy, writing something on a clipboard.

There was the anesthesiologist, glancing at the monitor, probably wondering what had caused the sudden surge in her heart rate.

There was Charlene, dabbing at the blood around Christy's ribs with a sponge.

There was Paul Bigoti, proudly executing the finest of his work as he chipped away.

Forgive them, for they know not what they do.

The thought must have come from her formative years, Christy thought.

Then she stepped up to the tray next to the surgeon, picked up the longest of three stainless surgical knives, leaned over the body on the table, and, using both hands on the handle, plunged the knife down with all of her strength.

She felt a jar as the blade struck a rib just below the breastbone before slipping past and sinking deep into the body's chest.

Into the heart.

The reaction was visceral, violent, and immediate, and it happened all around her, as if she'd stepped into a pack of rats feeding on a piece of cheese.

The body arched while her hand was still on the blade's handle. She didn't know if they could see the knife—they probably could—but they definitely saw the body spasm as the blade pinned its heart to the back of its ribcage.

As one, they jumped back, startled. How often did one see a blade plunge into a body of its own accord?

But it was as far as they got. The moment the monitor flatlined, the world around Christy changed. Not just a little bit, but a lot.

Kern Lawson was there one moment, eyes wide with the phone in his right hand, and gone the next. He simply vanished.

So did Nancy Wilkins. Just gone.

As was the surgeon. And Charlene. And the anesthesiologist.

The only thing left was the surgical table itself, with her bleeding dead body on its sheets. And then it was gone too. All of it, including the bed and the knife in her hand. It was as if someone had pulled the plug on a hologram.

Christy blinked and slowly looked around the room. It wasn't the hospital room. Where there had been an operating room with a checkerboard-tiled floor and all of the new equipment and instruments necessary to conduct the most advanced procedures, there was now only a small, very old, concrete room.

No sign of Alice.

She knew where she was immediately. This was the room that Nancy had helped her find, a secret place of fear deep in her mind. The basement room, though not as dark as before.

Directly ahead, vertical bars ran the length of the room, caging her in. In the center of that wall of bars, a door, also made of bars.

But this too was only an illusion, wasn't it? An illusion that no longer held any power over her.

Christy slowly walked up to the barred door, placed her hand on the old metal latch, and twisted the handle, knowing—hoping, pleading—that the door would open.

But it didn't. The handle simply vanished in her hand. And the bars with it. Even the concrete walls... All gone.

She stood alone in a large white room with freshly painted walls, dressed in a blue smock and matching pants. A single door stood in the far wall.

Her breath came steady, her pulse was strong, and she thought: *The illusion is gone. I am free.*

Her body began to tremble.

She stood there in the middle of the empty room for a long minute, drawing deep breaths, hardly able to contain the gratitude sweeping through her body. Tears broke from her eyes and slipped down her cheeks.

Be still and know. Know with your being, not your mind.

And she did. She knew as she had known nothing else, not even the love that Outlaw had shown her.

She knew that she was home. That she belonged, one with her Father. She was complete, wholly restored without even a hint of any need for further correction.

The only question that remained now was whether Austin knew as well.

Moving on feet that hardly felt connected to the floor, Christy walked to the door, opened it wide, and stepped into a vacant corridor that looked like it was freshly painted with gray paint and was newly carpeted. Patient rooms lined the hall, each with shiny new silver knobs.

She briefly wondered whether or not she and Austin had actually used those rooms, or if that, too, had been part of the illusion.

No, we actually used them, she thought.

She wasn't sure where she'd find Austin or if she'd find him at all—for all she knew, she'd only imagined him as well. But she'd last seen him with Lawson, and so she would start there, at what had been Lawson's office.

She headed toward the elevator at end of the hall, awash with amazement. Just a typical hospital corridor, newly upgraded and ready for occupancy.

She, on the other hand, was no longer typical. Because she, unlike most, had seen her true perfection.

She was seeing.

Lamps on.

Christy found the elevator working, as she knew she would. She exited it on the main level. Again she encountered the kind of hallway one would expect to see in a hospital wing that had just been remodeled.

She headed toward the administrator's office, indicated as such by a sign on the door.

Had Outlaw drawn her here? Was he even a real person?

It didn't matter, really. She was. Real and seeing things differently.

Her fear was gone, not only mostly, but completely, because it had been sustained by an illusion that was no longer part of her reality. The mere notion that she might be ugly or in any way less than perfectly beautiful felt as ludicrous as the claim that the world was really flat.

How long had she and Austin been here? The question dawned on her as she veered to the door that had led into the recreation room. Pushed through.

Inside was an empty room with counters on the far wall. A sink. A refrigerator. Scattered cans of soup and empty bags of chips were strewn on the counter and on the floor.

From a construction crew? Or had she eaten the food while in a state of delusion?

She walked up to the refrigerator. Beside it sat a white five-gallon pail with paint crusted on its surface. A trash pail left over from the construction. Austin's street clothes were stuffed into it. Next to it, his shoes.

So he was here. Or at least had been.

Christy reached into the pail and pulled his jeans and shirt out. Her own were wadded up underneath his. They'd put them here themselves, trapped in this illusion.

Her red blouse wasn't torn but it was dirty. Somehow the world had shifted when she'd opened the door into the boiler room—her shirt had torn getting out of the crawlspace. The illusion had begun then, when she'd crawled into the boiler room in the basement.

She opened the refrigerator. A nearly empty jug of water, nothing else. Maybe they'd eaten food from the refrigerator and cupboards, leftovers from whoever had used this room as a lunch room, likely a construction crew.

Christy closed the door and glanced over her shoulder to be sure that she really was alone, then quickly shed her smock and dressed in her own clothes, wondering where they'd found the blue uniforms.

Maybe the basement?

Ignoring their shoes, she grabbed Austin's shirt and jeans and walked back out into the hall toward the administrator's office, directly ahead.

She took a deep breath and pushed the door open, not sure what to expect.

A reception room, laid out exactly as she had always seen it, without the furniture. The door into what had been Lawson's office rested shut across the room. There then?

She crossed the room and pushed the door wide.

Like the rest of the wing, Lawson's office had no furniture. Unlike the outer office, however, it was not vacant. There was a person huddling in the far corner, arms wrapped around his knees, rocking slightly, whispering something she couldn't make out.

"Austin?"

He jerked his head up and gasped. For a full second he sat there staring, mouth parted and eyes wide. His eyes closed, then opened again.

"It's okay, Austin. It's me."

He cried out and scrambled to his feet, eyes darting this way and that, as if he couldn't see her.

"Christy? You're in here?" he asked, frantic.

"Yes."

"How... How did you get in? It's dark."

She suddenly understood. He was still trapped in his illusion, in a dark room. It was both strangely sad and absurd at once. The poor boy was lost in his suffering, groping in the darkness.

The human condition: lost in thought.

She crossed the room and reached for his hand. "It's okay, Austin. It's just an illusion."

His fingers were trembling and cold when she took them in her hand.

"What's an illusion?" he asked in a thin voice.

"You're not in a dark room. Lawson's not here. Everything Outlaw said is true."

"How did you get in? The door didn't open…"

He was hopelessly trapped. In his field of perception, she'd just walked through the wall—one that existed for him but not for her.

Aching with compassion, Christy put her arm around him and drew his trembling body close.

"It's okay, Austin," she whispered into his ear. "I'm going to take you out." She pressed her cheek against his neck and kissed it lightly. "It's okay. Trust me."

He couldn't stop shaking so she held him closer, until he finally began to settle. But his world was still pitch black, so he couldn't see her eyes. She wanted him to be able to look at her, and then maybe he would know.

"Put your clothes on," she whispered, pressing his jeans and shirt into his chest.

"My clothes?"

"I found them in a pail outside the door."

"He's setting us up…"

"No, Austin. I sent him away."

"Are you sure?"

"I'm here, aren't I?"

He hesitated.

"Yes, I'm very sure. Put your clothes on. We're getting out."

He took the clothes, quickly pulled his blue uniform off, then struggled into his jeans and shirt, still blind as a bat.

"Good. Take my hand."

He tentatively stuck out his hand, unsure where hers was.

She took his hand. "Just follow right behind me. Okay?"

"Are you sure?"

"I'm sure. Okay?"

He was still trying to get his eyes to adjust to the darkness. "Okay."

They got halfway to the door, a good start, but that's where it end-ed. Austin suddenly jerked back, released her hand, and grabbed his head as if struck.

"Ah! You walked me into the wall!"

A faint but distinct reddish bruise began to form on his forehead. He'd actually hit a wall. One of his own making, as real as the wall in his mind.

She looked around, trying to see what he saw. "No, there's no wall here."

Austin's eyes searched about, looking for her. "Christy?"

"Here, Austin. I'm right here."

"Christy! Are you there?"

He couldn't hear her?

No, she realized. He was on the other side of a sealed wall that was real to him. She had to go back into his room.

Christy walked up next to him and gently reached for his arm.

"I'm here, Austin."

He whipped his head toward her.

"It's dark," he said.

"There's no wall, Austin. It's only in your mind. Turn your lamps on and you'll see."

"I just ran into it!" he cried.

There's only a problem if you think there's a problem, and Austin definitely had a problem. He could no more walk through the wall in his mind than he could walk on water. His lamp was off. And this time there were no spectacles to save him.

What if he couldn't get out?

"Show me. Touch the wall, Austin."

"It's right there… You can't feel it?"

"No. It's not right there. It's nowhere."

"Then what did I hit?"

"Show me. Touch it."

He reached his hand out and she watched with some amazement as his palm flattened and whitened against a surface invisible to her. Like glass. A wall that only existed in Austin's world, where he was locked in a small black room at the back of Lawson's office.

"It's right here," he said.

Then how to get him out?

"What about the door? Show me where the door is. Show me the handle."

His hands groped along the invisible wall until they wrapped around a knob that she couldn't see.

"It's locked," he said.

It was all quite absurd, really, but she felt genuine compassion for him. She'd been caged in her own suffering as surely as he was now.

Only then did it occur to her that the answer might be a simple matter of trust. Even only a little.

She stepped up to him and took his hand. "Okay, Austin. It's okay. I assure you that I can walk through this wall. I got in, didn't I? So hold onto my hand and trust me. Don't try to see the wall, just trust me, because if I got in, I can get out. Can you do that?"

He didn't answer. She could see the wheels turning behind his eyes, grinding through the problem as he always did.

"Don't think. Close your eyes. Let it go. Just hold on to my hand tight and walk."

He gave a curt nod.

"Close your eyes."

He did.

"Forget everything but me. I'll lead you. Trust me, okay?"

He offered a slow nod.

Christy walked forward, leading him. This time they passed the point where his wall had been and she led him all the way to the door out into the hall.

"Open your eyes, Austin."

His eyes fluttered open. Then blinked. He spun back, wide eyed.

"Is it dark?" she asked.

"No. We... We're out."

"No more darkness?"

"No. We're in his office and the lights are on."

"His office? What do you see?"

He looked about. "What do you mean? His office. The desk, bookcase... I told you. Lawson's office."

He had already forgotten, just as Outlaw had warned them might happen. He was already back in his own illusion.

Austin's mind was too strong and too entrenched to step beyond its own understanding. She would have to lead him.

"Okay, Austin. We're going out. All the way to the front door. Just don't let go of my hand, okay?"

"You're sure?"

"Yes, I'm sure."

He nodded. "Okay."

"Okay. Let's go."

She led him out of the office and down the hall. She saw no one, but judging by the casting of his eyes, she knew that he did. Who or what, she could only imagine. Patients, attendants, maybe even Fisher.

"Don't let go of my hand, Austin. Whatever you do, just keep walking."

He walked faster and with each step seemed to grow a little more confident. Down the hall, then left and down the bottom corridor.

"No one's stopping us," he said.

"Of course they aren't," she said. "You're with me."

He didn't respond. His mind was too busy trying to figure it all out. He was still caught in the illusion. And that was okay too.

Holding Austin's hand in a firm grasp, she led him by the hand all the way to the main reception room, which, like the rest of the new ward, was empty. Then pushed through a door that led into the main hospital.

Christy pulled up and studied the wide hallway before her as the door behind clicked firmly closed.

Two nurses in white uniforms glanced up from a station twenty paces ahead. Beyond them, a man in a plaid shirt leaned against a wall, talking to a doctor who held a clipboard in his hand. Another nurse, this one in a green smock, stepped out of a patient's room and headed away from them toward a sign indicating that RADIOLOGY was to the left and the exit was to the right.

Christy looked over her shoulder at the large door they'd just used and saw that they'd broken through one of those three-inch plastic barriers with yellow and black stripes that warned the wayward not to enter. UNDER CONSTRUCTION.

The sign above the door identified the wing as PSYCH WARD B.

"Can I help you?"

One of the nurses at the station had stood and was approaching them, surprised to see two barefooted people in street clothes exiting from a ward that wasn't yet in use.

"We were just leaving," Austin said, walking forward.

"When does the wing open?" Christy asked.

The nurse eyed them curiously. "Who knows? Soon as they release the funding for furnishings. It's been completed for a month." Her eyes lowered to their bare feet. "You aren't supposed to be in there."

"Yeah... We got lost," Austin said and pulled Christy forward, headed for the exit sign.

She strode down the hall, aware of every sound and scent—the distant hum of the air conditioning, the clink of a spoon stirring tea in a glass, the soft laughter from a room down the hall, the scent of rubbing alcohol, and of perfume, and of Austin's sweat. They followed the arrows through two more turns that led them to the large glass door.

To Christy it all sounded and smelled exquisitely beautiful, like tiny bits of heaven sprinkled through the halls for their enjoyment.

But none of it compared to the overwhelming surge of wonder that met her as she pushed through the doors at Austin's side.

The first thing she saw was the sky—a brilliant gray so rich in hue and laced with such wispy strands of white that she gasped. She knew that anyone else might see the same sky and frown, but to her it was a staggering canvas, majestically painted just so.

They faced the eastern parking lot, filled with every kind of car imaginable—yes, mostly whites and blacks and various shades of gray, but to her eye they were strangely exotic. Who had conceived of such an incredible device as a car?

She stood next to Austin on the sidewalk ten feet from the side entrance to Saint Matthew's Hospital and soaked it all in. The fresh air, the sound of a car pulling into the parking lot, the distant sound of a horn, several birds chirping in a vibrant green tree to her right.

It was all so… *alive!*

"Wow," she finally said.

"Yeah." Austin looked at her. But there was a line of worry on his face.

"Do you hear that?"

"Hear what?" he asked.

"The birds…"

He nodded. "Yeah."

His tone didn't match her own wonder.

"Huh… What just happened?" he asked.

She thought about it for a moment, not remotely sure how to put it into words. She was even less sure what Austin was feeling.

"Everything," she said.

He nodded. "Crazy."

"Crazy doesn't begin to describe it."

"My head's killing me." His fingers felt his pocket, touched the pills he'd taken to carrying loose in his jeans, then quickly reached for his back pocket. He pulled out his cell phone.

It had been there the whole time.

Christy reached for her own and found that it had as well. She pulled it out and tapped the power button. Dead. So that much was real. So was the storage room, she guessed. Which meant her locket might still be where she'd lost it.

"Did you find my locket?"

"It's Wednesday," he said.

She looked up and saw that he was staring at his phone.

His eyes lifted to meet hers, mind spinning—she could practically see it.

"Ten days..." he said.

"Ten days?"

"We've been gone ten days. How is that possible?"

"There was food in the rec room. I think we were meant to be in there ten days. We had to learn to see."

He swallowed hard, turned away from her, and lifted his phone to his ear. Listened carefully. Thumbed it off.

"My doctor left me a message. I don't have a tumor, in case his assistant's call frightened me. It's something else he's never seen. That's why he wanted to see me." He paused. "Whatever it is, it's affecting my mind."

"You think? I don't have anything wrong with my brain. I was in there too."

He shifted his eyes, lost in thought. "I don't know. I just know that all of that was a hallucination caused by a physical anomaly in my brain. Nothing happened."

"Everything happened," she said. "We saw the truth."

"What truth? That we're insane?"

He really wasn't seeing, not the way she was.

And then it struck her: To some all of this was foolishness, to those who didn't get it. Boring, stupid, and plain nonsensical.

But to her, the simple awareness of her true identity was earth shattering. Nothing would ever be the same.

"The truth that if we have eyes to see, we can see we are beautiful. We've been put right, a long time ago. We've just forgotten that. There is no further need for correction and there's really nothing more to know. Everything Outlaw said is true. So is Outlaw."

"Outlaw? He's just a figment of your imagination." He shook his head. "Nope. Something's wrong with my head."

"The only thing wrong is that you're not seeing how it really is."

"But I am. I'm seeing just fine now. I'm seeing that I need to find out what's wrong with my head. This is the real world, Christy. Wake up!"

He was still trapped in the illusion, just like that dark room that had held him captive. What had just happened wasn't acceptable to his rational, scientific mind, and so he was putting up a wall. It was all too much for him.

And wasn't that what most people did?

All but the Outlaws, she thought.

I am an Outlaw.

"I have woken up, Austin. I'm wide awake for the first time in years."

For a brief moment, his eyes lingered on her, and she thought he was reconsidering. But then they seemed to harden and he started to turn.

"I have to get to the doctor's office."

"Austin?"

He strode away.

"Austin?"

"What?" he snapped, jerking around.

He was upset, but she felt none of his anxiety. Not even a hint.

She looked down at her body, her hands, her feet, and she found that they looked exactly as they always had. But she—like the gray sky and the cars in the parking lot and the birds singing in the tree—was beautiful.

She felt like laughing, like shouting, like singing this great, staggering truth to the whole world.

Instead, she only smiled.

"My locket," she said, looking up at Austin. "Did you get it?"

He stared at her, face flat. "It's still in the storage room."

WHY THE locket still seemed important to her, Christy didn't know. The reason felt oddly distant now, like a distant bird on the wind, chirping unseen. But she was curious to track down that bird, if only to see that it was free.

Or, perhaps more accurately, to know that she was free from that desperate search for identity that had imprisoned her. She was now complete, just as she was.

So she headed south over the grass lawn that bordered the hospital's eastern wall. She wasn't sure what she'd find in the storage room, and, feeling the cool grass between her toes, she didn't care.

How she'd managed to live for so long without being aware of the life all around her was a bit of a mystery. Did other people feel the kind of awe she did now? Was that normal, and she was only now catching up?

Or did most people stumble through most days, groping in the dark, lights off, eyes shut?

Eyes wide open, Christy.

And they were. Oh, how they were!

Overwhelmed by it all, Christy impulsively cried at the sky.

"I see!"

She didn't care who saw her—whatever they noticed was likely their own illusion of what should or shouldn't be. She spread her arms wide, threw her head back, and closed her eyes.

"I'm home! I belong!"

She stared up at the beautiful gray clouds and cried it again, face split by a smile that felt as wide as the sky itself. "I see, I see, I see!"

And then she was hurrying forward, skipping, tumbling once in the grass and springing to her feet.

She spun back and shouted it one last time in the direction that Austin had taken. "Do you hear me? I'm free! I'm home!"

The driver of a passing car had his window down and was staring at her.

She turned and walked briskly, normal on the outside, she imagined, but screaming with joy on the inside. Right to the corner of the old hospital.

Into the alleyway with the large garbage bins.

Straight to the storage room, through the still unlocked door, and right up to the casket which was still scooted away from the wall.

There lay her silver heart-shaped locket.

She reached down, mindful of the trapdoor, shoved the coffin back against the wall, exited the storage room, and headed up the alley the way she'd first come only a short time ago.

Even the bins looked beautiful to her. They simply were what they were and were doing a splendid job being just that.

She came out of the alley with long, even strides, a new woman who had no intention of ever looking back with old eyes.

Traffic hummed in song—how many pumping pistons and rolling tires collaborated to make up that orchestra? Thunder pealed to the south, like drums.

It all sounded so incredible. And the sights. The sidewalk, the street, the shops. The bench ahead to her left with the bum...

Christy pulled up and stared at the bench, heart suddenly in her throat. There was a man on the bench, yes, but it wasn't the bum.

It was Outlaw, leaning back with both of his arms up on the bench's backrest, one leg crossed over the other, staring directly ahead at the street.

For a long moment, she couldn't move. Once again, the world around her seemed to slow as her memories of their first encounter in the canyon streamed through her mind.

He was real. In the flesh. She knew it!

Without looking at her, Outlaw lowered his arms, set his boot on the ground, leaned forward, and rose to his feet. Only when he turned did he lift his eyes to meet hers.

He strode forward, coat lifting with the wind at his calves. His lips curved upward in a knowing grin, and his eyes twinkled with mystery.

"Hello again, Christy."

"Hello, Outlaw." She couldn't stop matching his grin.

He looked into her eyes, searching.

"Austin?"

Yes. There was the matter of Austin.

"He's not seeing so clearly," she said.

"He will. Sooner or later. The more intelligent ones come to lean exclusively on their own understanding. They tend to be so entrenched in their own dogma they can't see beyond their own minds. He's trapped in a prison with much thicker walls than you might guess. His greatest gift is as much a curse in this world."

Christy offered a simple nod. The love she'd felt in his presence before was back. Her fingertips tingled with it.

"It's time you knew more about where you grew up," he said.

She blinked, freshly desperate to know. But not in a way that caused her anxiety. She was home already. In some ways, where she grew up no longer mattered.

"It was called Project Showdown," he said. "Thirty-six orphans were taken to a monastery deep in the canyon you saw, hidden from the world and raised by good Christian monks to accept and follow the path of light. You were taught all the right things, said all the right prayers, embraced it all as best you knew how with all of your heart."

Christy's head swam. "I grew up in a monastery?"

"So did Austin."

"Not just in a dream, but for real?"

"Yes."

"Why can't we remember any of it?"

"The children were twelve or thirteen years old when the project failed. Your memories were wiped clean and you were integrated back into the world."

"You said thirty-six…"

"Thirty-six. The idea was based on an ancient mystical Jewish tradition that claims there are thirty-six righteous pillars in the world, uniquely gifted individuals who carry the weight of humanity. The *Lamed-Vav*. It's their existence, the legend goes, that holds back the great wrath."

"The other patients in the psych ward?" Christy asked.

"Alice and Jacob were among the thirty-six, none of the others. They know more than some, less than others, but they are still trapped in their own hells. You're the first to see. A Seer."

Strange, she thought. She'd grown up in a monastery surrounded by teachers of the highest virtue. Details of that time began to prick the edges of her memory.

She'd said all the right prayers, learned and accepted all the right things about Jesus and religion, argued dogma with the best, written papers on why this and why that, and followed the master. Her world had once been neat and buttoned up, a perfect bundle of beliefs and certainties.

But under all of it there was her. Still believing that she was ugly and broken.

And that was the lie she'd become.

A lie! Just like the lie even the most well-meaning people clung to.

"I'm the first?" she asked.

Outlaw shifted his gaze to the horizon. "The first. And the rest may not respond to this kind of experience. All in good time. You don't have to understand everything just yet. When the time is right, I'll share my own story with you. In the meantime, don't forget who you are."

"Lawson is dead," she said, smiling.

His blue eyes found hers again. "Deader than dead."

"I am *Outlaw*."

He nodded. "It's not only the thirty-six. Share your story with any who have ears to hear and eyes to see. All who would step out of the law of sin and death and into the light. All who would live as Outlaws."

Outlaw took her hand. "We will show them the way, Christy. We and all those who hear the call."

"The call to see," she said.

He smiled. "The call to hear the drum beating in the heartland and awaken. They will come."

"Home," she said. "To a place of beauty and perfection where there is no more need for correction."

"Home. Where we all belong."

"What about Alice?"

"Alice has gone missing and is a long way from here, escaping into dreams because she knows no better. She's next."

"And Jacob?"

"Not yet. When the time is right, he will see. As will Austin."

For his sake, she hoped so.

"You drew me to the storage room?"

"I created a thin space to help you see." He glanced at the hand in which she held her pendant. "You retrieved the locket?"

She opened her hand and showed him the silver heart.

He withdrew a round medallion on a leather cord. Nearly identical to the one that hung from his neck.

"Join me," he said.

Christy lifted the medallion from his palm and rubbed the embossed *O* with her thumb.

DEDITIO.

Surrender. Surrender her old vision of the world to reality. To seeing who she really was, no longer bound by rules of perception that had locked her in a prison of suffering. She would wear it always to remember that she, too, was now an outlaw.

He'd said he'd grown up in a jungle far away. It made her wonder what events had made him Outlaw. They were in the book he carried embossed with the large 'O'. His story.

"Here," she said, placing her necklace in his palm. "I don't need this anymore. I know who I am now."

He winked at her, then took the locket and casually dropped it into his pocket.

"And so the journey begins." He lifted his hand and brought it to the side of her face. Brushed her cheek with his thumb. "Join me, Christy."

She felt a hot tear slide from her eye.

"I already have."

"Yes, you have. Whole and perfect, as you are."

She nodded. "Loved."

"Don't forget who you already are, fully restored. Whole. If you find yourself forgetting, surrender again to who you are and embrace your Father with whom you are one."

"Deditio," she said.

"Deditio."

He leaned forward, and placed a kiss on her forehead. "I'll come for you soon."

Then he offered her one final nod and turned to leave.

"Do you ever forget?" she asked.

He turned back and for a few seconds only looked at her.

"Too often, my dear. Far too often." His lips nudged upward. "And then I remember."

"Do you have a name?"

Outlaw hesitated only a moment.

"Stephen," he said. And then he dipped his head, and walked away, like that man who knew where he was going but had nowhere to be.

Stephen.

The Outlaw.

Eyes wide open.

Nothing would ever be the same.

ACKNOWLEDGMENTS

A massive shout-out to my friend, brother, and partner in crime, Kevin Kaiser, without whom I would be lost. Together we take a journey into all things spiritual, together we concoct wild scenarios that find their way into these stories, and together we imagine and commune with the tribe of Outlaws who gather in the world of story, both on paper and in cyberspace. I can't adequately convey my gratitude for your partnership and creativity, so I'll just go with thank you. *Eyes Wide Open* would not be what it is without you. Neither would my life. Thank you, from the bottom of my heart, thank you.

Gary Dorsey, artist extraordinaire. Thank you for joining me on this journey and giving flesh to the unseen world through visionary artwork that we would all be proud to hang on our walls. Your genius and talent is truly a gift to the world. Your incredible imagination has helped me see life through a new lens more times than you realize. For that I will always be grateful. The best is yet to come, brother. Deditio.

ABOUT THE AUTHOR

Ted Dekker is a New York Times best-selling author with more than five million books in print. Heralded as a "master of suspense" by *Library Journal*, Dekker has sold millions worldwide. Dekker's upbringing as the child of missionaries who lived among the headhunter tribes of Indonesia gives him a unique perspective outside the cultural bubble, enabling him to craft provocative insights, unforgettable characters, and adrenaline-laced plots in his fiction. Two of his thirty-plus novels, *Thr3e* and *House*, have been made into movies, with more in production.

Dekker resides in Austin, Texas, with his wife and children. You can find him at Teddekker.com and Facebook.com/teddekker.

WORTHY*
PUBLISHING

If you enjoyed this book, will you consider
sharing the message with others?

- Mention the book in a Facebook post, Twitter update, Pinterest pin, or blog post.

- Recommend this book to those in your small group, book club, workplace, and classes.

- Head over to www.facebook.com/TedDekker, "LIKE" the page, and post a comment as to what you enjoyed the most..

- Tweet "I recommend reading #EyesWideOpen by @TedDekker // @worthypub"

- Pick up a copy for someone you know who would be challenged and encouraged by this message.

- Write a book review online.

You can subscribe to Worthy Publishing's newsletter at worthypublishing.com

WORTHY PUBLISHING
FACEBOOK PAGE

WORTHY PUBLISHING
WEBSITE